DAMON KNIGHT, who has been a freelance writer since 1950, is the author and editor of over thirty books, including anthologies, translations, novels and short stories. In 1956 he won the 'Hugo' award for science fiction criticism and is at present editor of the *Orbit* series of original collections of science fiction stories. He is the founder and first President (1965–6) of the Science Fiction Writers of America and a Director of the Milford Science Fiction Writers' Conference.

Born in 1922, Damon Knight now lives with his wife, authoress Kate Wilhelm, in Florida.

Also available in Pan Books

ONE HUNDRED YEARS OF SCIENCE FICTION
(Book Two)

Edited by Damon Knight

ONE HUNDRED YEARS OF SCIENCE FICTION

Book One

Edited by Damon Knight

PAN BOOKS LTD : LONDON

Books One and Two of
One Hundred Years of Science Fiction
first published in one volume in Great Britain 1969
by Victor Gollancz Ltd.
This edition first published 1972 by Pan Books Ltd,
33 Tothill Street, London, SW1.

ISBN 0 330 02982 7

Printed and bound in England by
Hazell Watson & Viney Ltd,
Aylesbury, Bucks

CONTENTS

ACKNOWLEDGEMENTS

'With the Night Mail', by Rudyard Kipling, is reprinted from 'Actions and Reactions' by kind permission of Mrs George Bembridge and Macmillan & Co. Ltd.

'Mr Murphy of New York', by Thomas McMorrow, copyright 1930 by Curtis Publishing Company. Reprinted by permission from the *Saturday Evening Post*.

'New Apples in the Garden', by Kris Neville, copyright © 1963 by The Condé Nast Publications, Inc. Reprinted by permission of the author's agents, Scott Meredith Literary Agency, Inc.

'Sanity', by Fritz Leiber, copyright 1944 by Street & Smith Publications, Inc. Reprinted by permission of the author's agent, Robert P. Mills, Ltd.

'The Shapes', by J.-H. Rosny *aîné*. English translation copyright © 1967 by Mercury Press, Inc. Reprinted by permission of Robert Borel-Rosny.

'The Other Celia', by Theodore Sturgeon, copyright © 1957 by Galaxy Publishing Corp. Reprinted by permission of the author's agent, Robert P. Mills, Ltd.

'Black Charlie', by Gordon R. Dickson, copyright 1954 by Galaxy Publishing Corp. Reprinted by permission of the author's agent, Robert P. Mills, Ltd.

'A Subway Named Mobius', by A. J. Deutsch, copyright 1950 by Street & Smith Publications, Inc. Reprinted by permission of The Condé Nast Publications, Inc.

'The Man Who Came Early', by Poul Anderson, copyright © 1956 by Fantasy House, Inc. Reprinted by permission of the author's agents, Scott Meredith Literary Agency, Inc.

'The Other Now', by Murray Leinster, copyright 1951 by World Editions, Inc. Reprinted by permission of the author.

INTRODUCTION

One of the curious things about science fiction is that its history has been consistently misunderstood by its own practitioners. For years we all believed that SF had been virtually invented by Hugo Gernsback in the 1920s. (We knew about Wells and Verne, but considered them anomalies.) We now learn from H. Bruce Franklin, an associate professor of English at Stanford, that SF stories were published as a matter of course in American literary magazines all through the nineteenth century, and that 'there was no major nineteenth-century American writer of fiction, and indeed few in the second rank, who did not write some science fiction or at least one utopian romance'.

Science fiction probably fell from grace in the general twentieth-century decline of romantic fiction. The nineteenth century was quite prepared to believe in marvels, scientific or otherwise; the first half of the twentieth was the day of the hard-headed businessman, when any display of interest in Martians, robots, atom bombs or spaceships was taken as evidence of weakmindedness, if not insanity.

The importance of the Gernsback era is in the enormous impetus it gave to the writing of short science fiction. Donald B. Day's *Index to the Science Fiction Magazines, 1926–1950*, now sadly out of date, lists ten thousand stories. From these, and from the three hundred new SF stories published every year, anthologists compile some twenty collections a year in this country alone. To the editors of the SF magazines and to the talented writers they have attracted in increasing numbers since about 1940 we owe much of the vitality and richness of modern science fiction. At the same time, all through this period, mainstream writers have continued to produce occasional SF novels whose literary quality has generally set them apart from the works of coterie writers; this distinction is no longer so clearly marked, and there is reason to believe that the two streams are about to merge. If they do, it will be over the dead bodies of some SF writers and editors, who continue to insist, in concert with the enemies of science fiction, that SF is a *genre*, a special and limited form which cannot be judged by ordinary literary standards.

This brings us to another odd thing about science fiction; its practitioners have never been able to agree on what it is. I know of no more fruitless argument, and will not bore you with any of the tormented Teutonic constructions in which critics have tried to capture science fiction while excluding all its near neighbours. Basil Davenport, in his *Inquiry into Science Fiction*, very sensibly refers us to Quiller-Couch's definition of a ballad: 'A ballad is *Sir Patrick Spens* and *The Lass of Lochroyan* and *The Bonnie Mill-Dams of Binnorie*, and things of that sort'. A similar definition of science fiction will serve us very well. Science fiction, as C. S. Lewis has pointed out, is not one thing but many. It is Captain Nemo and Richard Seaton and John Carter; it is Perelandra and Dune and Trenco; it is *1984* and *Flowers for Algernon* and *The Incredible Shrinking Man*. A science fiction story always postulates a world changed in some way from the everyday world we know, but these changes are of many different kinds and are made for different ends. They may be as sweeping as the creation of a whole imaginary world, with its mountains, cities and people, or as narrow as the invention of a new weapon. Since science is a way of describing the world, these changes often involve science – but they need not do so. Much of what is carelessly called science in SF from the 'spacewarps' and 'overdrives' beloved of all writers of space-opera, to the 'positronic brains' of Isaac Asimov's robots, is really word-magic – what Davenport calls 'jiggery-pokery'; moreover this is not only legitimate but necessary. The alternative would be to use only known principles and inventions in science fiction, as Jules Verne did ('I sent my characters to the Moon with gunpowder, a thing one may see every day. Where does M. Wells find his cavourite? Let him show it to me!'). If there is anything we can be sure of about the future, it is that it will be full of inventions and principles now unknown. The whole history of science in the last fifty years is a series of ghastly upsets of the known and the reasonable; even today, in particle physics and in astronomy, it begins to appear that current ideas about the universe, although they are crazy, are not crazy enough.

I have said elsewhere that science fiction and prophecy are two different things. Science fiction deals with what may be, not what will be. It is true that we can now afford to smile at those who once dismissed SF as 'Buck Rogers stuff', while our astronauts orbit the earth, our space probes photograph the moon, Mars, and Venus; while computers take over banking, commerce and industry, and electron microscopes unlock the secrets of the genetic code. But to value science fiction merely because of its predictive quality is as absurd as to reject it, as some unimaginative readers do, because it is 'not true'. Science fiction stories allow us to enter worlds that exist nowhere else. We prize them for that, not for the irrelevant coincidence that may later make them seem prophetic. *The War of the Worlds* is no less a great story because the Martians have not landed; neither is *Out of the Silent Planet* diminished if there are no *sorns*.

The stories in this book are those that have given me enduring pleasures of this kind. I have chosen and arranged them in an attempt to give a cross section of SF, parallel to but not overlapping the similar cross section in *A Century of Science Fiction*. In the introduction to that volume, published six years ago, I said, 'So many people have written good SF during the last century that a book twice this size could not represent them all'. This is as true as ever, but here, at any rate, are twenty of the best, from Kipling to Ballard.*

I wish to acknowledge my debt to older anthologists, particularly to Groff Conklin, Raymond J. Healy, and Frederik

* Please see also *One Hundred Years of Science Fiction*, Book Two.

Pohl, whose work made mine possible; and to the compilers of all the reference works listed in *A Century of Science Fiction*, plus two more: *A Checklist of Science-Fiction Anthologies*, compiled by W. R. Cole (published by the author, New York, 1964), and *Index to the Science Fiction Magazines, 1951–1965* (published by the Massachusetts Institute of Technology Science Fiction Society, Cambridge, 1966).

DAMON KNIGHT

The Anchorage
Milford, Pennsylvania
April 1968

1 WORLDS OF TOMORROW

WITH THE NIGHT MAIL (AD 1908)

A STORY OF AD 2000

RUDYARD KIPLING

(*Together with extracts from the magazine in which it appeared*)

At nine o'clock of a gusty winter night I stood on the lower stages of one of the GPO outward mail towers. My purpose was a run to Quebec in 'Postal Packet 162 or such other as may be appointed'; and the Postmaster-General himself countersigned the order. This talisman opened all doors, even those in the dispatching-caisson at the foot of the tower, where they were delivering the sorted Continental mail. The bags lay packed close as herrings in the long grey underbodies which our GPO still calls 'coaches'. Five such coaches were filled as I watched, and were shot up the guides to be locked on to their waiting packets three hundred feet nearer the stars.

From the dispatching-caisson I was conducted by a courteous and wonderfully learned official – Mr L. L. Geary, Second Dispatcher of the Western Route – to the Captains' Room (this wakes an echo of old romance), where the mail captains come on for their turn of duty. He introduces me to the captain of '162' – Captain Purnall, and his relief, Captain Hodgson. The one is small and dark; the other large and red; but each has the brooding sheathed glance characteristic of eagles and aeronauts. You can see it in the pictures of our racing professionals, from L. V. Rautsch to little Ada Warrleigh – that fathomless abstraction of eyes habitually turned through naked space.

On the notice-board in the Captains' Room, the pulsing arrows of some twenty indicators register, degree by geographical degree, the progress of as many homeward-bound packets. The word 'Cape' rises across the face of a dial; a gong strikes: the South African mid-weekly mail is in at the Highgate Receiving Towers. That is all. It reminds one comically of the traitorous little bell which in pigeon-fanciers' lofts notifies the return of a homer.

'Time for us to be on the move,' says Captain Purnall, and we are shot up by the passenger-lift to the top of the dispatch-towers. 'Our coach will lock on when it is filled and the clerks are aboard . . .'

'No 162' waits for us in Slip E of the topmost stage. The great curve of her back shines frostily under the lights, and some minute alteration of trim makes her rock a little in her holding-down slips.

Captain Purnall frowns and dives inside. Hissing softly, '162' comes to rest as level as a rule. From her North Atlantic Winter nosecap (worn bright as diamond with boring through uncounted leagues of hail, snow, and ice) to the inset of her three built-out propeller-shafts is some two hundred and forty feet. Her extreme diameter, carried well forward, is thirty-seven. Contrast this with the nine hundred by ninety-five of any crack liner, and you will realize the power that must drive a hull through all weathers at more than the emergency speed of the *Cyclonic*!

The eye detects no joint in her skin plating save the sweeping hair-crack of the bow-rudder – Magniac's rudder that assured us the dominion of the unstable air and left its inventor penniless and half-blind. It is calculated to Castelli's 'gull-wing' curve. Raise a few feet of that all but invisible plate three-eighths of an inch and she will yaw five miles to port or starboard ere she is under control again. Give her full helm and she returns on her track like a whip-lash. Cant the whole forward – a touch on the wheel will suffice – and she sweeps at your good direction up or down. Open the complete circle and she presents to the air a mushroom head that will bring her up all standing within a half mile.

'Yes,' says Captain Hodgson, answering my thought, 'Castelli thought he'd discovered the secret of controlling aeroplanes when he'd only found out how to steer dirigible balloons. Magniac invented his rudder to help war-boats ram each other; and war went out of fashion and Magniac he went out of his mind because he said he couldn't serve his country any more. I wonder if any of us ever know what we're really doing.'

'If you want to see the coach locked you'd better go aboard. It's due now,' says Mr Geary. I enter through the door amidships. There is nothing here for display. The inner skin of the gas-tanks comes down to within a foot or two of my head and turns over just short of the turn of the bilges. Liners and yachts disguise their tanks with decoration, but the GPO serves them raw under a lick of grey official paint. The inner skin shuts off fifty feet of the bow and as much of the stern, but the bow-bulkhead is recessed for the lift-shunting apparatus as the stern is pierced for the shaft-tunnels. The engine-room lies almost amidships. Forward of it, extending to the turn of the bow tanks, is an aperture – a bottomless hatch at present – into which our coach will be locked. One looks down over the coamings three hundred feet to the dispatching-caisson whence voices boom upwards. The light below is obscured to a sound of thunder, as our coach rises on its guides. It enlarges rapidly from a postage stamp to a playing-card; to a punt and last a pontoon. The two clerks, its crew, do not even look up as it comes into place. The Quebec letters fly under their fingers and leap into the docketed racks, while both captains and Mr Geary satisfy themselves that the coach is locked home. A clerk passes the way-bill over the hatch-coaming. Captain Purnall thumb-marks and passes it to Mr Geary. Receipt has been given and taken. 'Pleasant run,' says Mr Geary, and disappears through the door which a foot-high pneumatic compressor locks after him.

'A-ah!' sighs the compressor released. Our holding-down clips part with a tang. We are clear.

Captain Hodgson opens the great colloid underbody porthole through which I watch over-lighted London slide eastwards as the gale gets hold of us. The first of the low winter clouds cuts off the well-known view and darkens Middlesex. On the south edge of it I can see a postal packet's light ploughing through the white fleece. For an instant she gleams like a star ere she drops toward the Highgate Receiving Towers. 'The Bombay Mail,' says Captain Hodgson, and looks at his watch. 'She's forty minutes late.'

'What's our level?' I ask.

'Four thousand. Aren't you coming up on the bridge?'

The bridge (let us ever praise the GPO as a repository of ancientest tradition!) is represented by a view of Captain Hodgson's legs where he stands on the Control Platform that runs thwart-ships overhead. The bow colloid is unshuttered and Captain Purnall, one hand on the wheel, is feeling for a fair slant. The dial shows 4,300 feet.

'It's steep tonight,' he mutters, as tier on tier of cloud drops under. 'We generally pick up an easterly draught below three thousand at this time o' the year. I hate slathering through fluff.'

'So does Van Cutsem. Look at him huntin' for a slant!' says Captain Hodgson. A fog-light breaks cloud a hundred fathoms below. The Antwerp Night Mail makes her signal and rises between two racing clouds far to port, her flanks blood-red in the glare of Sheerness Double Light. The gale will have us over the North Sea in half an hour, but Captain Purnall lets her go composedly – nosing to every point of the compass as she rises.

'Five thousand – six, six thousand eight hundred' – the dip-dial reads ere we find the easterly drift, heralded by a flurry of snow at the thousand fathom level. Captain Purnall rings up the engines and keys down the governor on the switch before him. There is no sense in urging machinery when Æolus himself gives you good knots for nothing. We are away in earnest now – our nose notched home on our chosen star. At this level the lower clouds are laid out, all neatly combed by the dry fingers of the East. Below that again is the strong westerly blow through which we rose. Overhead, a film of southerly drifting mist draws a theatrical gauze across the firmament. The moonlight turns the lower strata to silver without a stain except where our shadow underruns us. Bristol and Cardiff Double Lights (those statelily-inclined beams over Severnmouth) are dead ahead of us; for we keep the Southern Winter Route. Coventry Central, the pivot of the English system, stabs upward once in ten seconds its spear of diamond light to the north; and a point or two off our starboard bow The Leek, the great cloud-breaker of Saint David's Head, swings its unmistakable green beam twenty-five degrees each way. There must be half a mile of fluff over it in this weather, but it does not affect The Leek.

'Our planet's over–lighted if anything,' says Captain Purnall at the wheel, as Cardiff-Bristol slides under. 'I remember the old days of common white verticals that 'ud show two or three hundred feet up in a mist, if you knew where to look for 'em. In really fluffy weather they might as well have been under your hat. One could get lost coming home then, an' have some fun. Now it's like driving down Piccadilly.'

He points to the pillars of light where the cloud-breakers bore through the cloud-floor. We see nothing of England's outlines: only a white pavement pierced in all directions by these manholes of variously coloured fire – Holy Island's white and red – St Bee's interrupted white, and so on as far as the eye can reach. Blessed be Sargent, Ahrens, and the Dubois brothers, who invented the cloud-breakers of the world whereby we travel in security!

'Are you going to lift for The Shamrock?' asks Captain Hodgson. Cork Light (green, fixed) enlarges as we rush to it. Captain Purnall nods. There is heavy traffic hereabouts – the cloud-bank beneath us is streaked with running fissures of flame where the Atlantic boats are hurrying Londonward just clear of the fluff. Mail-packets are supposed, under the Conference rules, to have the five-thousand-foot lanes to themselves, but the foreigner in a hurry is apt to take liberties with English air. 'No 162' lifts to a long-drawn wail of the breeze in the fore-flange of the rudder and we make Valencia (white, green, white) at a safe 7,000 feet, dipping our beam to an incoming Washington packet.

There is no cloud on the Atlantic, and faint streaks of cream round Dingle Bay show where the driven seas hammer the coast. A big SATA liner (*Société Anonyme des Transports Aëriens*) is diving and lifting half a mile below us in search of some break in the solid west wind. Lower still lies a disabled Dane: she is telling the liner all about it in International. Our General Communication dial has caught her talk and begins to eavesdrop. Captain Hodgson makes a motion to shut it off but checks himself. 'Perhaps you'd like to listen,' he says.

'*Argol* of St Thomas,' the Dane whimpers. 'Report owners three starboard shaft collar-bearings fused. Can make Flores as we are, but impossible further. Shall we buy spares at Fayal?'

The liner acknowledges and recommends inverting the bearings. The *Argol* answers that she has already done so without effect, and begins to relieve her mind about cheap German enamels for collar-bearings. The Frenchman assents cordially, cries, '*Courage, mon ami,*' and switches off.

Their lights sink under the curve of the ocean.

'That's one of Lundt & Blcamers' boats,' says Captain Hodgson. 'Serves 'em right for putting German compos in their thrust-blocks. *She* won't be in Fayal tonight! By the way, wouldn't you like to look round the engine-room?'

I have been waiting eagerly for this invitation and I follow Captain Hodgson from the Control Platform, stooping low to avoid the bulge of the tanks. We know that Fleury's gas can lift anything, as the world-famous trials of '89 showed, but its almost indefinite powers of expansion necessitate vast tank room. Even in this thin air the lift-shunts are busy taking out one-third of its normal lift, and still '162' must be checked by an occasional downdraw of the rudder or our flight would become a climb to the stars. Captain Purnall prefers an overlifted to an underlifted ship; but no two captains trim ship alike. 'When *I* take the bridge,' says Captain Hodgson, 'you'll see me shunt forty per cent of the lift out of the gas and run her on the upper rudder. With a swoop upwards instead of a swoop downwards, *as* you say. Either way will do. It's only habit. Watch our dip-dial! Tim fetches her down once every thirty knots as regularly as breathing.'

So is it shown on the dip-dial. For five or six minutes the arrow creeps from 6,700 to 7,300. There is the faint 'szgee' of the rudder, and back slides the arrow to 6,000 on a falling slant of ten or fifteen knots.

'In heavy weather you jockey her with the screws as well,' says Captain Hodgson, and, unclipping the jointed bar which divides the engine-room from the bare deck, he leads me on to the floor.

Here we find Fleury's Paradox of the Bulk-headed Vacuum – which we accept now without thought – literally in full blast. The three engines are HT&T assisted-vacuo Fleury turbines running from 3,000 to the Limit – that is to say, up to the point when the blades make the air 'bell' – cut out a vacuum for themselves precisely as over-driven marine propellers used to do. '162's' Limit is low on account of the small size of her nine screws, which, though handier than the old colloid Thelussons, 'bell' sooner. The midships engine, generally used as a reinforce, is not running; so the port and starboard turbine vacuum chambers draw direct into the return-mains.

The turbines whistle reflectively. From the low-arched expansion-tanks on either side the valves descend pillarwise to the turbine-chests, and thence the obedient gas whirls through the spirals of blades with a force that would whip the teeth out of a power-saw. Behind, is its own pressure held in leash or spurred on by the lift-shunts; before it, the vacuum where Fleury's Ray dances in violet-green bands and whirled turbillons of flame. The jointed U-tubes of the vacuum-chamber are pressure-tempered colloid (no glass would endure the strain for an instant) and a junior engineer with tinted spectacles watches the Ray intently. It is the very heart of the machine – a mystery to this day. Even Fleury who begat it and, unlike Magniac, died a multi-millionaire, could not explain how the restless little imp shuddering in the U-tube can, in the fractional fraction of a second, strike the furious blast of gas into a chill greyish-green liquid that drains (you can hear it trickle) from the far end of the vacuum through the eduction-pipes and the mains back to the bilges. Here it returns to its gaseous, one had almost written sagacious, state and climbs to work afresh. Bilge-tank, upper tank, dorsal-tank, expansion-chamber, vacuum, main-return (as a liquid), and bilge-tank once more is the ordained cycle. Fleury's Ray sees to that; and the engineer with the tinted spectacles sees to Fleury's Ray. If a speck of oil, if even the natural grease of the human finger touch the hooded terminals, Fleury's Ray will wink and disappear and must be laboriously built up again. This means half a day's work for all hands and an expense of 170-odd pounds to the GPO for radium-salts and such trifles.

'Now look at our thrust-collars. You won't find much German compo there. Full-jewelled, you see,' says Captain Hodgson as the engineer shunts open the top of a cap. Our shaft-bearings are CMC (Commercial Minerals Company) stones, ground with as much care as the lens of a telescope. They cost £37 apiece. So far we have not arrived at their term of life. These bearings came from 'No 97', which took them over from the old *Dominion of Light* which had them out of the wreck of the *Perseus* aeroplane in the years when men still flew wooden kites over oil engines!

They are a shining reproof to all low-grade German 'ruby' enamels, so-called 'boort' facings, and the dangerous and unsatisfactory alumina compounds which please dividend-hunting owners and turn skippers crazy.

The rudder-gear and the gas lift-shunt, seated side by side under the engine-room dials, are the only machines in visible motion. The former sighs from time to time as the oil plunger rises and falls half an inch. The latter, cased and guarded like the U-tube aft, exhibits another Fleury Ray, but inverted and more green than violet. Its function is to shunt the lift out of the gas, and this it will do without watching. That is all! A tiny pump-rod wheezing and whining to itself beside a sputtering green lamp. A hundred and fifty feet aft down the flat-topped tunnel of the tanks a violet light, restless and irresolute. Between the two, three white-painted turbine-trunks, like eel-baskets laid on their side, accentuate the empty perspectives. You can hear the trickle of the liquefied gas flowing from the vacuum into the bilge-tanks and the soft *gluck-glock* of gas-locks closing as Captain Purnall brings '162' down by the head. The hum of the turbines and the boom of the air on our skin is no more than a cotton-wool wrapping to the universal stillness. And we are running an eighteen-second mile.

I peer from the fore end of the engine-room over the hatch-coamings into the coach. The mail-clerks are sorting the Winnipeg, Calgary, and Medicine Hat bags; but there is a pack of cards ready on the table.

Suddenly a bell thrills; the engineers run to the turbine-valves and stand by; but the spectacled slave of the Ray in the U-tube never lifts his head. He must watch where he is. We are hard-braked and going astern; there is language from the Control Platform.

'Tim's sparking badly about something,' says the unruffled Captain Hodgson. 'Let's look.'

Captain Purnall is not the suave man we left half an hour since, but the embodied authority of the GPO. Ahead of us floats an ancient, aluminium-patched, twin-screw tramp of the dingiest, with no more right to the 5,000-foot lane than has a horse-cart to a modern road. She carries an obsolete 'barbette' conning-tower – a six-foot affair with railed platform forward – and our warning beam plays on the top of it as a policeman's lantern flashes on the area sneak. Like a sneak-thief, too, emerges a shock-headed navigator in his shirtsleeves. Captain Purnall wrenches open the colloid to talk with him man to man. There are times when Science does not satisfy.

'What under the stars are you doing here, you sky-scraping chimney-sweep?' he shouts as we two drift side by side. 'Do you know this is a Mail-lane? You call yourself a sailor, sir? You ain't fit to peddle toy balloons to an Esquimaux. Your name and number! Report and get down, and be—!'

'I've been blown up once,' the shock-headed man cries, hoarsely, as a dog barking. 'I don't care two flips of a contact for anything *you* can do, Postey.'

'Don't you, sir? But I'll make you care. I'll have you towed stern first to Disko and broke up. You can't recover insurance if you're broke for obstruction. Do you understand *that*?'

Then the stranger bellows: 'Look at my propellers! There's been a wulli-wa down below that has knocked us into umbrella-frames! We've been blown up about forty thousand feet! We're all one conjuror's watch inside! My mate's arm's broke; my engineer's head's cut open; my Ray went out when the engines smashed; and . . . and . . . for pity's sake give me my height, Captain! We doubt we're dropping.'

'Six thousand eight hundred. Can you hold it?' Captain Purnall overlooks all insults, and leans half out of the colloid, staring and snuffing. The stranger leaks pungently.

'We ought to blow into St John's with luck. We're trying to plug the fore-tank now, but she's simply whistling it away,' her captain wails.

'She's sinking like a log,' says Captain Purnall in an undertone. 'Call up the Banks Mark Boat, George.' Our dip-dial shows that we, keeping abreast the tramp, have dropped five hundred feet the last few minutes.

Captain Purnall presses a switch and our signal beam begins to swing through the night, twizzling spokes of light across infinity.

'That'll fetch something,' he says, while Captain Hodgson watches the General Communicator. He has called up the

North Banks Mark Boat, a few hundred miles west, and is reporting the case.

'I'll stand by you,' Captain Purnall roars to the lone figure on the conning-tower.

'Is it as bad as that?' comes the answer. 'She isn't insured. She's mine.'

'Might have guessed as much,' mutters Hodgson. 'Owner's risk is the worst risk of all!'

'Can't I fetch St John's – not even with this breeze?' the voice quavers.

'Stand by to abandon ship. Haven't you *any* lift in you, fore or aft?'

'Nothing but the midship tanks, and they're none too tight. You see, my Ray gave out and—' he coughs in the reek of the escaping gas.

'You poor devil!' This does not reach our friend. 'What does the Mark Boat say, George?'

'Wants to know if there's any danger to traffic. Says she's in a bit of weather herself, and can't quit station. I've turned in a General Call, so even if they don't see our beam some one's bound to help – or else we must. Shall I clear our slings? Hold on! Here we are! A Planet liner, too! She'll be up in a tick!'

'Tell her to have her slings ready,' cries his brother captain. 'There won't be much time to spare . . . Tie up your mate,' he roars to the tramp.

'My mate's all right. It's my engineer. He's gone crazy.'

'Shunt the lift out of him with a spanner. Hurry!'

'But I can make St John's if you'll stand by.'

'You'll make the deep, wet Atlantic in twenty minutes. You're less than fifty-eight hundred now. Get your papers.'

A Planet liner, east-bound, heaves up in a superb spiral and takes the air of us humming. Her underbody colloid is open and her transporter-slings hang down like tentacles. We shut off our beam as she adjusts herself – steering to a hair – over the tramp's conning-tower. The mate comes up, his arm strapped to his side, and stumbles into the cradle. A man with a ghastly scarlet head follows, shouting that he must go back and build up his Ray. The mate assures him that he will find a nice new Ray all ready in the liner's engine-room. The bandaged head goes up wagging excitedly. A youth and a woman follow. The liner cheers hollowly above us, and we see the passengers' faces at the saloon colloid.

'That's a pretty girl. What's the fool waiting for now?' says Captain Purnall.

The skipper comes up, still appealing to us to stand by and see him fetch St John's. He dives below and returns – at which we little human beings in the void cheer louder than ever – with the ship's kitten. Up fly the liner's hissing slings; her underbody crashes home and she hurtles away again. The dial shows less than 3,000 feet.

The Mark Boat signals we must attend to the derelict, now whistling her death-song, as she falls beneath us in long sick zigzags.

'Keep our beam on her and send out a General Warning,' says Captain Purnall, following her down.

There is no need. Not a liner in air but knows the meaning of that vertical beam and gives us and our quarry a wide berth.

'But she'll drown in the water, won't she?' I ask.

'Not always,' is his answer. 'I've known a derelict up-end and sift her engines out of herself and flicker round the Lower Lanes for three weeks on her forward tanks only. We'll run no risks. Pith her, George, and look sharp. There's weather ahead.'

Captain Hodgson opens the underbody colloid, swings the heavy pithing-iron out of its rack which in liners is generally cased as a smoking-room settee, and at two hundred feet releases the catch. We hear the whir of the crescent-shaped arms opening as they descend. The derelict's forehead is punched in, starred across, and rent diagonally. She falls stern first, our beam upon her; slides like a lost soul down that pitiless ladder of light, and the Atlantic takes her.

'A filthy business,' says Hodgson. 'I wonder what it must have been like in the old days?'

The thought had crossed my mind, too. What if that wavering carcass had been filled with the men of the old days, each one of them taught (*that* is the horror of it!) that after death he would very possibly go for ever to unspeakable torment?

And scarcely a generation ago, we (one knows now that we are only our fathers re-enlarged upon the earth), *we*, I say, ripped and rammed and pithed to admiration.

Here Tim, from the Control Platform, shouts that we are to get into our inflators and to bring him his at once.

We hurry into the heavy rubber suits – the engineers are already dressed – and inflate at the air-pump taps. GPO inflators are thrice as thick as a racing man's 'flickers', and chafe abominably under the armpits. George takes the wheel until Tim has blown himself up to the extreme of rotundity. If you kicked him off the cp to the deck he would bounce back. But it is '162' that will do the kicking.

'The Mark Boat's mad – stark ravin' crazy,' he snorts, returning to command. 'She says there's a bad blow-out ahead and wants me to pull over to Greenland. I'll see her pithed first! We wasted half an hour fussing over that dead duck down under, and now I'm expected to go rubbin' my back all round the Pole. What does she think a postal packet's made of? Gummed silk? Tell her we're coming on straight, George.'

George buckles him into the Frame and switches on the Direct Control. Now under Tim's left toe lies the port-engine Accelerator; under his left heel the Reverse, and so with the other foot. The lift-shunt stops stand out on the rim of the steering-wheel where the fingers of his left hand can play on them. At his right hand is the midships engine-lever ready to be thrown into gear at a moment's notice. He leans forward in his belt, eyes glued to the colloid, and one ear cocked toward the General Communicator. Henceforth he is the strength and direction of '162', through whatever may befall.

The Banks Mark Boat is reeling out pages of ABC Directions to the traffic at large. We are to secure all 'loose objects'; hood up our Fleury Rays; and 'on no account to attempt to clear snow from our conning-towers till the weather abates.' Under-powered craft, we are told, can ascend to the limit of their lift, mail-packets to look out for them accordingly; the lower lanes westward are pitting very badly, 'with frequent blow-outs, vortices, laterals, etc.'.

Still the clear dark holds up unblemished. The only warning is the electric skin-tension (I feel as though I were a lace-maker's pillow) and an irritability which the gibbering of the General Communicator increases almost to hysteria.

We have made eight thousand feet since we pithed the tramp and our turbines are giving us an honest two hundred and ten knots.

Very far to the west an elongated blur of red, low down, shows us the North Banks Mark Boat. There are specks of fire round her rising and falling – bewildered planets about an unstable sun – helpless shipping hanging on to her light for company's sake. No wonder she could not quit station.

She warns us to look out for the backlash of the bad vortex in which (her beam shows it) she is even now reeling.

The pits of gloom about us begin to fill with very faintly luminous films – wreathing and uneasy shapes. One forms itself into a globe of pale flame that waits shivering with eagerness till we sweep by. It leaps monstrously across the blackness, alights on the precise tip of our nose, pirouettes there an instant, and swings off. Our roaring bow sinks as though that light were lead – sinks and recovers to lurch and stumble again beneath the next blow-out. Tim's fingers on the lift-shunt strike chords of numbers – 1: 4: 7: – 2: 4: 6: – 7: 5: 3, and so on; for he is running by his tanks only, lifting or lowering her against the uneasy air. All three engines are at work, for the sooner we have skated over this thin ice the better. Higher we dare not go. The whole upper vault is charged with pale krypton vapours, which our skin–friction may excite to unholy manifestations. Between the upper and lower levels – 5,000 and 7,000, hints the Mark Boat – we may perhaps bolt through if . . . Our bow clothes itself in blue flame and falls like a sword. No human skill can keep pace with the changing tensions. A vortex has us by the beak and we dive down a two-thousand foot slant at an angle (the dip-dial and my bouncing body record it) of thirty-five. Our turbines scream shrilly; the propellers cannot bite on the thin air. Tim shunts the lift out of five tanks at once and by sheer weight drives her bullet-wise through the maelstrom till she cushions with a jar on an up-gust, three thousand feet below.

'*Now* we've done it,' says George in my ear. 'Our skin-friction, that last slide, has played Old Harry with the tensions! Look out for laterals, Tim; she'll want some holding.'

'I've got her,' is the answer. 'Come *up*, old woman.'

She comes up nobly, but the laterals buffet her left and right like the pinions of angry angels. She is jolted off her course four ways at once, and cuffed into place again, only to be swung aside and dropped into a new chaos. We are never without a corposant grinning on our bows or rolling head over heels from nose to midships, and to the crack of electricity around and within us is added once or twice the rattle of hail – hail that will never fall on any sea. Slow we must or we may break our back, pitch-poling.

'Air's a perfectly elastic fluid,' roars George above the tumult. 'About as elastic as a head sea off the Fastnet, ain't it?'

He is less than just to the good element. If one intrudes on the Heavens when they are balancing their volt-accounts; if one disturbs the High Gods' market-rates by hurling steel hulls at ninety knots across tremblingly adjusted electric tensions, one must not complain of any rudeness in the reception. Tim met it with an unmoved countenance, one corner of his under lip caught up on a tooth, his eyes fleeting into the blackness twenty miles ahead, and the fierce sparks flying from his knuckles at every turn of the hand. Now and again he shook his head to clear the sweat trickling from his eyebrows, and it was then that George, watching his chance, would slide down the life-rail and swab his face quickly with a big red handkerchief. I never imagined that a human being could so continuously labour and so collectedly think as did Tim through that Hell's half-hour when the flurry was at its worst. We were dragged hither and yon by warm or frozen suctions, belched up on the tops of wulli-was, spun down by vortices and clubbed aside by laterals under a dizzying rush of stars in the company of a drunken moon. I heard the rushing click of the midships engine-lever sliding in and out, the low growl of the lift-shunts, and, louder than the yelling winds without, the scream of the bow-rudder gouging into any lull that promised hold for an instant. At last we began to claw up on a cant, bow-rudder and port-propeller together; only the nicest balancing of tanks saved us from spinning like the rifle-bullet of the old days.

'We've got to hitch to windward of that Mark Boat somehow,' George cried.

'There's no windward,' I protested feebly, where I swung shackled to a stanchion. 'How can there be?'

He laughed – as we pitched into a thousand foot blow-out – that red man laughed beneath his inflated hood!

'Look!' he said. 'We must clear those refugees with a high lift.'

The Mark Boat was below and a little to the sou'west of us, fluctuating in the centre of her distraught galaxy. The air was thick with moving lights at every level. I take it most of them were trying to lie head to wind, but, not being hydras, they failed. An under-tanked Moghrabi boat had risen to the limit of her lift, and, finding no improvement, had dropped a couple of thousand. There she met a superb wulli-wa, and was blown up spinning like a dead leaf. Instead of shutting off she went astern and, naturally, rebounded as from a wall almost into the Mark Boat, whose language (our GC took it in) was humanly simple.

'If they'd only ride it out quietly it 'ud be better,' said George in a calm, while we climbed like a bat above them all. 'But some skippers *will* navigate without enough lift. What does that Tad-boat think she is doing, Tim?'

'Playin' kiss in the ring,' was Tim's unmoved reply. A Trans-Asiatic Direct liner had found a smooth and butted into it full power. But there was a vortex at the tail of that smooth, so the TAD was flipped out like a pea from off a fingernail, braking madly as she fled down and all but over-ending.

'Now I hope she's satisfied,' said Tim. 'I'm glad I'm not a Mark Boat . . . Do I want help?' The General Communicator dial had caught his ear. 'George, you may tell that gentleman with my love – love, remember, George – that I do not want help. Who *is* the officious sardine-tin?'

'A Rimouski drogher on the look-out for a tow.'

'Very kind of the Rimouski drogher. This postal packet isn't being towed at present.'

'Those droghers will go anywhere on a chance of salvage,' George explained. 'We call 'em kittiwakes.'

A long-beaked, bright steel ninety-footer floated at ease for one instant within hail of us, her slings coiled ready for rescues, and a single hand in her open tower. He was smoking. Surrendered to the insurrection of the airs through which we tore our way, he lay in absolute peace. I saw the smoke of his pipe ascend untroubled ere his boat dropped, it seemed, like a stone in a well.

We had just cleared the Mark Boat and her disorderly neighbours when the storm ended as suddenly as it had begun. A shooting-star to northward filled the sky with the green blink of a meteorite dissipating itself in our atmosphere.

Said George: 'That may iron out all the tensions.' Even as he spoke, the conflicting winds came to rest; the levels filled; the laterals died out in long, easy swells; the air-ways were smoothed before us. In less than three minutes the covey round the Mark Boat had shipped their power-lights and whirred away upon their businesses.

'What's happened?' I gasped. The nerve-storm within and the volt-tingle without had passed: my inflators weighed like lead.

'God, He knows!' said Captain George soberly. 'That old shooting-star's skin-friction has discharged the different levels. I've seen it happen before. Phew! What a relief!'

We dropped from ten to six thousand and got rid of our clammy suits. Tim shut off and stepped out of the Frame. The Mark Boat was coming up behind us. He opened the colloid in that heavenly stillness and mopped his face.

'Hello, Williams!' he cried. 'A degree or two out o' station, ain't you?'

'May be,' was the answer from the Mark Boat. 'I've had some company this evening.'

'So I noticed. Wasn't that quite a little draught?'

'I warned you. Why didn't you pull out north? The east-bound packets have.'

'Me? Not till I'm running a Polar consumptives' sanatorium boat. I was squinting through a colloid before you were out of your cradle, my son.'

'I'd be the last man to deny it,' the captain of the Mark Boat replies softly. 'The way you handled her just now – I'm a pretty fair judge of traffic in a volt-hurry – it was a thousand revolutions beyond anything even I've ever seen.'

Tim's back supples visibly to this oiling. Captain George on the cp winks and points to the portrait of a singularly attractive maiden pinned up on Tim's telescope bracket above the steering-wheel.

I see. Wholly and entirely do I see!

There is some talk overhead of 'coming round to tea on Friday', a brief report of the derelict's fate, and Tim volunteers as he descends: 'For an ABC man young Williams is less of a high-tension fool than some. . . Were you thinking of taking her on, George? Then I'll just have a look round that port-thrust – seems to me it's a trifle warm – and we'll jog along.'

The Mark Boat hums off joyously and hangs herself up in her appointed eyrie. Here she will stay a shutterless observatory; a life-boat station; a salvage tug; a court of ultimate appeal-cum-meteorological bureau for three hundred miles in all directions, till Wednesday next when her relief slides across the stars to take her buffeted place. Her black hull, double conning-tower, and ever-ready slings represent all that remains to the planet of that odd old word authority.

She is responsible only to the Aerial Board of Control – the ABC of which Tim speaks so flippantly. But that semi-elected, semi-nominated body of a few score of persons of both sexes, controls this planet. 'Transportation is Civilization', our motto runs. Theoretically, we do what we please so long as we do not interfere with the traffic *and all it implies*. Practically, the ABC confirms or annuls all international arrangements and, to judge from its last report, finds our tolerant, humorous, lazy little planet only too ready to shift the whole burden of public administration on its shoulders.

I discuss this with Tim, sipping maté on the cp while George fans her along over the white blur of the Banks in beautiful upward curves of fifty miles each. The dip-dial translates them on the tape in flowing freehand.

Tim gathers up a skein of it and surveys the last few feet, which record '162's' path through the volt-flurry.

'I haven't had a fever-chart like this to show up in five years,' he says ruefully.

A postal packet's dip-dial records every yard of every run. The tapes then go to the ABC, which collates and makes composite photographs of them for the instruction of captains. Tim studies his irrevocable past, shaking his head.

'Hello! Here's a fifteen-hundred-foot drop at fifty-five degrees! We must have been standing on our heads then, George.'

'You don't say so,' George answers. 'I fancied I noticed it at the time.'

George may not have Captain Purnall's catlike swiftness but he is an artist to the tips of the broad fingers that play on the shunt-stops. The delicious flight-curves come away on the tape with never a waver. The Mark Boat's vertical spindle of light lies down to eastward, setting in the face of the following stars. Westward, where no planet should rise, the triple verticals of Trinity Bay (we keep still to the Southern route) make a low-lifting haze. We seem the only thing at rest under all the heavens; floating at ease till the earth's revolution shall turn up our landing-towers.

And minute by minute our silent clock gives us a sixteen-second mile.

'Some fine night,' says Tim, 'we'll be even with that clock's Master.'

'He's coming now,' says George, over his shoulder. 'I'm chasing the night west.'

The stars ahead dim no more than if a film of mist had been drawn under unobserved, but the deep air-boom on our skin changes to a joyful shout.

'The dawn-gust,' says Tim. 'It'll go on to meet the Sun. Look! Look! There's the dark being crammed back over our bows! Come to the after-colloid. I'll show you something.'

The engine-room is hot and stuffy; the clerks in the coach are asleep, and the Slave of the Ray is ready to follow them. Tim slides open the aft colloid and reveals the curve of the world – the ocean's deepest purple – edged with fuming and intolerable gold. Then the Sun rises and through the colloid strikes out our lamps. Tim scowls in his face.

'Squirrels in a cage,' he mutters. 'That's all we are. Squirrels in a cage! He's going twice as fast as us. Just you wait a few years, my shining friend, and we'll take steps that will amaze you. *We*'ll Joshua you!'

Yes, that is our dream: to turn all earth into the Vale of Ajalon at our pleasure. So far, we can drag out the dawn to twice its normal length in these latitudes. But some day – even on the Equator – we shall hold the Sun level in his full stride.

Now we look down on a sea thronged with heavy traffic. A big submersible breaks water suddenly. Another and another follows with a swash and a suck and a savage bubbling of relieved pressures. The deep-sea freighters are rising to lung up after the long night, and the leisurely ocean is all patterned with peacock's eyes of foam.

'We'll lung up, too,' says Tim, and when we return to the cp George shuts off, the colloids are opened, and the fresh air sweeps her out. There is no hurry. The old contracts (they will be revised at the end of the year) allow twelve hours for a run which any packet can put behind her in ten. So we breakfast in the arms of an easterly slant which pushes us along at a languid twenty.

To enjoy life, and tobacco, begin both on a sunny morning half a mile or so above the dappled Atlantic cloud-belts and after a volt-flurry which has cleared and tempered your nerves. While we discussed the thickening traffic with the superiority that comes of having a high level reserved to ourselves, we heard (and I for the first time) the morning hymn on a Hospital boat.

She was cloaked by a skein of ravelled fluff beneath us and we caught the chant before she rose into the sunlight. '*Oh, ye Winds of God,*' sang the unseen voices: '*bless ye the Lord! Praise Him and magnify Him for ever!*'

We slid off our caps and joined in. When our shadow fell across her great open platforms they looked up and stretched out their hands neighbourly while they sang. We could see the doctors and the nurses and the white-button-like faces of the cot-patients. She passed slowly beneath us, heading northward, her hull, wet with the dews of the night, all ablaze in the sunshine. So took she the shadow of a cloud and vanished, her song continuing. '*Oh, ye holy and humble men of heart, bless ye the Lord! Praise Him and magnify Him for ever.*'

'She's a public lunger or she wouldn't have been singing the *Benedicite*; and she's a Greenlander or she wouldn't have snow-blinds over her colloids,' said George at last. 'She'll be bound for Frederikshavn or one of the Glacier sanatoriums for a month. If she was an accident ward she'd be hung up at the eight-thousand-foot level. Yes – consumptives.'

'Funny how the new things are the old things. I've read in books,' Tim answered, 'that savages used to haul their sick and wounded up to the tops of hills because microbes were fewer there. We hoist 'em into sterilized air for a while. Same idea. How much do the doctors say we've added to the average life of a man?'

'Thirty years,' says George with a twinkle in his eye. 'Are we going to spend 'em all up here, Tim?'

'Flap ahead, then. Flap ahead. Who's hindering?' the senior captain laughed, as we went in.

We held a good lift to clear the coastwise and Continental shipping; and we had need of it. Though our route is in no sense a populated one, there is a steady trickle of traffic this way along. We met Hudson Bay furriers out of the Great Preserve, hurrying to make their departure from Bonavista with sable and black fox for the insatiable markets. We over-crossed Keewatin liners, small and cramped; but their captains, who see no land between Trepassy and Blanco, know what gold they bring back from West Africa. Trans-Asiatic Directs we met, soberly ringing the world round the Fiftieth Meridian at an honest seventy knots; and white-painted Ackroyd & Hunt fruiters out of the south fled beneath us, their ventilated hulls whistling like Chinese kites. Their market is in the North among the northern sanatoria where you can smell their grape-fruit and bananas across the cold snows. Argentine beef boats we sighted too, of enormous capacity and unlovely outline. They, too, feed the northern health stations in ice-bound ports where submersibles dare not rise.

Yellow-bellied ore-flats and Ungava petrol-tanks punted down leisurely out of the north, like strings of unfrightened wild duck. It does not pay to 'fly' minerals and oil a mile farther than is necessary; but the risks of transhipping to submersibles in the ice-pack off Nain or Hebron are so great that these heavy freighters fly down to Halifax direct, and scent the air as they go. They are the biggest tramps aloft except the Athabasca grain-tubs. But these last, now that the wheat is moved, are busy, over the world's shoulder, timber-lifting in Siberia.

We held to the St Lawrence (it is astonishing how the old waterways still pull us children of the air), and followed his broad line of black between its drifting ice-blocks, all down the Park that the wisdom of our fathers – but every one knows the Quebec run.

We dropped to the Heights Receiving Towers twenty minutes ahead of time, and there hung at ease till the Yokohama Intermediate Packet could pull out and give us our proper slip. It was curious to watch the action of the holding-down clips all along the frosty river front as the boats cleared or came to rest. A big Hamburger was leaving Pont Levis and her crew, unshipping the platform railings, began to sing *Elsinore* – the oldest of our chanteys. You know it of course:

Mother Rugen's tea-house on the Baltic –
Forty couples waltzing on the floor!
And you can watch my Ray,
For I must go away
And dance with Ella Sweyn at Elsinore!

Then, while they sweated home the covering-plates:

Nor-Nor-Nor-Nor-
West from Sourabaya to the Baltic –
Ninety knot an hour to the Skaw!
Mother Rugen's tea-house on the Baltic
And a dance with Ella Sweyn at Elsinore!

The clips parted with a gesture of indignant dismissal, as though Quebec, glittering under her snows, were casting out these light and unworthy lovers. Our signal came from the Heights. Tim turned and floated up, but surely then it was with passionate appeal that the great tower arms flung open – or did I think so because on the upper staging a little hooded figure also opened her arms wide toward her father?

In ten seconds the coach with its clerks clashed down to the receiving-caisson; the hostlers displaced the engineers at the idle turbines, and Tim, prouder of this than all, introduced me to the maiden of the photograph on the shelf. 'And by the way,' said he to her, stepping forth in sunshine under the hat of civil life, 'I saw young Williams in the Mark Boat. I've asked him to tea on Friday.'

AERIAL BOARD OF CONTROL

Lights

No changes in England Inland lights for week ending Dec. 18th.

CAPE VERDE – Week ending Dec. 18th. Verde inclined guide-light changes from 1st proximo to triple flash – green white green – in place of occulting red as heretofore. The warning light for Harmattan winds will be continuous vertical glare (white) on all oases of trans-Saharan NE by E. Main Routes.

INVERCARGIL (NZ) – From 1st prox.: extreme southerly light (double red) will exhibit white beam inclined 45 degrees on approach of Southerly Buster. Traffic flies high off this coast between April and October.

TABLE BAY – Devil's Peak Glare removed to Simonsberg. Traffic making Table Mountain coastwise keep all lights from Three Anchor Bay at least two thousand feet under, and do not round to till East of E. shoulder Devil's Peak.

SANDHEADS LIGHT – Green triple vertical marks new private landing-stage for Bay and Burma traffic only.

SNAEFELL JOKUL – White occulting light withdrawn for winter.

PATAGONIA – No summer light south Cape Pilar. This includes Staten Island and Port Stanley.

C. NAVARIN – Quadruple fog flash (white), one minute intervals (new).

EAST CAPE – Fog flash – single white with single bomb, 30-sec intervals (new).

MALAYAN ARCHIPELAGO – Lights unreliable owing eruptions. Lay from Cape Somerset to Singapore direct, keeping highest levels.

FOR THE BOARD:

Catterthun }
St Just } *Lights.*
Van Hedder }

Casualties

Week ending Dec. 18th.

SABLE ISLAND – Green single barbette-tower freighter, number indistinguishable, up-ended, and fore-tank pierced after collision, passed 300-ft level 2 PM Dec. 15th. Watched to water and pithed by Mark Boat.

NF BANKS – Postal Packet 162 reports *Halma* freighter (Fowey–St John's) abandoned, leaking after weather, 46° 15′ N 50° 15′ W. Crew rescued by Planet liner *Asteroid*. Watched to water and pithed by Postal Packet, Dec. 14th.

KERGUELEN, MARK BOAT reports last call from *Cymena* freighter (Gayer Tong Huk & Co) taking water and sinking in snow-storm South McDonald Islands. No wreckage recovered. Messages and wills of crew at all ABC offices.

FEZZAN – TAD freighter *Ulema* taken ground during Harmattan on Akakus Range. Under plates strained. Crew at Ghat where repairing Dec. 13th.

BISCAY, MARK BOAT reports *Carducci* (Valandingham Line) slightly spiked in western gorge Point de Benasque. Passengers transferred *Andorra* (Fulton Line). Barcelona Mark Boat salving cargo Dec. 12th.

ASCENSION, MARK BOAT – Wreck of unknown racing-plane, Parden rudder, wire-stiffened xylonite vans, and Harliss engine-seating, sighted and salved 7° 20′ S 18° 41′ W. Dec. 15th. Photos at all ABC offices.

Missing

No answer to General Call having been received during the last week from following overdues, they are posted as missing:

Atlantis, W. 17630 . .	Canton – Valparaiso
Audhumla, W. 889 . .	Stockholm – Odessa
Berenice, W. 2206 . .	Riga – Vladivostock
Draco, E. 446	Coventry – Puntas Arenas
Tontine, E. 3068 . . .	C. Wrath – Ungava
Wu-Sung, E. 41776 . .	Hankow – Lobito Bay

General Call (all Mark Boats) out for:

Jane Eyre, W. 6990 . .	Port Rupert – City of Mexico
Santander, W. 5514 . .	Gobi Desert – Manila
V. Edmundsun, E. 9690	Kandahar – Fiume

Broke for Obstruction, and Quitting Levels

VALKYRIE (racing plane), A. J. Hartley owner, New York (twice warned).

GEISHA (racing plane), S. van Cott owner, Philadelphia (twice warned).

MARVEL OF PERU (racing plane), J. X. Peixoto owner, Rio de Janeiro (twice warned).

FOR THE BOARD:
Lazareff
McKeough } *Traffic*
Goldblatt

NOTES

High-level Sleet

The Northern weather so far shows no sign of improvement. From all quarters come complaints of the unusual prevalence of sleet at the higher levels. Racing-planes and digs alike have suffered severely – the former from unequal deposits of half-frozen slush on their vans (and only those who have 'held up' a badly balanced plane in a cross-wind know what that means), and the latter from loaded bows and snow-cased bodies. As a consequence, the Northern and North-western upper levels have been practically abandoned, and the high fliers have returned to the ignoble security of the Three, Five, and Six hundred foot levels. But there remain a few undaunted sun-hunters who, in spite of frozen stays and ice-jammed connecting rods, still haunt the blue empyrean.

Bat-boat Racing

The scandals of the past few years have at last moved the yachting world to concerted action in regard to 'bat' boat racing.

We have been treated to the spectacle of what are practically keeled racing-planes driven a clear five foot or more above the water, and only eased down to touch their so-called 'native element' as they near the line. Judges and starters have been conveniently blind to this absurdity, but the public demonstration off St Catherine's Light at the Autumn Regattas has borne ample, if tardy, fruit. In the future the 'bat' is to be a boat, and the long-unheeded demand of the true sportsman for 'no daylight under mid-keel in smooth water' is in a fair way to be conceded. The new rule severely restricts plane area and lift alike. The gas compartments are permitted both fore and aft, as in the old type, but the water-ballast central tank is rendered obligatory. These things work, if not for perfection, at least for the evolution of a sane and wholesome *water-borne cruiser*. The type of rudder is unaffected by the new rules, so we may expect to see the Long-Davidson make (the patent on which has just expired) come largely into use henceforward, though the strain on the stern-post in turning at speeds over forty miles an hour is admittedly very severe. But bat-boat racing has a great future before it.

Crete and the ABC

The story of the recent Cretan crisis, as told in the *ABC Monthly Report*, is not without humour. Till October 25th, Crete, as all our planet knows, was the sole surviving European repository of 'autonomous institutions', 'local self-government', and the rest of the archaic lumber devised in the past for the confusion of human affairs. She has lived practically on the tourist traffic attracted by her annual pageants of Parliaments, Boards, Municipal Councils, etc., etc. Last summer the islanders grew wearied, as their premier explained, of 'playing at being savages for pennies', and proceeded to pull down all the landing-towers on the island and shut off general communication till such time as the ABC should annex them. For side-splitting comedy we would refer our readers to the correspondence between the

Board of Control and the Cretan premier during the 'war'. However, all's well that ends well. The ABC have taken over the administration of Crete on normal lines; and tourists must go elsewhere to witness the 'debates', 'resolutions', and 'popular movements' of the old days. The only people to suffer will be the Board of Control, which is grievously overworked already. It is easy enough to condemn the Cretans for their laziness; but when one recalls the large, prosperous, and presumably public-spirited communities which during the last few years have deliberately thrown themselves into the hands of the ABC, one cannot be too hard upon St Paul's old friends.

CORRESPONDENCE

Skylarking on the Equator

To the Editor: Only last week, while crossing the Equator (W. 26–15), I became aware of a furious and irregular cannonading some fifteen or twenty knots S. 4 E. Descending to the 500-ft level, I found a party of Transylvanian tourists engaged in exploding scores of the largest pattern atmospheric bombs (ABC standard) and, in the intervals of their pleasing labours, firing bow and stern smoke-ring swivels. This orgy – I can give it no other name – went on for at least two hours, and naturally produced violent electric derangements. My compasses, of course, were thrown out, my bow was struck twice, and I received two brisk shocks from the lower platform-rail. On remonstrating, I was told that these 'professors' were engaged in scientific experiments. The extent of their 'scientific' knowledge may be judged by the fact that they expected to produce (I give their own words) 'a little blue sky' if 'they went on long enough'. This in the heart of the Doldrums at 450 feet! I have no objection to any amount of blue sky in its proper place (it can be found at the 4,000 level for practically twelve months out of the year), but I submit, with all deference to the educational needs of Transylvania, that 'skylarking' in the centre of a main-travelled road where, at the best of times, electricity literally drips off one's stanchions and screw blades, is unnecessary. When my friends had finished, the road was seared, and blown, and pitted with unequal pressure-layers, spirals, vortices, and readjustments for at least an hour. I pitched badly twice in an upward rush – solely due to these diabolical throw-downs – that came near to wrecking my propeller. Equatorial work at low levels is trying enough in all conscience without the added terrors of scientific hooliganism in the Doldrums.

Rhyl. J. VINCENT MATHEN

[We entirely sympathize with Professor Mathen's views, but till the Board sees fit to further regulate the Southern areas in which scientific experiments may be conducted, we shall always be exposed to the risk which our correspondent describes. Unfortunately, a chimera bombinating in a vacuum is, nowadays, only too capable of producing secondary causes. – *Editor*.]

Answers to Correspondents

VIGILANS – The Laws of Auroral Derangements are still imperfectly understood. Any overheated motor may of course 'seize' without warning; but so many complaints have reached us of accidents similar to yours while shooting the Aurora that we are inclined to believe with Lavalle that the upper strata of the Aurora Borealis are practically one big electric 'leak', and that the paralysis of your engines was due to complete magnetization of all metallic parts. Low-flying planes often 'glue up' when near the Magnetic Pole, and there is no reason in science why the same disability should not be experienced at higher levels when the Auroras are 'delivering' strongly.

INDIGNANT – On your own showing, you were not under control. That you could not hoist the necessary NUC lights on approaching a traffic-lane because your electrics had short-circuited is a misfortune which might befall any one. The ABC, being responsible for the planet's traffic, cannot, however, make allowance for this kind of misfortune. A reference to the Code will show that you were fined on the lower scale.

PLANISTON – (1) The Five Thousand Kilometre (overland) was won last year by L. V. Rautsch; R. M. Rautsch, his brother, in the same week pulling off the Ten Thousand (oversea). R. M.'s average worked out at a fraction over 500 kilometres per hour, thus constituting a record. (2) Theoretically, there is no limit to the lift of a dirigible. For commercial and practical purposes 15,000 tons is accepted as the most manageable.

PATERFAMILIAS – None whatever. He is liable for direct damage both to your chimneys and any collateral damage caused by fall of bricks into garden, etc, etc. Bodily inconvenience and mental anguish may be included, but the average courts are not, as a rule, swayed by sentiment. If you can prove that his grapnel removed *any* portion of your roof, you had better rest your case on decoverture of domicile (see Parkins *v* Duboulay). We sympathize with your position, but the night of the 14th was stormy and confused, and – you may have to anchor on a stranger's chimney yourself some night. *Verbum sap!*

ALDEBARAN – (1) War, as a paying concern, ceased in 1967. (2) The Convention of London expressly reserves to every nation the right of waging war so long as it does not interfere with the traffic *and all that implies.* (3) The ABC was constituted in 1949.

LMD – (1) Keep her full head-on at half power, taking advantage of the lulls to speed up and creep into it. She will strain much less this way than in quartering across a gale. (2) Nothing is to be gained by reversing into a following gale, and there is always risk of a turn-over. (3) The formulæ for stun'sle brakes are uniformly unreliable, and will continue to be so as long as air is compressible.

PEGAMOID – (1) Personally we prefer glass or flux compounds to any other material for winter work nose-caps as being absolutely non-hygroscopic. (2) We cannot recommend any particular make.

PULMONAR – (1) For the symptoms you describe, try the

Gobi Desert Sanatoria. The low levels of most of the Saharan Sanatoria are against them except at the outset of the disease. (2) We do not recommend boarding-houses or hotels in this column.

BEGINNER – On still days the air above a large inhabited city being slightly warmer – *ie,* thinner – than the atmosphere of the surrounding country, a plane drops a little on entering the rarefied area, precisely as a ship sinks a little in fresh water. Hence the phenomena of 'jolt' and your 'inexplicable collisions' with factory chimneys. In air, as on earth, it is safest to fly high.

EMERGENCY – There is only one rule of the road in air, earth, and water. Do you want the firmament to yourself?

PICCIOLA – Both Poles have been overdone in Art and Literature. Leave them to Science for the next twenty years. You did not send a stamp with your verses.

NORTH NIGERIA – The Mark Boat was within her right in warning you off the Reserve. The shadow of a low-flying dirigible scares the game. You can buy all the photos you need at Sokoto.

NEW ERA – It is not etiquette to overcross an ABC official's boat without asking permission. He is one of the body responsible for the planet's traffic, and for that reason must not be interfered with. You, presumably, are out on your own business or pleasure, and must leave him alone. For humanity's sake don't try to be 'democratic'.

EXCORIATED – All inflators chafe sooner or later. You must go on till your skin hardens by practice. Meantime Vaseline.

REVIEW

The Life of Xavier Lavalle

(REVIEWED BY RÉNÉ TALLAND.
ÉCOLE AËRONAUTIQUE, PARIS)

Ten years ago Lavalle, 'that imperturbable dreamer of the heavens', as Lazareff hailed him, gathered together the fruits of a life-time's labour, and gave it, with well-justified contempt, to a world bound hand and foot to Barald's Theory of Vertices and 'compensating electric nodes'. 'They shall see,' he wrote – in that immortal postscript to *The Heart of the Cyclone* – 'the Laws whose existence they derided written in fire *beneath* them.'

'But even here,' he continues, 'there is no finality. Better a thousand times my conclusions should be discredited than that my dead name should lie across the threshold of the temple of Science – a bar to further inquiry.'

So died Lavalle – a prince of the Powers of the Air, and even at his funeral Céllier jested at 'him who had gone to discover the secrets of the Aurora Borealis.'

If I choose thus to be banal, it is only to remind you that Céllier's theories are today as exploded as the ludicrous deductions of the Spanish school. In the place of their fugitive and warring dreams we have, definitely, Lavalle's Law of the Cyclone which he surprised in darkness and cold at the foot of the overarching throne of the Aurora Borealis. It is there that I, intent on my own investigations, have passed and re-passed a hundred times the worn leonine face, white as the snow beneath him, furrowed with wrinkles like the seams and gashes upon the North Cape; the nervous hand, integrally a part of the mechanism of his flighter; and above all, the wonderful lambent eyes turned to the zenith.

'Master,' I would cry as I moved respectfully beneath him, 'what is it you seek today?' and always the answer, clear and without doubt, from above: 'The old secret, my son!'

The immense egotism of youth forced me on my own path, but (cry of the human always!) had I known – if I had known – I would many times have bartered my poor laurels for the privilege, such as Tinsley and Herrera possess, of having aided him in his monumental researches.

It is to the filial piety of Victor Lavalle that we owe the two volumes consecrated to the ground-life of his father, so full of the holy intimacies of the domestic hearth. Once returned from the abysms of the utter North to that little house upon the outskirts of Meudon, it was not the philosopher, the daring observer, the man of iron energy that imposed himself on his family, but a fat and even plaintive jester, a farceur incarnate and kindly, the co-equal of his children, and, it must be written, not seldom the comic despair of Madame Lavalle, who, as she writes five years after the marriage, to her venerable mother, found 'in this unequalled intellect whose name I bear the abandon of a large and very untidy boy.' Here is her letter:

'Xavier returned from I do not know where at midnight, absorbed in calculations on the eternal question of his Aurora – *la belle Aurore*, whom I begin to hate. Instead of anchoring – I had set out the guide-light above our roof, so he had but to descend and fasten the plane – he wandered, profoundly distracted, above the town with his anchor down! Figure to yourself, dear mother, it is the roof of the mayor's house that the grapnel first engages! That I do not regret, for the mayor's wife and I are not sympathetic; but when Xavier uproots my pet araucaria and bears it across the garden into the conservatory I protest at the top of my voice. Little Victor in his night-clothes runs to the window, enormously amused at the parabolic flight without reason, for it is too dark to see the grapnel, of my prized tree. The Mayor of Meudon thunders at our door in the name of the Law, demanding, I suppose, my husband's head. Here is the conversation through the megaphone – Xavier is two hundred feet above us:

'"Mons. Lavalle, descend and make reparation for outrage of domicile. Descend, Mons. Lavalle!"

'No one answers.

'"Xavier Lavalle, in the name of the Law, descend and submit to process for outrage of domicile."

'Xavier, roused from his calculations, comprehending only the last words: "Outrage of domicile? My dear mayor, who is the man that has corrupted thy Julie?"

'The mayor, furious, "Xavier Lavalle –"

'Xavier, interrupting: "I have not that felicity. I am only a dealer in cyclones!"

'My faith, he raised one then! All Meudon attended in the

streets, and my Xavier, after a long time comprehending what he had done, excused himself in a thousand apologies. At last the reconciliation was effected in our house over a supper at two in the morning – Julie in a wonderful costume of compromises, and I have her and the mayor pacified in bed in the blue room.'

And on the next day, while the mayor rebuilds his roof, her Xavier departs anew for the Aurora Borealis, there to commence his life's work. M. Victor Lavalle tells us of that historic collision (*en plane*) on the flank of Hecla between Herrera, then a pillar of the Spanish school, and the man destined to confute his theories and lead him intellectually captive. Even through the years, the immense laugh of Lavalle as he sustains the Spaniard's wrecked plane, and cries: 'Courage! *I* shall not fall till I have found Truth, and I hold *you* fast!' rings like the call of trumpets. This is all Lavalle whom the world, immersed in speculations of immediate gain, did not know nor suspect – the Lavalle whom they adjudged to the last a pedant and a theorist.

The human, as apart from the scientific, side (developed in his own volumes) of his epoch-making discoveries is marked with a simplicity, clarity, and good sense beyond praise. I would specially refer such as doubt the sustaining influence of ancestral faith upon character and will to the eleventh and nineteenth chapters, in which are contained the opening and consummation of the Tellurionical Records extending over nine years. Of their tremendous significance be sure that the modest house at Meudon knew as little as that the Records would one day be the planet's standard in all official meteorology. It was enough for them that their Xavier – this son, this father, this husband – ascended periodically to commune with powers, it might be angelic, beyond their comprehension, and that they united daily in prayers for his safety.

'Pray for me,' he says upon the eve of each of his excursions, and returning, with an equal simplicity, he renders thanks 'after supper in the little room where he kept his barometers.'

To the last Lavalle was a Catholic of the old school, accepting – he who had looked into the very heart of the lightnings – the dogmas of papal infallibility, of absolution, of confession – of relics great and small. Marvellous – enviable contradiction!

The completion of the Tellurionical Records closed what Lavalle himself was pleased to call the theoretical side of his labours – labours from which the youngest and least impressionable planeur might well have shrunk. He had traced through cold and heat, across the deeps of the oceans, with instruments of his own invention, over the inhospitable heart of the polar ice and the sterile visage of the deserts, league by league, patiently, unweariedly, remorselessly, from their ever-shifting cradle under the magnetic pole to their exalted death-bed in the utmost ether of the upper atmosphere – each one of the Isoconical Tellurions – Lavalle's Curves, as we call them today. He had disentangled the nodes of their intersections, assigning to each its regulated period of flux and reflux. Thus equipped, he summons Herrera and Tinsley, his pupils, to the final demonstration as calmly as though he were ordering his flighter for some mid-day journey to Marseilles.

'I have proved my thesis,' he writes. 'It remains now only that you should witness the proof. We go to Manila tomorrow. A cyclone will form off the Pescadores S. 17 E. in four days, and will reach its maximum intensity twenty-seven hours after inception. It is there I will show you the Truth.'

A letter heretofore unpublished from Herrera to Madame Lavalle tells us how the Master's prophecy was verified.

I will not destroy its simplicity or its significance by any attempt to quote. Note well, though, that Herrera's preoccupation throughout that day and night of superhuman strain is always for the Master's bodily health and comfort. 'At such a time,' he writes, 'I forced the Master to take the broth'; or 'I made him put on the fur coat as you told me.' Nor is Tinsley (see pp 184, 185) less concerned. He prepares the nourishment. He cooks eternally, imperturbably, suspended in the chaos of which the Master interprets the meaning.

Tinsley, bowed down with the laurels of both hemispheres, raises himself to yet nobler heights in his capacity of a devoted *chef*. It is almost unbelievable! And yet men write of the Master as cold, aloof, self-contained. Such characters do not elicit the joyous and unswerving devotion which Lavalle commanded throughout life. Truly, we have changed very little in the course of the ages! The secrets of earth and sky and the links that bind them, we felicitate ourselves we are on the road to discover; but our neighbours' heart and mind we misread, we misjudge, we condemn – now as ever. Let all, then, who love a man read these most human, tender, and wise volumes.

MISCELLANEOUS

WANTS

REQUIRED IMMEDIATELY, for East Africa, a thoroughly competent Plane and Dirigible Driver, acquainted with Petrol Radium and Helium motors and generators. Low-level work only, but must understand heavy-weight digs.

MOSSAMEDES TRANSPORT ASSOC.
84 Palestine Buildings, E.C.

MAN WANTED—DIG DRIVER for Southern Alps with Saharan summer trips. High levels, high speed, high wages.

Apply M. SIDNEY
Hotel San Stefano. Monte Carlo.

FAMILY DIRIGIBLE. A COMpetent, steady man wanted for slow speed, low level Tangye dirigible. No night work, no sea trips. Must be member of the Church of England, and make himself useful in the garden.

M. R.,
The Rectory, Gray's Barton, Wilts.

COMMERCIAL DIG, CENTRAL and Southern Europe. A smart, active man for a L.M.T. Dig. Night work only. Headquarters London and Cairo. A linguist preferred.

BAGMAN
Charing Cross Hotel, W. C. (urgent.)

FOR SALE—A BARGAIN—Single plane, narrow-gauge vans, Pinke motor. Restayed this autumn. Hansen air-kit, 38 in. chest, 15½ collar. Can be seen by appointment.

N.2650. This office.

The Bee-Line Bookshop

BELT'S WAY-BOOKS, giving town lights for all towns over 4,000 pop. as laid down by A.B.C.

THE WORLD. Complete 2 vols. Thin Oxford, limp back. 12s. 6d.

BELT'S COASTAL ITINERARY. Shore Lights of the World. 7s. 6d.

THE TRANSATLANTIC AND MEDITERRANEAN TRAFFIC LINES. (By authority of the A.B.C.) Paper, 1s.6d.: cloth, 2s. 6d. Ready Jan. 15.

ARCTIC AEROPLANING. Siemens and Galt. Cloth, bds. 8s. 6d.

LAVALLE'S HEART OF THE CYCLONE, with supplementary charts. 4s. 6d.

RIMINGTON'S PITFALLS IN THE AIR, and Table of Comparative Densities. 3s. 6d.

ANGELO'S DESERT IN A DIRIGIBLE. New edition, revised. 5s. 9d.

VAUGHAN'S PLANE RACING IN CALM AND STORM. 2s. 6d.

VAUGHAN'S HINTS TO THE AIR-MATEUR. 1s.

HOFMAN'S LAWS OF LIFT AND VELOCITY. With diagrams, 3s. 6d.

DE VITRE'S THEORY OF SHIFTING BALLAST IN DIRIGIBLES. 2s. 6d.

SANGER'S WEATHERS OF THE WORLD. 4s.

SANGER'S TEMPERATURES AT HIGH ALTITUDES. 4s.

HAWKIN'S FOG AND HOW TO AVOID IT. 3s.

VAN ZUYLANS' SECONDARY EFFECTS OF THUNDERSTORMS. 4s. 6d.

DAHLGREN'S AIR CURRENTS AND EPIDEMIC DISEASES. 5s. 6d.

REDMAYNE'S DISEASE AND THE BAROMETER. 7s. 6d.

WALTON'S HEALTH RESORTS OF THE GOBI AND SHAMO. 3s. 6d.

WALTON'S THE POLE AND PULMONARY COMPLAINTS. 7s. 6d.

MUTLOW'S HIGH LEVEL BACTERIOLOGY. 7s. 6d.

HALLIWELL'S ILLUMINATED STAR MAP, with clockwork attachment, giving apparent motion of heavens, boxed, complete with clamps for binnacle, 36 inch size, only £2. 2. 0. (Invaluable for night work.) With A.B.C. certificate, £3. 10s. 0d.

Zalinski's Standard Works:
PASSES OF THE HIMALAYAS, 5s.
PASSES OF THE SIERRAS, 5s.
PASSES OF THE ROCKIES, 5s.
PASSES OF THE URALS, 5s.
The four boxed, limp cloth, with charts, 15s.

GRAY'S AIR CURRENTS IN MOUNTAIN GORGES, 7s. 6d.

A. C. BELT & SON, READING

SAFETY WEAR FOR AERONAUTS

Flickers! **Flickers!** **Flickers!**

High Level Flickers

"He that is down need fear no fall"
Fear not! You will fall lightly as down!

¶ Hansen's air-kits are down in all respects. Tremendous reductions in prices previous to winter stocking. Pure para kit with cellulose seat and shoulder-pads, weighted to balance. Unequalled for all drop-work.

Our trebly resilient heavy kit is the *ne plus ultra* of comfort and safety.

Gas-buoyed, waterproof, hail-proof, non-conducting Flickers with pipe and nozzle fitting all types of generator. Graduated tap on left hip.

Hansen's Flickers Lead the Aerial Flight
197 Oxford Street

The new weighted Flicker with tweed or cheviot surface cannot be distinguished from the ordinary suit till inflated.

Flickers! **Flickers!** **Flickers!**

APPLIANCES FOR AIR PLANES

What

"SKID"

was to our forefathers on the ground.

"PITCH"

is to their sons in the air.

The popularity of the large, unwieldy, slow, expensive Dirigible over the light, swift, Plane is mainly due to the former's immunity from pitch.

Collison's forward-socketed Air Van renders it impossible for any plane to pitch. The C.F.S. is automatic, simple as a shutter, certain as a power hammer, safe as oxygen. Fitted to any make of plane.

COLLISON

186 Brompton Road

Workshops, *Chiswick*

LUNDIE & MATHERS

Sole Agts for East'n Hemisphere

Starters and Guides

Hotel, club, and private house plane-starters, slips and guides affixed by skilled workmen in accordance with local building laws.

Rackstraw's forty-foot collapsible steel starters with automatic release at end of travel—prices per foot run, clamps and crampons included. The safest on the market.

Weaver & Denison
Middleboro

AIR PLANES AND DIRIGIBLE GOODS

Remember

Planes are swift—so is Death
Planes are cheap—so is Life

Why does the plane builder insist on the safety of his machines?

Methinks the gentleman protests too much.

The Standard Dig Construction Company do not build kites.

They build, equip and guarantee dirigibles.

Standard Dig Construction Co.

Millwall and Buenos Ayres

HOVERS

POWELL'S
Wind Hovers

for 'planes lying-to in heavy weather, save the motor and strain on the forebody. Will not send to leeward. "Albatross" wind-hovers, rigid-ribbed; according to h.p. and weight.

We fit and test free to 40° east of Greenwich

L. & W. POWELL
196 Victoria Street, W.

Remember

We shall always be pleased to see you.

We build and test and guarantee our dirigibles for all purposes. They go up when you please and they do not come down till you please.

You can please yourself, but—you might as well choose a dirigible.

STANDARD DIRIGIBLE CONSTRUCTION CO.
Millwall *and* Buenos Ayres

Gayer & Hutt

Birmingham Eng. AND **Birmingham Ala.**

Towers, Landing Stages, Slips and Lifts

public and private

Contractors to the A.B.C., South-Western European Postal Construction Dept.

Sole patentees and owners of the Collison anti-quake diagonal tower-tie. Only gold medal Kyoto Exhibition of Aerial Appliances, 1997.

AIR PLANES AND DIRIGIBLES

C.M.C.

Our Synthetical Mineral

BEARINGS

are chemically and crystallogically identical with the minerals whose names they bear. Any size, any surface.

Diamond, Rock-Crystal, Agate and Ruby Bearings—cups, caps and collars for the higher speeds.

For tractor bearings and spindles—Imperative.

For rear propellers—Indispensable.

For all working parts—Advisable.

Commercial Minerals Co.
107 Minories

Resurgam!

IF YOU HAVE NOT CLOTHED YOURSELF IN A

Normandie Resurgam

YOU WILL PROBABLY NOT BE INTERESTED IN OUR NEXT WEEK'S LIST OF AIR-KIT.

Resurgam Air-Kit Emporium

HYMANS & GRAHAM

1198

Lower Broadway, New York

Remember!

It is now nearly a generation since the Plane was to supersede the Dirigible for all purposes.

TO-DAY *none* of the Planet's freight is carried *en plane*.

Less than two per cent of the Planet's passengers are carried *en plane*.

We design, equip and guarantee Dirigibles for all purposes.

Standard Dig Construction Company
MILLWALL and BUENOS AYRES

BAT-BOATS

Flint & Mantel

Southampton

FOR SALE

at the end of Season the following Bat-Boats:

GRISELDA, 65 knt., 42 ft., 430 (nom.) Maginnis Motor. under-rake rudder.

MABELLE, 50 knt., 40 ft., 310 Hargreaves Motor, Douglas' lock-steering gear.

IVEMONA, 50 knt., 35 ft., 300 Hargreaves (Radium accelerator), Miller keel and rudder.

The above are well known on the South Coast as sound, wholesome knockabout boats, with ample cruising accommodation. *Griselda* carries spare set of Hofman racing vans and can be lifted three foot clear in smooth water with ballast-tank swung aft. The others do not lift clear of water, and are recommended for beginners.

Also by private treaty, racing B. B. *Tarpon* (76 winning flags) 120 knt., 60 ft.; Long-Davidson double under-rake rudder, new this season and unstrained. 850 nom. Maginnis motor, Radium relays and Pond generator. Bronze breakwater forward and treble reinforced forefoot and entry. Talfourd rockered keel. Triple set of Hofman vans, giving maximum lifting surface of 5327 sq. ft.

Tarpon has been lifted *and held* seven feet for two miles between touch and touch.

Our Autumn List of racing and family Bats ready on the 9th January.

AIR PLANES AND STARTERS

Hinks's Moderator

¶ Monorail overhead starter for family and private planes up to twenty-five foot over all

Absolutely
Safe

Hinks & Co., Birmingham

J. D. ARDAGH

I AM NOT CONCERNED WITH YOUR PLANE AFTER IT LEAVES MY GUIDES, BUT *TILL THEN* I HOLD MYSELF PERSONALLY RESPONSIBLE FOR YOUR LIFE, SAFETY, AND COMFORT. MY HYDRAULIC BUFFER-STOP *CANNOT* RELEASE TILL THE MOTORS ARE WORKING UP TO BEARING SPEED, THUS SECURING A SAFE AND GRACEFUL FLIGHT WITHOUT PITCHING.

Remember our motto, "*Upward and Outward,*" and do not trust yourself to so-called "rigid" guide-bars

J. D. ARDAGH, BELFAST AND TURIN

ACCESSORIES AND SPARES

CHRISTIAN WRIGHT & OLDIS

ESTABLISHED 1924

Accessories and Spares

Hooded Binnacles with dip-dials automatically recording change of level (illuminated face).

All heights from 50 to 15,000 feet £2 10 0

With Aerial Board of Control certificate £3 11 0

Foot and Hand Fog-horns; Sirens toned to any club note; with air-chest belt-driven from motor £6 8 0

Wireless installations syntonised to A.B.C. requirements, in neat mahogany case, hundred mile range £3 3 0

Grapnels, mushroom-anchors, pithing-irons, winches, hawsers, snaps, shackles and mooring ropes, for lawn, city, and public installations.

Detachable under-cars, aluminium or stamped steel.

Keeled under-cars for planes: single-action detaching-gear, turning car into boat with one motion of the wrist. Invaluable for sea trips.

Head, side, and riding lights (by size) Nos. 00 to 20 A.B.C. Standard. Rockets and fog-bombs in colours and tones of the principal clubs (boxed).

A selection of twenty £2 17 6

International night-signals (boxed) £1 11 6

Spare generators guaranteed to lifting power marked on cover (prices according to power).

Wind-noses for dirigibles—Pegamoid, cane-stiffened, lacquered cane or aluminium and flux for winter work.

Smoke-ring cannon for hail storms, swivel mounted, bow or stern.

Propeller blades: metal, tungsten backed; papier-mache; wire stiffened; ribbed Xylonite (Nickson's patent); all razor-edged (price by pitch and diameter).

Compressed steel bow-screws for winter work.

Fused Ruby or Commercial Mineral Co. bearings and collars. Agate-mounted thrust-blocks up to 4 inch.

Magniac's bow-rudders—(Lavalle's patent grooving).

Wove steel beltings for out-board motors (non-magnetic).

Radium batteries, all powers to 150 h.p. (in pairs).

Helium batteries, all powers to 300 h.p. (tandem).

Stun'sle brakes worked from upper or lower platform.

Direct plunge-brakes worked from lower platform only, loaded silk or fibre, wind-tight.

Catalogues free throughout the Planet

THOMAS McMORROW

MR MURPHY OF NEW YORK

'New York,' said Cohen bitterly, 'is dying of enlargement of the heart.'

'Well said,' I nodded, surveying this czar of an industry employing 250,000 New Yorkers.

'The great building, the skyscraper,' he continued with a touch of fanaticism, 'is a natural and necessary feature of a modern city! How can keymen meet one another otherwise? If they're going to be miles apart and communicate only by televistor, why, you don't need a city at all. The reason why Canabec is the new metropolis of North America—'

'By George,' exclaimed Mr Bligh, of Canabec, making a show of consulting his watch, 'if I miss the St Lawrence express on the Controlane, I'll not get home till this afternoon. Don't let me hurry you, gentlemen, but if you've decided to do this thing, let's do it. As I've told you, I can give you ten acres, which will be enough to house your industry for all purposes; you are aware that we will require you to go up not less than one hundred floors, sixty per cent to be residential. But I dare say that Mr Craig here' – looking at me – 'who is going to build for you, is familiar with our code.'

'Quite,' I said curtly, and readdressed myself to Cohen. 'Were you in New York when the Americus Tower fell?'

'I had my residence on the roof of the Americus,' interposed the futile Mr Murphy, producing blueprints, 'and the cosiest home I ever lived in. If you'll give me your attention now, Mr Craig, I'll show you what I want you to build for me in the way of a residence atop your new Central Unit in Canabec, and I'll take a twenty-year lease at eighty thousand per year.'

He was of just enough importance to us to be admitted to the fringes of our conference, but that wasn't Mr Murphy's conception of his status. He had a great deal of inherited money.

'You weren't at home, I take it, Mr Murphy,' said Cohen soberly, 'when the Americus fell?'

'Oh, I would have been killed!' expostulated Mr Murphy. 'As a matter of fact, gentlemen, I was at my shore home in Maine.' He became weightily informative. 'I was in the recreation hall of my place there, superintending the refinishing of the bowling alley – Mrs Murphy and I are both very fond of bowling – when my man Rogers came to me with a sheet from the Radio News, and showed me the flash from New York to the general effect that the Americus Tower had fallen. I took it very easily at first; it seemed more likely to me that the news service had been misinformed than that so unprecedented an event had come to pass. "Nonsense, Rogers!" I said, dismissing it as lightly as that. However, gentlemen, later in the day – Rogers had come to me about twenty-three o'clock – Mrs Murphy came home to lunch from the country club, and the first thing she said to me, gentlemen, was "Darius, have you heard —" '

'That the Americus Tower has fallen,' finished Cohen. We were on a topic of inexhaustible interest to New Yorkers, but Mr Murphy was taking us too far afield, as usual.

'Ah, exactly!' said Mr Murphy, turning approving blue eyes on the black-browed manufacturer. 'Or in effect, Mr Cohen.'

'Post mortem, gentlemen,' said Mr Bligh restively. He looked out my window at moribund New York. 'It was the fall of the Americus Tower that brought about your Safe-and-Sane Law, limiting the height of buildings to ten storeys, but that law was justified in any event. Your skyscrapers were creating such a traffic problem—'

'No such thing!' snapped Cohen. 'Pardon me, Mr Bligh.

I'll tell you what created that traffic problem – it was our transportation system. Go back there to 1930, when the building of skyscrapers really began in earnest, and see what they were doing about transportation. They were building the first Hudson River bridge, for one thing, and landing it in New York at One Hundred and Seventy-eighth Street. There's city planning for you – who wanted to go to One Hundred and Seventy-eighth Street? The commuters wanted to go to the mid-town, and they had to travel about seven miles down through Manhattan Island to get there. I suppose it was easier to land away up there – which reminds me of a new joke I heard last night on the Home Circuit . . . Do you subscribe to the Home Circuit, Mr Bligh? They have all the latest . . . About an intoxicated man who lost his watch one night on Fourteenth Street, but went to look for it on Forty-second because the light was better up there. Ha-ha! . . . That was the bridge; and look at the way they ran the city into debt by building north-and-south subways, all long haul, when they could have run short lines into Long Island and Jersey and made the city spread east and west. What gave you people the jump on us, in my opinion—'

'You New Yorkers,' sighed Mr Bligh. 'Let's get to business, gentlemen, please.'

'In my opinion,' repeated Cohen, 'Canabec is the world centre today because she had the vision to accommodate herself to facts. Skyscrapers – absolutely! But mostly residential – that's the point. Canabec, with six million population, has no traffic problem. Her people live where they work, and that's the end of it. We were working towards it here, until the fall of the Americus gave the little people their chance.'

He brooded. 'We had executive ability, but no imagination. We spent a billion dollars to bring water into the city, emptying puddles a hundred miles away, when the vast Hudson River was right beside us! When the last puddle was drained dry, somebody noticed the Hudson and thought of narrowing it at Spuyten Duyvil and raising it above salt-water level. Why, it's only two years since we used to sewer into it. New York wasn't a city; it was a big Indian village.'

'Gas-proof casements and an aerating plant,' said Mr Murphy. 'I must insist on that, the same as I had in my home on the Americus Tower, because with Russia only six hours away, you never can tell. It might have been all right when the United States was the only great nation, but now there are three – four, if you count Canada – and I was reading an article in last Sunday's paper describing the next war, and it was enough to make a man thoughtful. And Mrs Murphy won't have glass curtain walls; she says it never gives the same sense of privacy. She says she can't have every Tom, Dick, and Harry looking into her apartment, as they do when somebody leaves the cap off the televistor. There's that; and also—'

'Mr Craig, you're a builder,' said Cohen. 'I've often wondered if there was anything in that talk about the iron erectors planning to wreck the Americus Tower because the builder had been a strike-breaker out West.'

'Poppycock. You mean that they put the steel frame together in such a way that it would collapse later? It couldn't be done, Mr Cohen. We had a building department in New York, with a competent force of inspectors, and the company that made the building loan had its own inspectors. And I knew the steel engineer who designed that job, and he was one of the best. His plans are still on file with the city.'

'I understand that you saw the building go down, Mr Craig.'

'I did,' I said, with slowly kindling enthusiasm for an oft-told tale. 'And it was only the mercy of heaven that I didn't go down with it, because I was one of the tenants ... If you remember, the building fell on the day that the first Controlane landed in New York, and that's why so few people were killed – only a hundred odd. Almost everybody had gone over to see the ship come down on the landing field in Welfare Island in the East River. You'll remember that it was a Saturday, and the mayor proclaimed a municipal holiday, suspending business.

'I was over there on the Queensboro Bridge at eleven o'clock that morning, talking to a chap who told me a lot about the new ship and what a wonderful advance in transportation it was; it wasn't much bigger than old Robert Fulton's first steamboat. He told me about the lanes of control, and how the ship is lifted and propelled by power sent through the air by the stations; he said that those stations could lift a locomotive and train of cars and drive them through the air, and I was old-fashioned enough to marvel.

'There was some delay, and I didn't wait to see the ship arrive. If I recall what the trouble was, the power wasn't selective at that time, and some skylarkers were throwing things down from the bridge into the power lane for the fun of watching them vanish as the power seized them and flung them across the ocean. Word came that the ship was being held in Islip, England, until the bombardment was stopped. Fortunately, the cushion was working over there and nobody was seriously hurt, except in his dignity; the American ambassador, in the midst of his speech, was hit with watermelon rind, and then came cucumbers and other edibles, none very choice or welcome. The New York police came up on the bridge to stop the rowdies' sport, and somebody cried out that the bridge was getting into the lane, and there was a panic. Somebody jostled me while somebody else snatched my watch, and I decided to go back to my office and to see the ship another day.

'I walked, of course. That was the quickest way to get around New York in those days, just before they gave out the taxi franchise. You remember the streets? Wheel to wheel – twice as many cars as could be accommodated, and everybody free to add still another. They didn't have then even the thousand-dollar licence fee to operate a private car within the five boroughs.'

'All cure and no prevention,' rasped Cohen. 'That was New York.'

'I came up Forty-second Street and looked over at the Americus Tower across Bryant Park, and wished I owned it; it was a magnificent property. It was two hundred feet wide at the base, by half the block, and ninety storeys high; an office building only six months old and with a gross rental of three million dollars a year. A very sweet proposition, I thought enviously, and Tweed is a lucky dog – Tweed, you remember, was the owner. One big success like that building, I thought, and I'd be satisfied. Tweed had chosen a fine neighbourhood – a neighbourhood of professional clubs. His building towered over them all; ninety storeys of tapestry brick and Indiana limestone, with the new gold-plated gambrel roof, not a flaw nor a hairline crack, all rented and pulling for Tweed like a Percheron.

'A dirt truck was staggering up out of the lot adjoining the Americus on the east. A new skyscraper was to go there; the excavator was working on a bonus against time, and he wasn't bothering with the Controlane ship.

'I was at Forty-second Street and Fifth Avenue, and was stepping from the kerb to cross the street when I heard that first crash. It wasn't so loud; a door banged beside me would have startled me more. There was a rumbling as of a subway train heard over-ground.'

I paused to light a cigarette. It was an old story, but one of unfailing interest to New Yorkers, with the fascination of the unsolved and perhaps unsolvable. The quiet streets of Manhattan could be fairly covered with the paper that has been blackened with discussions of the fall of the Americus Tower.

'Twelve rooms and five baths,' said Mr Murphy, 'and you can use all the glass you like in the bathrooms. Suction glass, isn't it, Mr Craig? We had a studio living-room thirty-five feet long and twenty feet high; I think nothing has quite the tone of a real high ceiling. But don't forget the gas-proof casements closing all openings to the air. Mrs Murphy and I couldn't rest in peace if we thought we might be smothered in our beds. Who could, now, really?

'Pardon me, Mr Craig; I didn't intend to interrupt you. Yes, we were at our shore place in Maine when the building fell. We had left our home atop the Americus in the middle of May, and had been some six weeks at the shore when this terrible thing happened. How little we think! I can still see Mrs Murphy waiting for me at the elevator. "Darius," she said, "are you positively sure you closed and fastened all the windows, and left all the interior doors open? You are so absent-minded." We had been troubled with mice, and when you're troubled with mice it is very wise to leave open all the interior doors in your home when going away, or the little villains will gnaw through the doors. You can prevent that sort of thing by using steel doors, but I don't think they're ever quite the same as fireproofed wood. So cold and institutionlike. Don't you think so?'

'Yes, indeed, Mr Murphy ... And then came that steady and deafening grinding and squealing. My eyes were on the Americus, and I can tell you they popped. The windows of the showrooms on the ground floor were gone; I hadn't seen them go, nor heard them; you could hear nothing but that merciless grating and wrenching. The limestone ashlar between window openings fell out and I saw red iron. The building was— Up shot my gaze to the roof. The shining surfaces up there seemed to be undulating in the sunlight.

'The building was— The great Americus Tower— No, I didn't believe it. Like our friend Mr Murphy here, though with less excuse, I couldn't believe it. I stood there. The three storeys of ashlar were undulating, buckling, and they seemed as pliable and elastic as rubber. They didn't disintegrate; they didn't fall. And then they fell – three storeys of cut limestone – into the street. But so incredulous was I that they seemed to fall slowly, like sheets of paper wafting down.

'The building was falling. The Americus Tower was falling. The brickwork of the whole twenty-fifth floor – some say it was first the eighteenth, but I say it was the twenty-fifth – came away and swept down, slowly, floating. It was a steel-bearing job, of course; the walls were carried on the steel.

'The Americus was tilting. Its façade was dissolving. I claim that the steel failed first at the twenty-fifth floor. No matter now, but it was once thought very important, before the public took the bit in its teeth and brought in the verdict in advance of the evidence. I testified to it, telling what I saw; let other people tell what they saw. The façade below the twenty-fifth floor seemed to stand still while the upper twenty floors bowed toward the street. And then the whole vast fabric moved from its place in the sky – moved outwards, slowly, so slowly; gathering speed.

'I turned and bolted for dear life. I never ran so; I didn't feel myself running; I was only intent on getting away, and I everlastingly got! I shot up Fifth Avenue. Flashing a look about, to see whence destruction would rush upon me now, I saw the people on the Elevated station on Sixth Avenue, agape, hands in air. I met a man last February in Sebring who was on that Elevated station that day; he told me that he was not conscious of being frightened, but that his heart stopped beating. I wasn't like that; I was stampeded. I'm told that the air was full of a vast roaring and whistling, but I didn't hear it. When the Americus came flailing down across Bryant Park and the blocks north – Mr Murphy's private residence landed in Forty-fifth Street, knocking a ten-storey loft into a cocked hat – the noise was heard in Irvington-on-the-Hudson and in Summit, in New Jersey; but I didn't hear it, upon my word. I was running.

'I was pretty heavy then, and I lost my first burst about Forty-fifth Street; a policeman had me by the shoulder. I was sobbing so for breath that I couldn't talk. I knew him and he knew me, and he told me that he thought I was running away after setting off a bomb, but he didn't tell me until months later, and then it had come out in the investigation that he had fired a shot at me. All he said at first was, "It's Mr Craig."

' "Did you see it?" I gasped.

' "What? I heard it, God knows. What was it?"

'We were up to our ankles in water that was pouring down Forty-fifth Street; a main had been broken evidently. The street was level with water from building line to line.

' "Let's go back," I urged. And with him beside me, I ran

the other way, as if a wave had caught me and swept me to Forty-fifth Street and was now receding with equally compelling sweep.

'Yes, there are a great many people in New York who have the mayor's holiday and the ballyhoo over the new Controlane to thank for their lives. Seven thousand people would have been at work in the Americus that was now lying across Bryant Park like a wrecked and beached steamer. Not since the last earthquake below a modern city has anyone seen the like; and not even then, let me say. Why, sixty years ago, at San Francisco, the steel-framed buildings stood; the outcry against them after the Americus disaster was reactionary panic. As well condemn steel ships because of the Titanic or Burgundia sinkings; the Burgundia was ninety thousand tons, and it went down like a tin cup. An accident is an accident, and such will happen to the end of time. The Americus disaster might have been much worse. I believe not more than a hundred and fifty people were killed in all, which was wonderful luck, speaking from the viewpoint of the rest of us.

'It took the Northard and the Hennesy wrecking companies four months to cut up the wreck and ride it away; they were two weeks clearing Forty-fifth Street of the metal roof. The Metropolitan, I understand, realized only two thousand dollars from the sale of the roof as junk – something queer about that. The Tyng process for deep mining had knocked the bottom out of the price of roofing metal, but scrap gold was still worth a dollar ten a pound; and there was the aluminium alloy. However, that's a small matter; I mention it because it was wrangled over during the investigation.'

'That was a great investigation,' said Cohen. 'Some of those witnesses should have left the chamber under arrest, for they certainly violated the P. & P. Act.'

'Publicity,' I nodded. 'Harrigan's testimony, that such a time was made over, is a fair example – barefaced publicity for the new striated steel process. I myself had sometimes thought that designers were going too far in lightening structural steel, but I'm no steel engineer, and I guess Hendricks knew his business; he designed the Americus steel. He exposed Harrigan's animus later on when he proved that the eccentrically loaded columns were braced laterally, bringing the thrust below the bracing; and that was accepted practice. As for the carrying capacity, those columns were rolled steel, and it's sound construction to impose a working stress per square inch of sectional area of ten tons. Harrigan's stuff was all laboratory stuff, theorizing; practice is what I go by, and I don't want anybody to stand around and tell me how to pick up the mule's hind foot, especially if he's selling crutches.'

'They believed Harrigan.'

'I tell you he was selling the striated steel process! Go look at the fifty-storey Federal Building on Mail Street, and you'll see so-called settlement cracks. Settlement cracks, my eye; they're caused by the buckling of the striated steel columns. The material has tremendous tensile strength, and is fine for framing and connecting – trimmers, headers and tail beams – but I'd prefer even cast iron for compression. I'm no steel engineer, but I'm betting my money every day on my notions of construction. The steel didn't fail until the Americus was away out of plumb – when the masonry flaked off – and then it began at the splice plates. That was what let in the lurid yarn about the erectors neglecting to rivet.

'Excited and puzzled people will listen to anything; you remember the amateur detective who rushed in and told them that the first-floor columns were not steel at all but cast pottery! What started the wheels in his head was my testimony that the building had failed first at the street; that pointed inquiry at the base columns, and it was discovered that one of them had been eaten nearly through by sulphuric acid. The explanation was that a canister of the acid had leaked into the channel; the tenants of the ground floor were industrial chemists.'

'Gentlemen, gentlemen,' said Mr Bligh.

'I believe, Mr Craig,' said Mr Murphy, spreading his blueprints, 'that you builders calculate your costs by the cubic foot; correct me if I err. Now, including the observation room and garage, I had about one hundred and ten thousand cubic feet in my residence atop the Americus Tower, and if I pay you eighty thousand dollars per year—'

'Hendricks insisted to the day of his death that the bearing stresses had shifted. He was the best steel engineer in New York, but he got his reputation, of course, by shaving the margin of safety. Any dub can design steel if he is given a free hand to thicken it, but the engineer who gets the business is the one who can lighten it. When the Americus was built, steel was selling for about a hundred per ton erected, and a difference of a thousand tons was worth saving. I do think his forty-per-cent aluminium alloy was too much, in columns, but it was accepted practice.

'The steel failed somewhere, changing into thrusts what were meant to be compressions. Steel-framed buildings will stand a shaking, such as by earthquake, much better than an old-style, wall-bearing job, but they won't stand a lateral thrust so well. Speaking of wartime risks, like Mr Murphy, a bomb exploding by a masonry wall will knock a hole in it and let the rest of the wall stand, but if that bomb knocked out a column of a steel-bearing job, the whole building would pull that way. That's my opinion, though I'm no engineer. Hendricks said that the loadings had shifted, bringing stresses to bear on columns that they weren't designed to carry, but he couldn't explain how it came about. His plans are still on file, and many competent engineers have passed on them.'

'What about the foundations?'

'There was a loose end. That excavation beside the Americus might have had something to do with the catastrophe. Too bad that the excavator and all his men were killed when the gable wall fell on them. Dan Derry, better known as Dynamite Dan, was the excavator. He had been shooting several holes at a time, and that's not so wise, because an unexploded charge is likely to be left in the rock. If he detonated a forgotten charge under one of the piers of the Americus Tower, it might have brought the building down. The footings were examined after the water was pumped out, but nothing was learned.'

'The water?' said Mr Murphy, frowning.

'The main intake had been broken, naturally.'

'Mrs Murphy—'

'The footings were on bed rock and there was no evidence that they had shifted. You remember the report of the investigating committee; after reviewing all the guesses, they favoured that of a theorizing engineer and guessed with him that the collapse was due to fatigue of materials.'

'In other words,' smiled Cohen, 'they brought in a verdict of death by suicide; that the Americus Tower had become tired of life.'

'May I venture to hope, gentlemen,' said Mr Bligh, 'that we may soon find time to attend to our affair? If you can use this ten acres at Canabec—'

'Now there's an idea,' said Mr Murphy brightly. 'Perhaps you can settle a domestic controversy, Mr Craig. I have often debated with Mrs Murphy – and not always in the best of temper – her use of my razors.

'Take a razor. If you use the same razor all the time, it grows fatigued and will not hold an edge. Lay it aside and let it rest, and it will pick up again. Or again, you have watched a man breaking a rock with a sledge; he hits it a dozen times without effect, and then the next blow breaks it apart.'

'How interesting! You'll pardon me, Mr Bligh, but I've always been tremendously interested in science.'

'Fatigue of materials, Mr Murphy,' said I, 'is a subject as to which scientists are still somewhat in the dark. They know it's a fact. And we may take it as a fact that if there was no margin of safety in the Americus Tower, if the steel was loaded to the limit of its strength, it would hold for a certain time and then get tired and let go.'

'What you say about the water main having burst, Mr Craig,' said Mr Murphy intently, 'bears out my own contention at the time. Following the disaster, the city presented me with a perfectly preposterous bill for water, and I had to make an affidavit that I had not been in residence at the Americus Tower for a matter of at least six weeks. You can't imagine how insistent and disobliging the chaps were.'

Cohen took the contracts that Mr Bligh was thrusting at him, glanced at them and laid them down. 'Skyscrapers, Mr Craig!'

'Positively,' said I. 'A necessity of modern business; the big unit.'

'What were you telling me, Mr Bligh, about the Education Law in Canabec?'

'We're up to date,' said Mr Bligh contentedly. 'Our young people must leave the schools and find gainful employment at the age of eighteen.'

'I was twenty-four when I graduated from college,' said Mr Murphy. 'Surely, Mr Bligh, a boy can't complete the study of Latin, Greek—'

'Nor Sanskrit, either, Mr Murphy; and every argument for the universal study of Latin and Greek holds for Sanskrit. It's the basic language and has a great literature. And, to most people, astrology is a more colourful and interesting study than the higher mathematics, and just as useful. You people made the mistake of letting professional educators decide what the children should learn; by limiting the school age we persuade our people to take interest in the education of their children and to see that their time isn't wasted. You people let lawyers make your laws, teachers control your education, soldiers plan your military establishment, and the general population plan your cities.'

'Say rather the taxpayers,' amended Cohen. 'It was the majority of taxpayers who took advantage of the fall of the Americus to clap on a height limit. Their interests certainly, were being injured by the erection of skyscrapers. That the process was inevitable, biological, was no satisfaction to them. We are builders, like ants – your Canabec is still not as tall in proportion as the cities raised by African ants; our cities are part of our life processes, and while we may ameliorate their effects on the individual, we cannot choke down the biological urge to federate, to cooperate, to build – skyscrapers!'

'Surely you don't compare a human being to an ant, Mr Cohen,' objected Mr Murphy. 'He's ever so much more intelligent, you know.'

'Which?'

'Eh? The human being! My goodness.'

'Unproved, Mr Murphy. First comes division of labour, then adaptation to the job, and then division of thinking. The ants have gone the whole route.'

Cohen was extravagant, bitter, inclined to gibe; I knew what he was feeling. I, too, was a New Yorker of many generations, and I had come to see my city slipping towards decay. The country dweller finds a dearness in the familiar hill and stream; even the tree – mere springing vegetables – that shades his house is dear to him. Would not his pride be greater, more deeply to be wounded, if his people had built every foot of that landscape, if that tree were a giant edifice raised by his people? Cohen and I, obeying the will to live which is stronger than love, fiercer than pride, were here to arrange for a vast migration to the city that was supplanting our incomparable New York.

'It is not a matter of sentiment,' exclaimed Cohen, as if sensible of my thoughts. 'The big building is a necessity and ordained! If we live we must grow; other times, other ways. Not a thing did they allege against the skyscraper that was the skyscraper's fault. Congestion of traffic? But the big building immobilizes traffic, gathers a multitude of people in one place. They say it turns the street into a canyon; but doesn't it turn the house into a hill? It's all morbid opposition to change; people want things to be as they are, as they were. Look at our antique collectors – my wife paid six thousand dollars yesterday for a brass bed, circa 1910; and she puts in our living-room, where I have the best electric heating, an antique oil stove that smells to high heaven. Gordon Gin bottles with those quaint bootleg labels, phonograph records, cuspitoons and door keys. She calls me a barbarian. I have no love for the beautiful and artistic.'

'Your wife collects G. G. bottles, Mr Cohen?' said Mr Murphy with new respect. 'I'd love to have her opinion on the few that I've got hold of; I believe they are authentic bootleg, but there is so much faking done nowadays. Has she any American Scotch bottles? I have one with Just Off the Ship blown in the glass, and the dealer gave me his word—'

'Now, gentlemen, please,' breathed Mr Bligh. 'Do remember that I'm a thousand miles from home and haven't had any lunch yet. Well, I shall have to call up.' He took out his pocketell. 'Are you there? Bill calling ... Hello, Molly I just called you to say that I can't possibly get home— What's that, sweetheart? ... Oh, no, no ... But I say that I am not! I am in New York at a conference ... Yes, business ... Why don't I— Now, Molly, how can you ask me to be so rude? ... Oh, very well, my dear; in a moment.' He turned to us, colouring, and said, 'Will you permit?' We were married men ourselves; we smiled and got to our feet and bowed to his lady when she appeared; her eyes swept us vigilantly. 'I'm sorry this had to happen, gentlemen,' said Mr Bligh, blanking her. 'May we proceed now with our affair?'

'I know how you feel, Mr Bligh,' said Mr Murphy, 'and I speak as a fellow sufferer and not a physician. Last week I went down to the Chesapeake for a day's sport – clam digging. Nothing of any size in those waters but jellyfish, and I can't see them as game. I had a good day and got my full bag and was showing the shelly beauties to Mrs Murphy when I chanced to lay down my pocketell and forgot it there. I tell you I caught it proper when I arrived home for being out of sight so long; besides losing a first-chop pocketell. It isn't as though I were often forgetful. A great game country, that. Robins, moles, even woodchuck. And frogs? In plenty. It's the sort of country our ancestors—

'But that reminds me, Mr Craig, of something that's been bothering me off and on for the last twenty years, ever since I got that ridiculous bill from the city for a hundred thousand cubic feet of water. It's not of the least importance, I'm sure, but if the money was due and owing, I'd pay it even yet. You are quite sure the main was broken?'

'Certainly ... Mr Cohen, we might as well get to it. If we sign up at once, I'll take the St Lawrence express with Mr Bligh, together with my superintendent, and I'll put an air blast into the lot tomorrow morning. You'll have to decide at once whether you'll use brick or glass; on that point, the mason machinists are talking strike against the new machines that lay a thousand bricks a minute. Glass will cost you a little more, but you don't need windows, and you have in every way a more modern building.'

'I like brick walls for the homes,' said Cohen. 'Brick seems more homelike somehow. Lay up thirty-five floors in glass, and the upper sixty-five in brick. What about the lighting?'

'The good old lumen bulb is still my first choice. If I were you, I'd leave the Radio-light alone for the present; the service is very unsatisfactory more than three hours after sunset. For heating we'll use Silver Bar, the same as you have in your own home; the first cost is high, but then it becomes cheap and foolproof.'

'We shall use gaslight and steam,' said Mr Murphy with innocent vanity. 'These modern inventions are all a bit vulgar, don't you think? Give me the soft and mellow flickering of the gas mantle and the cheerful knocking of the steam in the radiators! It may cost quite a little more, but—I don't know; we like antique effects. They give a home such atmosphere. And we have authentic Hoover Period radiator enclosures for all the rooms.' He smiled cosily. 'It's a small matter, Mr Craig, but I'm glad to be assured that I turned off the water in the bathtub in our residence in the Americus Tower. Mrs Murphy always insisted that I didn't, and I always insisted that I did. And while we were still debating, the building fell down, so that it seemed that the issue would never be decided between us.'

Cohen poised the pen; the responsibility of the moment pressed on him. It was fifteen years since New York had ceased to grow; twelve since it had registered its first loss in population. The movement away, to cities that had not adopted the arbitrary height limit, had slowly gathered volume, but ours would be the first large-scale desertion. It would be imitated.

'Our fault,' he said, striving for definition, 'was rating administration too highly; our chosen leader was the able executive. Executive ability didn't make America the first power on earth, and didn't save the other nations. It was imagination! It was private enterprise. Imagination is the gift of the few, and private enterprise welcomes it. Government – administration – does not welcome imagination, is hostile to it. Government expresses the mind of the unimaginative majority, and its first article of faith is that it is perfect. Private enterprise built New York, made it the world city; and then, because of a small catastrophe, it was shouldered aside, and the unimaginative majority, with its faces to the past, took charge. No more integration; no more striving upward; no more skyscrapers.'

'But, Mr Cohen,' said Mr Murphy with irritating patience, 'there were great cities before there were skyscrapers. Look at London; look at Paris, Rome.'

'They have their skyscrapers now,' said Mr Bligh. 'And they always did build as high as they could. The modern building was impossible before the invention of the lift, the elevator. Even so, Rome had its ten and twelve storey buildings – they must have had noble legs in those days. Well, Mr Cohen?'

Cohen dipped pen in ink. 'Look at the blood and tears that went into the building of the pyramids. And for what? One of the earliest stories of our race is of the men who tried to build a tower to reach the sky. I dare say they were stopped by the local taxpayers whose caves wouldn't rent any more.'

I had been doing some figuring. 'This may be of only historical value,' I said, looking at the result, 'but we're making history here. Mr Murphy, you say that the city sent you a bill for a hundred thousand cubic feet of water? That water couldn't have come from the broken main or it wouldn't have registered on your meter.'

'The city conceded that the meter had been put out of order by the crash, Mr Craig, when I pointed out to them that my residence had been shut up for more than six weeks.'

'You shut it up good and tight, did you?'

'Oh, yes. Mrs Murphy—'

'Mrs Murphy, of Chicago,' murmured Cohen, catching my point. His black eyes were intent.

'Of New York, Mr Cohen ... Yes, I made everything fast. I was in my room, drawing my bath – we'd sent the servants ahead – when my man Rogers sent down word that Washington Travel had notified him of an approaching disturbance, and that we'd better get going. Dressing rapidly—'

'Where was your bathroom?'

'On the mezzanine.' He turned to his blueprints again. 'We had five bathrooms in all. But I think, for our new residence at Canabec—'

'If you were drawing your bath,' I said sternly, 'you must have stopped the waste. And you think that, perhaps, you went away and left the water running.'

'A mere surmise, Mr Craig. But why are you so pressing? If you think that I should pay this bill even now—'

I drew a breath. 'A hundred thousand cubic feet of water, gentlemen, weighs more than three thousand tons. In my opinion, though I'm no engineer, the steel frame designed by Hendricks would not have stood under a superimposed load of three thousand tons – not without buckling somewhere. If it would stand any such overloading, Hendricks didn't know his business. It's late in the day to reopen the investigation into the fall of the Americus Tower.'

'Probably too late,' said Cohen briskly, snatching the televistor, 'but we can get an expert opinion in twenty minutes as to the engineering problem ... Hello, let me have the Building Department, and then the City Commissioner! ... Remain here, please, Mr Murphy. It seems that you kicked over the lamp, but perhaps the city is not yet destroyed. If there's a chance of scrapping the New York height limit within a reasonable time, and letting us build here as we should and must, my industry isn't moving to Canabec.'

'Gentlemen, gentlemen!' exclaimed Mr Bligh, of Canabec, vexedly.

KRIS NEVILLE

NEW APPLES IN THE GARDEN

Eddie Hibbs reported for work and was almost immediately called out on an emergency. It was the third morning in succession for emergencies.

This time a section of distribution cable had blown in West Los Angeles. Blown cable was routine, but each instance merited the attention of an assistant underground supervisor.

Eddie climbed down the manhole with the foreman of the maintenance crew. There were deep pull marks on the lead sheath above where the cable had blown.

'Where'd they get it?' he asked.

'It came in from a job on the East Side.'

'Sloppy work,' Eddie said. 'Water got in the splice?'

'These new guys . . .' the foreman said.

Eddie fingered the pull marks. 'I think she's about shot anyway. How much is like this?'

'A couple of hundred feet.'

'All this bad?'

'Yep.'

Eddie whistled. 'About fifteen thousand dollars worth. Well. Cut her back to here and make splices. Stand over them while they do it.'

'I'll need two men for a week.'

'I'll try to find them for you. Send through the paper.'

'I can probably find maybe another thousand miles or so that's about this bad.'

'Don't bother,' Eddie said.

That was Eddie's productive work during the morning. With traffic and two sections of street torn up by the water people, he did not get back to his office until just before lunch. He listened to the stock market reports while he drove.

He learned that spiralling costs had retarded the modernization programme of Hyspeed Electronics and much of their present equipment was obsolete in terms of current price factors. He was also told to anticipate that declining sales would lead to declining production, thereby perpetuating an unfortunate cycle. And finally he was warned that Hyspeed Electronics was an example of the pitfalls involved in investing in the so-called high growth stocks.

Eddie turned off the radio in the parking lot as the closing Dow-Jones report was starting.

During lunch, he succeeded in reading two articles in a six-week-old issue of *Electrical World*, the only one of the dozen technical journals he found time for now.

At 12.35 word filtered into the department that one of the maintenance crew, Ramon Lopez, had been killed. A forty-foot ladder broke while atop it Lopez was hosing down a pothead, and he was driven backward into the concrete pavement by the high-pressure water.

Eddie tried to identify the man. The name was distantly familiar but there was no face to go with it. Finally the face came. He smoked two cigarettes in succession. He stubbed the last one out angrily.

'That was a tough one,' his supervisor, Forester, said, sitting on the side of Eddie's desk. Normally exuberant, he was left melancholy and distracted by the accident. 'You know the guy?'

'To speak to.'

'Good man.'

'After I thought about it a little bit,' Eddie said, 'I remembered he was transferring tomorrow. Something like this brings a man up short, doesn't it?'

'A hell of a shame. Just a hell of a shame.'

They were silent for a minute.

'How was the market this morning?' Forester asked.

'Up again. I didn't catch the closing averages.'

'I guess that makes a new high.'

'Third straight day,' Eddie said.

'Hell of a shame,' Forester said.

'Yeah, Lopez was a nice guy.'

'Well . . .' Forester's voice trailed off in embarrassment.

'Yeah, well . . .'

'I wanted to remind you about the budget meeting.'

Eddie glanced at his watch. 'Hour and a half?'

'Yeah. You know, I feel like . . . never mind. What about the burial transformers, you get on it yet?'

'The ones we're running in the water mains for cooling? They're out of warranty. None of the local shops can rewind them until the manufacturer sends out a field engineer to set them up for the encapsulation process.'

'How long is that going to take?' Forester asked.

'They tell me several months. Still doesn't leave us with anything. The plant says they've fixed the trouble, but between them and the rewind shop, they can buck it back and forth for ever.'

'I guess we'll have to go back to the pad-mounted type.'

'People with the Gold Medallion Homes aren't going to like the pads by their barbecues.'

Forester uncoiled a leg. 'Draw up a memorandum on it, will you, Eddie?' He stood up. 'That thing sure got me today. There's just entirely too many of these accidents. A ladder breaking. I don't know.'

Eddie tried to find something intelligent to say. Finally he said, 'It was a rough one, all right.'

After Forester left, Eddie picked up listlessly from the top of the stack one of the preliminary reports submitted for his approval. The report dealt with three thousand capacitors purchased last year from an Eastern firm, now bankrupt. The capacitors were beginning to leak. Eddie called the electrical laboratory to see what progress was being made on the problem.

The supervisor refreshed his memory from the records. He reported: 'I don't have any adhesive man to work on it. Purchasing has half a dozen suppliers lined up – but none have any test data. I don't know when we'll get the time. We're on a priority programme checking out these new, low-cost terminations.'

'Can't we certify the adhesive to some AIEE spec or something?' Eddie asked.

'I don't know of any for sealing capacitors, Eddie. Not on the maintenance end, at least.'

'Maybe Purchasing can get a guarantee from one of the suppliers?'

'For the hundred dollars of compound that's involved? What good would that do us?'

Eddie thanked him and hung up. He signed the preliminary report.

He turned to the next one.

At 2.30 Forester came by and the two of them made their way between the jigsaw projections of maple and mahogany to the Conference Room.

Fourteen men were involved in the conference, all from operating departments. They shuffled in over a five-minute period, found seats, lit cigarettes, talked and joked with one another.

When one of the assistants to the manager came in, they fell silent.

'Gentlemen,' he said, 'I think I'd better get right to the point today. The Construction Programme in the Valley has now used up two bond issues. The voters aren't going to approve a third one.'

He paused for effect, then continued briskly. 'I see by the morning's *Times* that the mayor is appointing a watchdog commission. I guess you all saw it, too. The Department of Water and Power of the City of Los Angeles is going to be badly – and I mean badly – in the red at the end of the fiscal year.

'We're in hot water.

'We do not seem to be getting through to the operating departments regarding the necessity for cost reduction. I have here last month's breakdown on the Bunker Hill sub-station 115 KV installation. Most of you have seen it already, I think. I had it sent around. Now—'

The analysis continued for some ten minutes to conclude with an explosion. 'We've got to impose a ten-per-cent across-the-board cut on operating expenses.'

One of the listeners, more alert than the rest, asked, 'That go for salaries?'

'For personnel making more than eight hundred dollars a month it does.'

There was a moment of shocked silence.

'You can't make that stick,' one of the supervisors said. 'Half my best men will be out tomorrow looking for better offers – and finding them, too.'

'I'm just passing on what I was told.'

The men in the room shuffled and muttered under their breaths.

'Okay, that's the way they want it,' one of the supervisors said.

'I've brought along the notices for the affected personnel. Please see they're distributed when you leave.'

After the meeting, Forester walked with Eddie back to his desk.

'You be in tomorrow, Eddie?'

'I guess I will, Les. I really don't know yet.'

'I'd hate to lose you.'

'It's going to make it pretty tough. A man's fixed expenses don't come down.'

'I'll see what I can do for you, maybe upgrade the classification—'

'Thanks, Les.'

Back at his desk, Eddie looked at his watch. Nearly time for the Safety Meeting. Lost-time injuries had been climbing for the last four months.

While waiting, he signed a sixty-three page preliminary

report recommending a programme for the orderly replacement of all transmission and distribution cable installed prior to 1946. It was estimated that the savings, in the long run, would total some quarter of a billion dollars. The initial expense, however, was astronomical.

After the Safety Meeting, Eddie prepared another memorandum indicating the acute need for a better training programme and an increase in maintenance personnel. Shortage of qualified technicians was chronic.

At 4.25, the night supervisor phoned in to say he was having engine trouble with his new car and would be delayed until about six o'clock. Eddie agreed to wait for him.

Eddie dialled home to let his wife, Lois, know he would be late again. A modulated low-frequency note told him the home phone was out of order.

Ray Morely, one of the night-shift engineers, came in with coffee. 'You still here, Eddie?'

'Yeah, until Wheeler makes it. His car's down.'

'Market hit a new high.'

'Yeah. I guess you heard about the meeting today?'

Ray sipped coffee. 'Budget again? I missed the day crew. I got hung up in traffic and was a little late.'

'A pay cut goes with it this time.'

'You're kidding?'

'Been by your desk yet?'

'No.'

'I'm not kidding. Ten per cent for those making about eight hundred.'

'Nobody's going to put up with that,' Ray said. 'We're in an engineering shortage. We've got ICBMs rusting in their silos all over the country because we can't afford the engineering maintenance – that's how bad it is. Everybody'll quit.'

'I don't think they'll make it stick. Ramon Lopez, one of the truck crew, was killed today hosing down a high-voltage pothead.'

'No kidding?'

Eddie told him about the accident.

'That was a rough one to lose, wasn't it?'

The phone rang.

Ray said, 'I'll get it.'

He listened for a minute and hung up. 'There's an outage in the Silver Lake Area. The brakes on a bus failed and took out an overhead section.'

Eddie sat back. 'No sense in you going. With work traffic on the surface streets until the freeway gets fixed, they won't get the truck there until 6.30 or so.'

'Right.' Ray drank coffee reflectively. 'You going looking?'

'I'm an old-timer. I got a lot of seniority. How about you?'

'I got bills. It's going to cost me near a hundred a month – that's a steep bite.'

'I still think they'll back off.'

'They'll have to,' Ray said. 'If not right now, when the pressure gets on. You ask me, we've got them by the short hair.' He settled into the chair. 'I see it as an organic phenomenon. When society gets as complex as ours, it has to grow more and more engineers. But there's a feedback circuit in effect. The more engineers we grow, the more complex society becomes. Each new one creates the need for two more. I get a sort of feeling of – I don't know – vitality, I guess, when I walk into, say, an automated factory. All that machinery and all that electronic gear is like a single cell in a living organism – an organism that's growing every day, multiplying the bacteria. And it's always sick, and we're the doctors. That's job security. We're riding the wave of the future. I don't think they'll make a salary cut stick.'

'I hope you're right,' Eddie said.

Eddie checked out at 7.15, when the night supervisor finally arrived. As he left the building, he noted that a burglar alarm down the street had gone off, probably because of a short circuit. The clanking set his nerves on edge. Apprehensively he felt a rising wind against his cheeks.

At home, he was greeted with a perfunctory kiss at the door.

'Honey,' Lois told him, 'you took the chequebook, and I didn't have any money.'

'Something come up? I'm sorry.'

'We're all out of milk. The milk man didn't come today. Their homogenizing machinery broke down. I phoned the dairy about nine; and then, of course, the phone has been on the blink since about eleven or a little before, so I couldn't ask you to bring some home.'

'I kept trying to get you.'

'I figured you had to work late again, when you weren't here at six, and I knew you'd be here when you got here.'

Eddie sat down and she sat on the chair arm beside him. 'How did it go today?'

He started to tell her about the wage cut and Ramon Lopez; but then he didn't want to talk about it. 'So-so,' he said. 'There was an outage over in the Silver Lake Area just before I left.'

'Fixed yet?'

'I doubt it,' he said. 'Probably a couple of more hours.'

'Gee,' she said, 'when I think of all that meat in the deep freezer . . .'

'I wouldn't stock so much,' he said. 'I really wouldn't.'

She twisted away from him. 'Honey. I'm jittery. Something's . . . I don't know. In the air, I guess.'

The wind rattled the windows.

While Lois was warming dinner, his son came in.

'Hi, Eddie.'

'Hi, Larry.'

'Eddie, when we gonna get the TV fixed?'

Eddie put down the newspaper. 'We just don't have a hundred dollars or so right now.' He searched for matches on the table by the chair. 'Lois, oh, Lois, where're the matches?'

She came in. 'They were all out Friday at the store, and I

keep forgetting to lay in a supply. Use my lighter over there.'

'About the TV—'

Lois was wiping her hands on the paper towel she had brought with her. 'Replacement parts are hard to find for the older sets,' she said. 'Anyway, I read today Channel Three finally went off the air. That leaves only Two and Seven. And the programmes aren't any good, now, are they? All those commercials and all?'

'They do use a lot of old stuff I've already seen,' the son admitted, 'but every once in a while there's something new.'

'Let's talk about it some other time, Larry, okay?' Eddie said. 'How's that? It's almost your bedtime. Studies done?'

'All but the library report.'

'Well, finish it, and—'

'I got to read the book down there. Two classes assigned it and they don't have the copies to let us check out. And I want to ask you about something, Eddie.'

'Daddy's tired. His dinner's on. Come on, Eddie. I'll set it right now. And Larry, you've already eaten ...'

After dinner, Eddie got back to the paper, the evening *Times*. It was down to eight pages, mostly advertising. There was a front-page editorial reluctantly announcing a price increase.

'They raise the price once more, and we'll just quit taking it,' Lois said. 'You read about the aeroplane crash in Florida? Wasn't that terrible? What do you think caused it?'

'Metal fatigue, probably,' Eddie said. 'It was a twenty-year-old jet.'

'The company said it wasn't that at all.'

'They always do,' Eddie said.

'I don't guess the payroll cheque came today or you'd have mentioned it.'

'Payroll's still all balled up. Somebody pressed the wrong button on the new machine and some fifty thousand uncoded cards got scattered all over the office.'

'Oh, no! What do the poor people who don't have bank accounts do?'

'Just wait, like we wait.'

'You had a bad day,' Lois said. 'I can tell.'

'No . . .' Eddie said. 'Not really, I guess.'

'Still working on Saturday?'

'I guess so. Nothing was said. Maybe it'll get easier after the end of the month.'

'You said it was all the new construction work in the Valley that's making you so shorthanded.'

'That's part of it.'

'They're not scheduled to finish until . . . when, sometime next year, isn't it?'

'The end of '81 right now.'

'Eddie! Listen to me! I hardly ever see you any more. You're not going to have to put in all this overtime for the next two years!'

'Of course not,' Eddie said. 'Maybe after this month, that's all, and the work load will level off.'

Larry, dressed for bed, came in. 'Eddie?'

'Your father's tired.'

'I want to ask him something.'

'What is it, Larry?' Eddie asked.

'Eddie, you know the little culture I was running for science class? Something's wrong. Will you look at it?'

'Daddy's . . .'

'I'll look at it, Lois.' Eddie accompanied his son to his son's room.

'What do you think is wrong, Dad?'

'Well, let's see . . .'

'What is it?' Larry asked. 'What made it stop growing?'

Eddie did not answer for a minute. Then: 'You start with one or two . . . well, it's like this, Larry. I'm afraid it's dead. They grow exponentially. Figure out how much money you'd have at the end of a month if you started with just a penny and doubled your money every day. In just a little while, you'd have all the money in the world. Figure it out sometime. Things that grow exponentially, they just don't know when to quit. And your culture, here, it grew until the environment could no longer support it and all at once the food was eaten up and it died.'

'I . . . see . . . Something like that could just grow until it took over the whole world, couldn't it?'

Again Eddie was silent for a moment. Then he rumpled his son's hair. 'That's science fiction, Larry.'

Later, while they were listening to FM, there was a news break reporting a fire out of control in South Los Angeles.

'That's near Becky's, I'll bet,' she said. 'I better phone.'

The phone was still out of order.

'I sure feel cut off without a phone.'

After an interlude of music, Lois said, 'Larry wants to be an engineer, now. I guess after what you said, maybe that's a pretty good thing.'

Eddie looked up from his cigarette. 'Why this all of a sudden?'

'One of his teachers told him what you said – there's a growing engineering shortage.'

'I thought he wanted to be an astronaut.'

'You know Larry. That was last week. His teacher said we're not going to start up the space programme again. It's too expensive. We just don't have the technical manpower and materials to spare.'

'We are in . . . But these kids, young kids they're turning out – they aren't getting the education today. And if anything, I sometimes think it almost makes our jobs even worse, correcting their mistakes. I sometimes wonder where it's all going to stop.'

There was more news from the fire front.

Fire fighters were having a difficult time. Two water mains had broken and the pressure was dropping. The fire was reported to have been caused by the explosion of a gas main. Rising winds did not promise to abate until dawn.

'I sure wish I could get through to Beck,' Lois said. 'Oh,

I guess I told you, did I? Her sister has hypoglycemia, they found out. That's why she's been tired all the time.'

'Never heard of it.'

'Low blood sugar. It's caused by an overactive gland on the pancreas. And treatment is just the opposite of what you'd think, too. I'll bet you'd never guess. If you increase the amount of sugar in the diet, the gland becomes just that much more active to get rid of it and the hypoglycemia gets worse. It's what I'll bet you engineers call a feedback. Isn't that what you call it? Well . . . the way doctors treat it is to *reduce* the amount of sugar you eat. And after a little bit, the pancreas gets back its normal function, and the patient gets well. I told you you'd never guess!'

After a long time, Eddie said, very softly, 'Oh.'

Just after midnight, they went to bed.

'I've been . . .' Lois began and then stopped. 'I don't know. Jumpy. The market was up again today. Another all-time high. Do you think there'll be another crash? Like way back in 1929.'

She could feel him lying tense beside her in the darkness. 'No,' he said slowly, 'I don't think so. I don't think there'll be a crash.'

In spite of the warmth of the room, she could not suppress an involuntary shudder whose cause was nameless. Suddenly, she did not want to ask any more questions.

The wind was rattling the windows.

FRITZ LEIBER

SANITY

'Come in, Phy, and make yourself comfortable.'

The mellow voice – and the suddenly dilating doorway – caught the general secretary of the World playing with a blob of greenish gasoid, squeezing it in his fist and watching it ooze between his fingers in spatulate tendrils that did not dissipate. Slowly, crookedly, he turned his head. World Manager Carrsbury became aware of a gaze that was at once oafish, sly, vacuous. Abruptly the expression was replaced by a nervous smile. The thin man straightened himself, as much as his habitually drooping shoulders would permit, hastily entered, and sat down on the extreme edge of a pneumatically form-fitting chair.

He embarrassedly fumbled the blob of gasoid, looking around for a convenient disposal vent or a crevice in the upholstery. Finding none, he stuffed it hurriedly into his pocket. Then he repressed his fidgetings by clasping his hands resolutely together, and sat with downcast eyes.

'How are you feeling, old man?' Carrsbury asked in a voice that was warm with a benign friendliness.

The general secretary did not look up.

'Anything bothering you, Phy?' Carrsbury continued solicitously. 'Do you feel a bit unhappy, or dissatisfied, about your ... er ... transfer, now that the moment has arrived?'

Still the general secretary did not respond. Carrsbury leaned forward across the dully silver, semicircular desk and, in his most winning tones, urged, 'Come on, old fellow, tell me all about it.'

The general secretary did not lift his head, but he rolled up his strange, distant eyes until they were fixed directly on Carrsbury. He shivered a little, his body seemed to contract, and his bloodless hands tightened their interlocking grip.

'I know,' he said in a low, effortful voice. 'You think I'm insane.'

Carrsbury sat back, forcing his brows to assume a baffled frown under the mane of silvery hair.

'Oh, you needn't pretend to be puzzled,' Phy continued, swiftly now that he had broken the ice. 'You know what that word means as well as I do. Better – even though we both had to do historical research to find out.'

'Insane,' he repeated dreamily, his gaze wavering. 'Significant departure from the norm. Inability to conform to basic conventions underlying all human conduct.'

'Nonsense!' said Carrsbury, rallying and putting on his warmest and most compelling smile. 'I haven't the slightest idea of what you're talking about. That you're a little tired, a little strained, a little distraught – that's quite understandable, considering the burden you've been carrying, and a little rest will be just the thing to fix you up, a nice long vacation away from all this. But as for your being ... why, ridiculous!'

'No,' said Phy, his gaze pinning Carrsbury. 'You think I'm insane. You think all my colleagues in the World Management Service are insane. That's why you're having us replaced with those men you've been training for ten years in your Institute of Political Leadership – ever since, with my help and connivance, you became World Manager.'

Carrsbury retreated before the finality of the statement. For the first time his smile became a bit uncertain. He started to say something, then hesitated and looked at Phy, as if half hoping he would go on.

But that individual was once again staring rigidly at the floor.

Carrsbury leaned back, thinking. When he spoke it was in a more natural voice, much less consciously soothing and fatherly.

'Well, all right, Phy. But look here, tell me something, honestly. Won't you – and the others – be a lot happier when you've been relieved of all your responsibilities?'

Phy nodded sombrely. 'Yes,' he said, 'we will ... but' – his face became strained – 'you see—'

'But—?' Carrsbury prompted.

Phy swallowed hard. He seemed unable to go on. He had gradually slumped toward one side of the chair, and the pressure had caused the green gasoid to ooze from his pocket. His long fingers crept over and kneaded it fretfully.

Carrsbury stood up and came around the desk. His sympathetic frown, from which perplexity had ebbed, was now quite genuine.

'I don't see why I shouldn't tell you all about it now, Phy,' he said simply. 'In a queer sort of way I owe it all to you. And there isn't any point now in keeping it a secret ... there isn't any danger—'

'Yes,' Phy agreed with a quick bitter smile, 'you haven't been in any danger of a coup d'état for some years now. If ever we should have revolted, there'd have been' – his gaze shifted to a point in the opposite wall where a faint vertical crease indicated the presence of a doorway – 'your secret police.'

Carrsbury started. He hadn't thought Phy had known. Disturbingly, there loomed in his mind a phrase: *the cunning of the insane*. But only for a moment. Friendly complacency flooded back. He went behind Phy's chair and rested his hands on the sloping shoulders.

'You know, I've always had a special feeling towards you, Phy,' he said, 'and not only because your whims made it a lot easier for me to become World Manager. I've always felt that you were different from the others, that there were times when—' He hesitated.

Phy squirmed a little under the friendly hands. 'When I had my moments of sanity?' he finished flatly.

'Like now,' said Carrsbury softly, after a nod the other could not see. 'I've always felt that sometimes, in a kind of twisted, unrealistic way, you *understood*. And that has meant a lot to me. I've been alone, Phy, dreadfully alone, for ten whole years. No companionship anywhere. Not even among the men I've been training in the Institute of Political Leadership – for I've had to play a part with them too, keep them in ignorance of certain facts, for fear they would try to seize power over my head before they were sufficiently prepared. No companionship anywhere, except for my hopes – and for occasional moments with you. Now that it's over and a new régime is beginning for us both, I can tell you that. And I'm glad.'

There was silence. Then – Phy did not look around, but one lean hand crept up and touched Carrsbury's. Carrsbury cleared his throat. Strange, he thought, that there would be even a momentary rapport like this between the sane and the insane. But it was so.

He disengaged his hands, strode rapidly back to his desk, turned.

'I'm a throwback, Phy,' he began in a new, unused, eager voice. 'A throwback to a time when human mentality was far sounder. Whether my case was due chiefly to heredity, or to certain unusual accidents of environment, or to both, is unimportant. The point is that a person had been born who was in a position to criticize the present state of mankind in the light of the past, to diagnose its condition, and to begin its cure. For a long time I refused to face the facts, but finally my researches – especially those in the literature of the twentieth century – left me no alternative. The mentality of mankind had become – aberrant. Only certain technological advances, which had resulted in making the business of living infinitely easier and simpler, and the fact that war had been ended with the creation of the present world state, were staving off the inevitable breakdown of civilization. But only staving it off – delaying it. The great masses of mankind had become what would once have been called hopelessly neurotic. Their leaders had become . . . you said it first, Phy . . . insane. Incidentally, this latter phenomenon – the drift of psychological aberrants towards leadership – has been noted in all ages.'

He paused. Was he mistaken, or was Phy following his words with indications of a greater mental clarity than he had ever noted before, even in the relatively non-violent World Secretary? Perhaps – he had often dreamed wistfully of the possibility – there was still a chance of saving Phy. Perhaps, if he just explained to him clearly and calmly—

'In my historical studies,' he continued, 'I soon came to the conclusion that the crucial period was that of the Final Amnesty, concurrent with the founding of the present world state. We are taught that at that time there were released from confinement millions of political prisoners – and millions of others. Just who were those others? To this question, our present histories gave only vague and platitudinous answers. The semantic difficulties I encountered were exceedingly obstinate. But I kept hammering away. Why, I asked myself, have such words as insanity, lunacy, madness, psychosis, disappeared from our vocabulary – and the concepts behind them from our thought? Why has the subject "abnormal psychology" disappeared from the curricula of our schools? Of greater significance, why is our modern psychology strikingly similar to the field of abnormal psychology as taught in the twentieth century, and to that field alone? Why are there no longer, as there were in the twentieth century, any institutions for the confinement and care of the psychologically aberrant?'

Phy's head jerked up. He smiled twistedly. 'Because,' he whispered slyly, 'everyone's insane now.'

The cunning of the insane. Again that phrase loomed warningly in Carrsbury's mind. But only for a moment. He nodded.

'At first I refused to make that deduction. But gradually I reasoned out the why and wherefore of what had happened. It wasn't only that a highly technological civilization had subjected mankind to a wider and more swiftly tempoed range of stimulations, conflicting suggestions, mental strains, emotional wrenchings. In the literature of twentieth-century psychiatry there are observations on a kind of psychosis that results from success. An unbalanced individual keeps going so long as he is fighting something, struggling towards a goal. He reaches his goal – and goes to pieces. His repressed confusions come to the surface, he realizes that he doesn't know what he wants at all, his energies hitherto engaged in combatting something outside himself are turned against himself, he is destroyed. Well, when war was finally outlawed, when the whole world became one unified state, when social inequality was abolished . . . you see what I'm driving at?'

Phy nodded slowly. 'That,' he said in a curious, distant voice, 'is a very interesting deduction.'

'Having reluctantly accepted my main premise,' Carrsbury went on, 'everything became clear. The cyclic six-months' fluctuations in world credit – I realized at once that Morgenstern of Finance must be a manic-depressive with a six-months' phase, or else a dual personality with one aspect a spendthrift, the other a miser. It turned out to be the former. Why was thc Department of Cultural Advancement stagnating? Because Manager Hobart was markedly catatonic. Why the boom in Extraterrestrial Research? Because McElvy was a euphoric.'

Phy looked at him wonderingly. 'But naturally,' he said, spreading his lean hands, from one of which the gasoid dropped like a curl of green smoke.

Carrsbury glanced at him sharply. He replied, 'Yes, I know that you and several of the others have a certain warped awareness of the differences between your ... personalities, though none whatsoever of the basic aberration involved in them all. But to get on. As soon as I realized the situation, my course was marked out. As a sane man, capable of entertaining fixed realistic purposes, and surrounded by individuals of whose inconsistencies and delusions it was easy to make use, I was in a position to attain, with time and tact, any goal at which I might aim. I was already in the Managerial Service. In three years I became World Manager. Once there, my range of influence was vastly enhanced. Like the man in Archimedes' epigram, I had a place to stand from which I could move the world. I was able, in various guises and on various pretexts, to promulgate regulations the actual purpose of which was to soothe the great neurotic masses by curtailing upsetting stimulations and introducing a more regimented and orderly programme of living. I was able, by humouring my fellow executives and making the fullest use of my greater capacity for work, to keep world affairs staggering along fairly safely – at least stave off the worst. At the same time I was able to begin my Ten Years' Plan – the training, in comparative isolation, first in small numbers, then in larger, as those instructed could in turn become instructors, of a group of prospective leaders carefully selected on the basis of their relative freedom from neurotic tendencies.'

'But that—' Phy began rather excitedly, starting up.

'But what?' Carrsbury inquired quickly.

'Nothing,' muttered Phy dejectedly, sinking back.

'That about covers it,' Carrsbury concluded, his voice suddenly grown a little duller. 'Except for one secondary matter. I couldn't afford to let myself go ahead without any protection. Too much depended on me. There was always the risk of being wiped out by some ill-coordinated but nonetheless effective spasm of violence, momentarily uncontrollable by tact, on the part of my fellow executives. So, only because I could see no alternative, I took a dangerous step. I created' – his glance strayed toward the faint crease in the side wall – 'my secret police. There is a type of insanity known as paranoia, an exaggerated suspiciousness involving delusions of persecution. By means of the late-twentieth-century Rand technique of hypnotism, I inculcated a number of these unfortunate individuals with the fixed idea that their lives depended on me and that I was threatened from all sides and must be protected at all costs. A distasteful expedient, even though it served its purpose. I shall be glad, very glad, to see it discontinued. You can understand, can't you, why I had to take that step?'

He looked questioningly at Phy – and became aware with a shock that that individual was grinning at him vacuously and holding up the gasoid between his fingers.

'I cut a hole in my couch and a lot of this stuff came out,' Phy explained in a thick naïve voice. 'Ropes of it got all over my office. I kept tripping.' His fingers patted at it deftly, sculpturing it into the form of a hideous transparent green head, which he proceeded to squeeze out of existence. 'Queer stuff,' he rambled on, 'rarefied liquid. Gas of fixed volume. And all over my office floor, tangled up with the furniture.'

Carrsbury leaned back and shut his eyes. His shoulders slumped. He felt suddenly a little weary, a little eager for his day of triumph to be done. He knew he shouldn't be despondent because he had failed with Phy. After all, the main victory was won. Phy was the merest of side issues. He had always known that, except for flashes, Phy was as hopeless as the rest. Still—

'You don't need to worry about your office floor, Phy,' he said with a listless kindliness. 'Never any more. Your successor will have to see about cleaning it up. Already, you know, to all intents and purposes, you have been replaced.'

'That's just it!' Carrsbury started at Phy's explosive loudness. The World Secretary jumped up and strode towards him, pointing an excited hand. 'That's what I came to see you about! That's what I've been trying to tell you! I can't be replaced like that! None of the others can, either! It won't work! You can't do it!'

With a swiftness born of long practice, Carrsbury slipped behind his desk. He forced his features into that expression of calm, smiling benevolence of which he had grown unutterably weary.

'Now, now, Phy,' he said brightly, soothingly, 'if I can't do it, of course I can't do it. But don't you think you ought to tell me why? Don't you think it would be very nice to sit down and talk it over and you tell me why?'

Phy halted and hung his head, abashed.

'Yes, I guess it would,' he said slowly, abruptly falling back into the low, effortful tones. 'I guess I'll have to. I guess there just isn't any other way. I had hoped, though, not to have to tell you everything.' The last sentence was half question. He looked up wheedlingly at Carrsbury. The latter shook his head, continuing to smile. Phy went back and sat down.

'Well,' he finally began, gloomily kneading the gasoid, 'it all began when you first wanted to be World Manager. You weren't the usual type, but I thought it would be kind of fun – yes, and kind of helpful.' He looked up at Carrsbury. 'You've really done the World a lot of good in quite a lot of ways, always remember that,' he assured him. 'Of course,' he added, again focusing on the tortured gasoid, 'they weren't exactly the ways you thought.'

'No?' Carrsbury prompted automatically. *Humour him. Humour him.* The worn-out refrain droned in his mind.

Phy sadly shook his head. 'Take those regulations you promulgated to soothe people—'

'Yes?'

'—they kind of got changed on the way. For instance, your prohibition, regarding reading tapes, of all exciting literature . . . oh, we tried a little of the soothing stuff you suggested at first. Everyone got a great kick out of it. They laughed and laughed. But afterwards, well, as I said, it kind of got changed – in this case to a prohibition of all *unexciting* literature.'

Carrsbury's smile broadened. For a moment the edge of his mind had toyed with a fear, but Phy's last remark had banished it.

'Every day I coast past several reading stands,' Carrsbury said gently. 'The fiction tapes offered for sale are always in the most chastely and simply coloured containers. None of those wild and lurid pictures that one used to see everywhere.'

'But did you ever buy one and listen to it? Or project the visual text?' Phy questioned apologetically.

'For ten years I've been a very busy man,' Carrsbury answered. 'Of course I've read the official reports regarding such matters, and at times glanced through sample résumés of taped fiction.'

'Oh, sure, that sort of official stuff,' agreed Phy, glancing up at the wall of tape files beyond the desk. 'What we did, you see, was to keep the monochrome containers but go back to the old kind of contents. The contrast kind of tickled people. Remember, as I said before, a lot of your regulations have done good. Cut out a lot of unnecessary noise and inefficient foolishness, for one thing.'

That sort of official stuff. The phrase lingered unpleasantly in Carrsbury's ears. There was a trace of irrepressible suspicion in his quick over-the-shoulder glance at the tiered tape files.

'Oh, yes,' Phy went on, 'and that prohibition against yielding to unusual or indecent impulses, with a long listing of specific categories. It went into effect all right, but with a little rider attached: "unless you really want to". That seemed absolutely necessary, you know.' His fingers worked furiously with the gasoid. 'As for the prohibition of various stimulating beverages – well, in this locality they're still served under other names, and an interesting custom has grown up of behaving very soberly while imbibing them. Now when we come to that matter of the eight-hour working day—'

Almost involuntarily, Carrsbury had got up and walked over to the outer wall. With a flip of his hand through an invisible U-shaped beam, he switched on the window. It was as if the outer wall had disappeared. Through its near-perfect transparency, he peered down with fierce curiosity past the sleekly gleaming façades to the terraces and parkways below.

The modest throngs seemed quiet and orderly enough. But then there was a scurry of confusion – a band of people, at this angle all tiny heads with arms and legs, came out from a shop far below and began to pelt another group with what looked like foodstuffs. While, on a side parkway, two small ovoid vehicles, seamless drops of silver because their vision panels were invisible from the outside, butted each other playfully. Someone started to run.

Carrsbury hurriedly switched off the window and turned around. Those were just off-chance occurrences, he told himself angrily. Of no real statistical significance whatever. For ten years mankind had steadily been trending toward sanity despite occasional relapses. He'd seen it with his own eyes, seen the day-by-day progress – at least enough to know. He'd been a fool to let Phy's ramblings affect him – only tired nerves had made that possible.

He glanced at his timepiece.

'Excuse me,' he said curtly, striding past Phy's chair, 'I'd like to continue this conversation, but I have to get along to the first meeting of the new Central Managerial Staff.'

'Oh but you can't!' Instantly Phy was up and dragging at his arm. 'You just can't do it, you know! It's impossible!'

The pleading voice rose toward a scream. Impatiently Carrsbury tried to shake loose. The seam in the side wall widened, became a doorway. Instantly, both of them stopped struggling.

In the doorway stood a cadaverous giant of a man with a stubby dark weapon in his hand. Straggly black beard shaded into gaunt cheeks. His face was a cruel blend of suspicion and fanatical devotion, the first directed along the weapon at Phy, the second – and the somnambulistic eyes – at Carrsbury.

'He was threatening you?' the bearded man asked in a harsh voice, moving the weapon suggestively.

For a moment an angry, vindictive light glinted in Carrsbury's eyes. Then it flicked out. What could he have been thinking, he asked himself. This poor lunatic World Secretary was no one to hate.

'Not at all, Hartman,' he remarked calmly. 'We were discussing something and we became excited and allowed our voices to rise. Everything is quite all right.'

'Very well,' said the bearded man doubtfully, after a

pause. Reluctantly he returned his weapon to its holster, but he kept his hand on it and remained standing in the doorway.

'And now,' said Carrsbury, disengaging himself, 'I must go.'

He had stepped into the corridor slidewalk and had coasted halfway to the elevator before he realized that Phy had followed him and was plucking timidly at his sleeve.

'You can't go off like this,' Phy pleaded urgently, with an apprehensive backward glance. Carrsbury noted that Hartman had also followed – an ominous pylon two paces to the rear. 'You must give me a chance to explain, to tell you why, just like you asked me.'

Humour him. Carrsbury's mind was deadly tired of the drone, but mere weariness prompted him to dance to it a little longer. 'You can talk to me in the elevator,' he conceded, stepping off the slidewalk. His finger flipped through a U-beam and a serpentine movement of light across the wall traced the elevator's obedient rise.

'You see, it wasn't just that matter of prohibitory regulations,' Phy launched out hurriedly. 'There were lots of other things that never did work out like your official reports indicated. Departmental budgets for instance. The reports showed, I know, that appropriations for Extraterrestrial Research were being regularly slashed. Actually, in your ten years of office, they increased tenfold. Of course, there was no way for you to know that. You couldn't be all over the world at once and see each separate launching of suprastratospheric rockets.'

The moving light became stationary. A seam dilated. Carrsbury stepped into the elevator. He debated sending Hartman back. Poor babbling Phy was no menace. Still – *the cunning of the insane*. He decided against it, reached out and flipped the control beam at the sector that would bring them to the hundredth and top floor. The door snipped softly shut. The cage became a surging darkness in which floor numerals winked softly. Twenty-one. Twenty-two, Twenty-three.

'And then there was the Military Service. You had it sharply curtailed.'

'Of course I did.' Sheer weariness stung Carrsbury into talk. 'There's only one country in the world. Obviously, the only military requirement is an adequate police force. To say nothing of the risks involved in putting weapons into the hands of the present world population.'

'I know,' Phy's answer came guiltily from the darkness. 'Still, what's happened is that, unknown to you, the Military Service has been increased in size, and recently four rocket squadrons have been added.'

Fifty-seven. Fifty-eight. *Humour him.* 'Why?'

'Well, you see we've found out that Earth is being reconnoitred. Maybe from Andromeda. Maybe hostile. Have to be prepared. We didn't tell you ... well, because we were afraid it might excite you.'

The voice trailed off. Carrsbury shut his eyes. How long, he asked himself, how long? He realized with dull surprise that in the last hour people like Phy, endured for ten years, had become unutterably wearisome to him. For the moment even the thought of the conference over which he would soon be presiding, the conference that was to usher in a sane world, failed to stir him. Reaction to success? To the end of a ten years' tension?

'Do you know how many floors there are in this building?'

Carrsbury was not immediately conscious of the new note in Phy's voice, but he reacted to it.

'One hundred,' he replied promptly.

'Then,' asked Phy, 'just where are we?'

Carrsbury opened his eyes to the darkness. One hundred twenty-seven, blinked the floor numeral. One hundred twenty-eight. One hundred twenty-nine.

Something cold dragged at Carrsbury's stomach, pulled at his brain. He felt as if his mind were being slowly and irresistibly twisted. He thought of hidden dimensions, of unsuspected holes in space. Something remembered from elementary physics danced through his thoughts: if it were possible for an elevator to keep moving upwards with uniform acceleration, no one inside an elevator could determine whether the effects they were experiencing were due to acceleration or to gravity – whether the elevator were standing motionless on some planet or shooting up at ever-increasing velocity through free space.

One hundred forty-one. One hundred forty-two.

'Or as if you were rising through consciousness into an unsuspected realm of mentality lying above,' suggested Phy in his new voice, with its hint of gentle laughter.

One hundred forty-six. One hundred forty-seven. It was slowing now. One hundred forty-nine. One hundred fifty. It had stopped.

This was some trick. The thought was like cold water in Carrsbury's face. Some cunning childish trick of Phy's. An easy thing to hocus the numerals. Carrsbury groped irascibly about in the darkness, encountered the slick surface of a holster, Hartman's gaunt frame.

'Get ready for a surprise,' Phy warned from close at his elbow.

As Carrsbury turned and grabbed, bright sunlight drenched him, followed by a gripping, heart-stopping spasm of vertigo.

He, Hartman, and Phy, along with a few insubstantial bits of furnishings and controls, were standing in the air fifty storeys above the hundred-storey summit of World Managerial Centre.

For a moment he grabbed frantically at nothing. Then he realized they were not falling and his eyes began to trace the hint of walls and ceiling and floor and, immediately below them, the ghost of a shaft.

Phy nodded. 'That's all there is to it,' he assured Carrsbury casually. 'Just another of those charmingly odd modern notions against which you have legislated so persistently – like our incomplete staircases and roads to nowhere and those charming garden paths which ended in drops, not stairs, and the British called "ha-has". The Buildings and Grounds Committee decided to extend the range of the elevator for sightseeing purposes. The shaft was made air-transparent to avoid spoiling the form of the original building and to improve the view. This was achieved so satisfactorily that an electronic warning system had to be installed for the safety of passing airjets and other craft. Treating the surfaces of the cage like windows was an obvious detail.'

He paused and looked quizzically at Carrsbury. 'All very simple,' he observed, 'but don't you find a kind of symbolism in it? For ten years now you've been spending most of your life in that building below. Every day you've used this elevator. But not once have you dreamed of these fifty extra storeys. Don't you think that something of the same sort may be true of your observations of other aspects of contemporary social life?'

Carrsbury gaped at him stupidly.

Phy turned to watch the growing speck of an approaching aircraft. 'You might look at it too,' he remarked to Carrsbury, 'for it's going to transport you to a far happier, more restful life.'

Carrsbury parted his lips, wet them. 'But—' he said, unsteadily. 'But—'

Phy smiled. 'That's right, I didn't finish my explanation. Well, you might have gone on being World Manager all your life, in the isolation of your office and your miles of taped official reports and your occasional confabs with me and the others. Except for your Institute of Political Leadership and your Ten Years' Plan. That upset things. Of course, we were as much interested in it as we were in you. It had definite possibilities. We hoped it would work out. We would have been glad to retire from office if it had. But, most fortunately, it didn't. And that sort of ended the whole experiment.'

He caught the downward glance of Carrsbury's gaze.

'No,' he said, 'I'm afraid your pupils aren't waiting for you in the conference chamber on the hundredth storey. I'm afraid they're still in the Institute.' His voice became gently sympathetic. 'And I'm afraid that it's become . . . well . . . a somewhat different sort of institute.'

Carrsbury stood very still, swaying a little. Gradually his thoughts and his willpower were emerging from the waking nightmare that had paralyzed them. *The cunning of the insane* – he had neglected that trenchant warning. In the very moment of victory—

No! He had forgotten Hartman! This was the very emergency for which that counterstroke had been prepared.

He glanced sideways at the chief member of his secret police. The black giant, unconcerned by their strange position, was glaring fixedly at Phy as if at some evil magician from whom any malign impossibility could be expected.

Now Hartman became aware of Carrsbury's gaze. He divined his thought.

He drew his dark weapon from its holster, pointed it unwaveringly at Phy.

His black-bearded lips curled. From them came a hissing sound. Then, in a loud voice, he cried, 'You're dead, Phy! I disintegrated you.'

Phy reached over and took the weapon from his hand.

'That's another respect in which you completely miscalculated the modern temperament,' he remarked to Carrsbury, a shade argumentatively. 'All of us have certain subjects on which we're a trifle unrealistic. That's only human nature. Hartman's was his suspiciousness – a weakness for ideas involving plots and persecutions. You gave him the worst sort of job – one that catered to and encouraged his weaknesses. In a very short time he became hopelessly unrealistic. Why for years he's never realized that he's been carrying a dummy pistol.'

'But,' he added, 'give him the proper job and he'd function well enough – say something in creation or exploration or social service. Fitting a man to the job is an art with infinite possibilities. That's why we had Morgenstern in Finance – to keep credit fluctuating in a safe, predictable rhythm. That's why a euphoric is made manager of Extraterrestrial Research – to keep it booming. Why a catatonic is given Cultural Advancement – to keep it from tripping on its face in its haste to get ahead.'

He turned away. Dully, Carrsbury observed that the aircraft was hovering close to the cage and sidling slowly in.

'But in that case why—' he began stupidly.

'Why were you made World Manager?' Phy finished easily. 'Isn't that fairly obvious? Haven't I told you several times that you did a lot of good, indirectly? You interested us, don't you see? In fact, you were practically unique. As you know, it's our cardinal principle to let every individual express himself as he wants to. In your case, that involved letting you become World Manager. Taken all in all it worked out very well. Everyone had a good time, a number of constructive regulations were promulgated, we learned a lot – oh, we didn't get everything we hoped for, but one never does. Unfortunately, in the end, we were forced to discontinue the experiment.'

The aircraft had made contact.

'You understand, of course, why that was necessary?' Phy continued hurriedly, as he urged Carrsbury toward the opening port. 'I'm sure you must. It all comes down to a question of sanity. What is sanity – now, in the twentieth century, any time? Adherence to a norm. Conformity to certain basic conventions underlying all human conduct. In our age, departure from the norm has become the norm. Inability to conform has become the standard of conformity. That's quite clear, isn't it? And it enables you to understand, doesn't it, your own case and that of your protégés? Over a long period of years you persisted in adhering to a norm, in conforming to certain basic conventions. You were completely unable to adapt yourself to the society around you. You could only pretend – and your protégés wouldn't have been able to do even that. Despite your many engaging personal characteristics, there was obviously only one course of action open to us.'

In the port Carrsbury turned. He had found his voice at last. It was hoarse, ragged. 'You mean that all these years you've just been *humouring me*?'

The port was closing. Phy called, 'There was an Oglala Sioux Indian named Crazy Horse. He licked Crook and he licked Custer. Don't think I'm underestimating your strength, Carrsbury.'

As the aircraft edged out, he waved farewell with the blob of green gasoid.

'It'll be very pleasant where you're going,' he shouted encouragingly. 'Comfortable quarters, adequate facilities for exercise, and a complete library of twentieth-century literature to while away your time.'

He watched Carrsbury's rigid face, staring whitely from the vision port, until the aircraft had diminished to a speck.

Then he turned away, looked at his hands, noticed the gasoid, tossed it out the open door of the cage, studied its flight for a few moments, then flicked the downbeam.

'I'm glad to see the last of that fellow,' he muttered, more to himself than to Hartman, as they plummeted toward the roof. 'He was beginning to have a very disturbing influence on me. In fact, I was beginning to fear for my' – his expression became suddenly vacuous – 'insanity.'

II ALIENS, ON EARTH AND ELSEWHERE

J.-H. ROSNY aîné

THE SHAPES

Translated from the French
by Damon Knight

I

It was a thousand years before the beginning of that centre of civilization from which Nineveh, Babylon and Ecbatana were later to spring.

The nomadic tribe of Pjehu, with its horses, asses and cattle, was crossing the wild forest of Kzur towards the west, through a slanting curtain of light. The edge of the setting sun swelled, hovered, dropped from its graceful perches.

Everyone being weary, they were all silent, searching for a good clearing where the tribe might kindle the sacred fire, prepare the evening meal, and sleep in safety from wild animals, behind a double line of red-hot coals.

The clouds turned opalescent; illusory countrysides trailed away to the four horizons; the gods of night breathed their cradle song, and the tribe was still on the move. A scout came galloping back with word of a clearing and water, a pure spring.

The tribe gave three long shouts; everyone moved faster. Childish laughter rippled out; the very horses and asses, trained to recognize the nearness of a stopping place by the return of the scouts and the nomads' cheers, raised their necks proudly.

The clearing came into view. Here, where the delightful spring had hollowed out its bed among mosses and shrubs, a phantasmagoria met the nomads' eyes.

It was, first, a great circle of translucent bluish cones, point uppermost, each nearly half the bulk of a man. A few clear streaks, a few dark convolutions were scattered across their surfaces; each one had a dazzling star near its base.

Farther distant, equally strange, slabs stood on end, looking rather like birch-bark, and spotted with varicoloured ellipses. Other Shapes, here and there, were almost cylindrical – some tall and thin, others low and squat, all of a bronzed colour, tipped with green; and all, like the slabs, having the characteristic point of light.

The tribe stared in amazement. Even the bravest were frozen with superstitious fear, increasing still more when the Shapes began to sway in the twilight of the clearing. And suddenly, their stars wavering, flickering, the cones stretched higher, the cylinders and the slabs hissed like water thrown upon a flame, all of them moving towards the nomads with mounting speed.

Spellbound by the sight, the tribe did not move, but kept on watching. The Shapes fell upon them. The shock was terrible. Warriors, women and children fell in heaps, mysteriously struck down as if by lightning. Then the terrified survivors found strength to flee. And the Shapes, breaking their close ranks, spread out around the tribe, implacably pursuing those who fled. Nevertheless, the frightful attack was not infallible: it killed some, stunned others, wounded none. A few red drops spurted from the nostrils, eyes, and ears of the dying; but others, undamaged, soon arose and rejoined the fantastic rout, in the paling twilight.

Whatever might be the nature of the Shapes, they behaved like living creatures, not like elements of nature, having, like living creatures, an inconstancy and diversity of motion, evidently choosing their victims, not confounding the nomads with trees or shrubs, or even with animals.

In a short time the swiftest of the tribe noticed that no one was pursuing them any longer. Exhausted and in tatters, at last they dared retrace their steps towards the mystery. Far away, between the tree trunks flooded with shadow, the resplendent chase went on. And the Shapes, seemingly by choice, ran down and massacred the warriors, often disdaining to attack the feeble, or the women and children.

Seen thus at a distance, in the night that had now fallen, the scene was more supernatural, more overwhelming to barbarian minds. About to take up their flight once more, the warriors made a vital discovery. It was this: whatever the fugitives did, *the Shapes abandoned the pursuit at a fixed boundary*. However weary and powerless the victim might be, even if he were unconscious, once he had crossed that invisible frontier he was out of danger.

This reassuring discovery, soon confirmed by fifty observations, calmed the fugitives' frantic nerves. They dared to wait for their companions, their wives and their children who had escaped the butchery. One of them indeed, their Hero, who had been stunned at first, regained his spirit and lit a fire, blew on a buffalo horn to guide the fugitives.

Then one by one the pitiful survivors came. Many, crippled, dragged themselves by their hands. The mothers, with indomitable maternal strength, had protected, assembled, carried their children through the wild mêlée. And many asses, horses, and cattle reappeared, less frightened than their masters.

A dismal night followed, passed in sleepless silence, while the warriors felt shivers run up and down their spines. But the dawn came, stealing pale through the heavy foliage; then the auroral fanfare of colours, of echoing bird cries, exhorted them to live, to cast off the terrors of darkness.

The Hero, the natural leader, formed the crowd into groups and began counting the tribe. Half the warriors, two hundred, were missing. The loss of women was much less; of children, almost none.

When the counting was finished and the beasts of burden had been reassembled (few were missing, due to the superiority of instinct over reason during a crisis), the Hero formed up the tribe as usual. Then, ordering everyone to wait for him, he walked, pale and alone, towards the clearing. No one dared follow him, even at a distance.

He went to where the trees were spaced out widely, a little inside the limit observed yesterday, and looked.

Far across the clearing, in the cool transparency of morning, flowed the pretty spring. Around the edges, reunited, the fantastic troop of Shapes shone resplendently. Their colours had changed. The Cones were more compact, their turquoise tint had turned greenish; the Cylinders were streaked with violet and the Slabs looked like virgin copper. But each had its blazing star, dazzling even in daylight.

The outline of these phantasmagorical Entities had also changed. The Cones tended to enlarge into Cylinders, the Cylinders to flatten and spread, while the Slabs curled slightly.

But suddenly, as on the night before, the Shapes swayed, their stars began to flicker; the Hero, slowly, retreated beyond the borderline of safety.

II

The tribe of Pjehu halted at the doorway of the great nomad tabernacle, where only chiefs might enter. In the starry depths, under the virile image of the Sun, sat the three high priests. Below them on the gilded steps, the dozen under-priests.

The Hero stepped forward and recounted at length the fearful journey through the forest of Kzur; the priests listened very gravely, astonished, feeling their power dwindle before that inconceivable adventure.

The Supreme High Priest demanded that the tribe sacrifice to the Sun twelve bulls, seven onagers, three stallions. He recognized divine attributes in the Shapes, and, after the sacrifices, he resolved upon a hieratic expedition.

All the priests, all the chiefs of the Zahelal nation, were to take part.

And messengers were sent out over the mountains and the plains, for a hundred leagues around the place where later would rise Ecbatana of the mages. Everywhere the dark tale made men's hair stand on end; everywhere the chiefs responded quickly to the priestly call.

One autumn morning, the Male pierced the clouds, flooded the tabernacle, reached the altar where the bleeding heart of a bull lay smoking hot. The high priests, the under-priests, fifty tribal chiefs raised a cry of triumph. A hundred thousand nomads, standing in the dew outside, took up the clamour, turning their tanned faces towards the miraculous forest of Kzur and shivering a little. The omen was favourable.

Thus, with the priests at their head, a whole people marched through the trees. In the afternoon, at about the third hour, the Hero of Pjehu halted the throng. The great clearing lay spread out in its majesty, glowing with autumn, a torrent of dead leaves covering its mosses. On the banks of the spring, the priests saw the Shapes which they had come to worship and appease. They were pleasant to the eye, under the shade of the trees, with their trembling colour changes, the pure flames of their stars, their tranquil movements at the edge of the spring.

'We must make the offering here,' said the Supreme High Priest, 'that they may know we submit to their power!'

All the greybeards nodded. One voice was raised, nevertheless. It was Yushik, of the tribe of Nim, the young star-counter, the pale prophetic watchman, of recent fame, who boldly demanded to go nearer the Shapes.

But the old men, white-haired in their wisdom, prevailed. The altar was built, the victim led forward – a dazzling white stallion. Then, in the silence of the prostrate people, the bronze knife found the animal's noble heart. A great moan went up. And the High Priest:

'Art thou appeased, O god?'

Over there, among the silent trunks, the Shapes still moved in a ring, brightening themselves, preferring places where the sunbeams were thickest.

'Yea,' cried the enthusiast, 'they are appeased!'

And snatching up the stallion's warm heart, before the High Priest could say a word, he flung himself into the clearing. Shouting, other fanatics followed him. The Shapes gently swayed, crowding together, skimming the grass, then suddenly hurled themselves on the daring ones in a massacre that stunned the fifty tribes.

Six or seven fugitives, hotly pursued, managed to reach the boundary. The rest were dead, Yushik among them.

'These are relentless gods!' solemnly spoke the Supreme High Priest.

Then a council was held, the venerable council of priests, elders and chiefs. They decided to put up a row of stakes around the boundary line. In order to determine this line, they would force slaves to expose themselves to attack by the Shapes at one part of the perimeter after another.

And this was done. Under the threat of death, slaves entered the ring. So careful were the precautions taken that few of them perished. The boundary was firmly established, made visible to all by its line of stakes.

Thus the hieratic expedition ended successfully, and the Zahelals believed themselves safe from the enemy.

III

But the preventive system advocated by the council was not long in showing its flaws. The following spring, the tribes of Hertoth and Nazzum, carelessly passing near the ring of stakes and suspecting nothing, were cruelly assaulted and decimated by the Shapes.

The chiefs who escaped the massacre told the great Zahelal council that the Shapes were now much more numerous than they had been the preceding autumn. Their pursuit was still limited, but the boundary had been enlarged.

This news dismayed the people; there was great mourning and many sacrifices. Then the council resolved to destroy the forest of Kzur by fire.

In spite of all their efforts, they could burn no more than the borders of the forest.

Then the priests, in despair, consecrated the forest and forbade anyone to enter it. And many summers passed.

One autumn night, the sleeping encampment of the tribe of Zulf, ten bowshots from the forbidden forest, was invaded by the Shapes. Three hundred more warriors lost their lives.

From this day a dark, mysterious tale went from tribe to tribe, a thing whispered by night, under the wide starry skies of Mesopotamia. *Man was going to perish.* The *Others*, constantly expanding, in the forest, across the plains, indestructible, day by day would swallow up the overthrown race of man. And this dark, fearful secret haunted the brains of men, sapped their fighting strength and the confidence of their youth. The nomad, thinking such thoughts, no longer dared take pleasure in the lush pastures of his fathers. He turned his weary eyes upwards, waiting for the stars to halt in their courses. It was the millennial year of this childlike people, the world's knell.

And in their distress, these thinkers turned to a bitter cult, a cult of death preached by pale prophets, the cult of Darknesses more powerful than the Stars, the Darknesses which would engulf and devour the holy Light, the resplendent fire.

Everywhere at the edge of the wilderness were seen the emaciated, immobile figures of the inspired ones, the men of silence, who, passing from time to time among the tribes, told of their terrible dreams, the Twilight of the great Night to come, of the dying Sun.

IV

Now in those days there lived an extraordinary man called Bakhun, a member of the tribe of Ptuh and brother to the Supreme High Priest of the Zahelals. In his youth he had abandoned the nomadic life, had chosen a place in the wilderness, between four hills, in a narrow green valley where a spring poured out its pure song. He had built a fixed tent of stones, a cyclopean habitation. With patience and with the careful management of his horses and oxen, he had achieved the opulence of regular harvests. His four wives and thirty children lived the life of Eden there.

Bakhun professed unusual beliefs, for which he might have been stoned, save for the respect of the Zahelals for his elder brother, the Supreme High Priest.

First, he declared that the sedentary life was better than the life of the nomads, conserving man's strength to the profit of his spirit.

Second, he believed that the Sun, the Moon and the Stars were not gods, but luminous masses.

Third, he said that men should really believe only in those things tested by measurement.

The Zahelals credited him with magical powers, and the most daring of them sometimes risked consulting him. They never repented it. It was said that he had often helped unfortunate tribes by distributing food to them.

Now in this dark hour, when men were faced with the melancholy choice of giving up their green lands or being destroyed by the inexorable gods, the tribes thought of Bakhun, and the priests themselves, after a struggle with their pride, sent to him a deputation made up of three of the greatest among them.

Bakhun listened with close attention to their accounts, asking them to repeat certain parts, asking many detailed questions. He asked for two days to meditate. When the time was up, he announced simply that he would dedicate his life to the study of the Shapes.

The tribes were a little disappointed, for they had hoped Bakhun might be able to deliver the land by sorcery. Nevertheless, the chiefs expressed their happiness at his decision, and hoped that great things would come of it.

Then Bakhun took up his station at the edge of the forest of Kzur, leaving it only when night fell, and all day long, mounted on the swiftest stallion in Chaldea, he watched. Soon, convinced of the splendid animal's superiority over the most agile of the Shapes, he was able to begin his bold and painstaking study of the enemies of man, that study to which we owe the great antecuneiform book of sixty tablets, the finest stone book bequeathed by the nomadic age to modern civilization.

In this book, admirable for its restraint and its patient observation, is the description of a form of life absolutely distinct from our animal and vegetable kingdoms, a form which Bakhun humbly admitted he had been able to analyse only in its grossest and most superficial features. It is impossible for a man to read without shuddering this monograph on the beings Bakhun called the Xipehuz; these dispassionate notes, never forced to conform to any system, of their actions, their modes of locomotion, of combat, of procreation – these notes which demonstrate that the human race was once on the brink of Nothingness, that the earth nearly became the patrimony of a kingdom every trace of which has been lost.

The book should be read in Dessault's marvellous translation, full of unlooked-for discoveries in pre-Assyrian linguistics – discoveries unfortunately more admired in foreign countries, in England, in Germany, than in the author's native land. The eminent scholar has graciously made available salient passages of this precious work, which are given in the following pages; and it is hoped that these passages will inspire the reader to look further into Dessault's superb translation.[1]

V

The Xipehuz are evidently living beings. All their motions reveal the free will, impulsiveness, cooperation and partial independence which distinguish the Animal from the Plant and from nonliving matter. Although their mode of progression is impossible to describe in comparative terms – being a simple gliding motion across the ground – it is plain that it is under their voluntary control. We see them stop suddenly,

1. *The Precursors of Nineveh*, by B. Dessault (Calmann-Levy). In the interests of clarity, I have converted the following extract from the book of Bakhun into modern scientific language.

turn, pursue one another, stroll together by twos and threes; they display preferences which will make them leave one companion to join another at a distance. They are incapable of climbing trees, but they succeed in killing birds after *attracting them* by undiscoverable means. They are frequently seen to surround forest animals or to lie in wait for them behind a bush; these they invariably kill and consume. It may be stated as a rule that they kill *all animals without distinction*, whenever they can catch them, and this without any apparent motive, for they do not devour them, but merely reduce them to ashes.

In doing so they make use of no funeral pyre; the incandescent point which each has at its base suffices them for this purpose. They form a circle of ten or twenty around the carcass of a large animal and cause their rays to converge upon it. For small animals, birds for example, the rays of a single Xipehuz are sufficient to cause incineration. It should be noted that the heat they produce is not instantaneous in its effect. I have often received the irradiation of a Xipehuz upon my hand, and the skin began to feel warm only after a certain time.

I do not know if it is correct to say that the Xipehuz have different forms, for any one of them can successively transform itself into a cone, a cylinder and a slab, and this in the course of a single day. Their colours vary constantly, a fact which I believe can be attributed in general to the changes in the quality of the light from morning to evening and from evening to morning. Nevertheless certain variations seem to be due to the impulses of individuals, and in particular to their *passions*, if I may be permitted this term, and thus constitute genuine expressions of physiognomy, of which, in spite of ardent study, I have been utterly unable to identify any except by hypothesis. Thus I have never been able to distinguish between an angry tint and a calm one, which surely would be the primary discovery in this field.

I have spoken of their passions. I have also remarked earlier upon their preferences, which I might term their *friendships*. They also have their *hatreds*. One Xipehuz continually keeps his distance from another, and vice versa. They seem to experience violent rages. They hurl themselves upon one another with movements identical to those observed when they attack men or large animals, and in fact it was these combats which taught me they are not immortal, as I had been at first disposed to believe, for two or three times I have seen Xipehuz succumb in these encounters, that is to say *fall, shrink,* and *petrify.* I have carefully preserved some of these bizarre cadavers,[2] and perhaps at some future time they may serve to reveal the nature of the Xipehuz. They are yellowish crystals, arranged irregularly, and streaked with blue filaments.

From the fact that the Xipehuz are not immortal, I was able to deduce that it should be possible to attack and defeat them, and at that point I began the series of martial experiments of which I shall have to speak later.

Since the Xipehuz' radiance is always sufficient to make them visible through underbrush and even behind large tree trunks – a wide halo emanates from them in all directions and warns of their approach – I was able to venture often into the forest, trusting myself to the speed of my stallion.

There, I tried to find out if they built shelters, but I confess to having failed in that research. They move neither stones nor plants, and appear to be strangers to any form of *tangible* and *visible* industry, the only sort that can be distinguished by human observation. Consequently they have no weapons, in the usual sense of that word. It is certain that they cannot kill at a distance: every animal which has been able to flee without coming into *direct* contact with a Xipehuz, has invariably escaped, and I have witnessed this many times.

2. The Kensington Museum in London, and Professor Dessault himself, have in their possession certain mineral fragments, similar in every way to those described by Bakhun, which under chemical analysis have been found impossible to *decompose* or to *combine* with other substances, and which, in consequence, cannot be assigned a place in any conventional nomenclature.

As the unfortunate tribe of Pjehu has already observed, they cannot cross certain intangible barriers; thus their movements are limited. But these limits continually expand from year to year, from month to month. I had to try to discover the cause of this.

Well, this cause appears to be nothing other than a phenomenon of *collective growth,* and like most Xipehuzian things, it is incomprehensible to the human mind. In brief, the governing principle is this: The limits of Xipehuzian movement enlarge in proportion to the number of living individuals, that is to say that when new beings are propagated, the frontiers are extended; but so long as their number does not increase, each individual is totally incapable of leaving the habitat determined – by natural forces? – for the race as a whole. This principle suggests a closer correlation between the individual and the group than that observed among other animals and men. Later we saw the reciprocal of this principle in operation, for when the numbers of Xipehuz began to diminish, their frontiers shrank in proportion.

Concerning the phenomenon of propagation itself, I have little to say; but this little is characteristic. To begin with, this propagation takes place four times a year, a little before the equinoxes and solstices, and only on very clear nights. The Xipehuz join in groups of three, and these groups draw together little by little until there is only one, tightly amalgamated and arranged in a very long ellipse. They remain so all night long, and until the sun reaches the zenith on the following day. When they separate, vague forms arise, vaporous and *enormous.*

These forms slowly condense, dwindle, and transform themselves at the end of ten days into amber-tinted cones, considerably larger still than an adult Xipehuz. It takes them two months and several days to reach their maximum development, which is to say diminution. At the end of this time they become similar to other members of their race, their shapes and colours variable according to the weather, the time and the mood of the individual. A few days after their development or diminution is complete, the boundaries enlarge. Needless to say, it was shortly before this redoubtable moment that I kicked the flanks of my noble Kuath, in order to establish my camp farther away.

It is impossible to say whether the Xipehuz have senses as we understand the term. They certainly have organs which serve the same purpose.

The ease with which they detect the presence of animals, men above all, over great distances makes it evident that their organs of perception are at least as efficient as our eyes. I have never seen them mistake a plant for an animal, even under circumstances in which I might well have fallen into this error, deceived by the light filtering through leaves, the colour of the object, or its position. Their use of twenty to consume a large animal, whereas one alone incinerates a bird, indicates a correct understanding of proportions, and this understanding seems even more perfect when one considers that they make use of ten, twelve, fifteen, always in keeping with the relative size of the carcass. A still better argument, either for the existence of sense organs analogous to ours, or for their intelligence, is their manner of attacking our tribes, for while they mercilessly pursue the warriors, they give little or no attention to women and children.

Now, the most important question: do they have a language? I am able to reply without the slightest hesitation. Yes, they have a language. And this language is composed of signs, some of which I have even been able to decipher.

Suppose, for example, that a Xipehuz wishes to speak to another. To do this, it suffices for him to direct the radiation from his star toward the other, a thing which is always perceived instantly. The one who is hailed, if he is in motion, stops and waits. The speaker then traces rapidly on the very skin of the listener – and it makes no difference on which side – a series of short luminous characters made by directing the radiation from his base. These characters remain fixed a moment, then fade away.

The listener, after a short pause, responds.

As a preliminary to any action of combat or ambuscade,

I have always seen the Xipehuz employ the following characters:

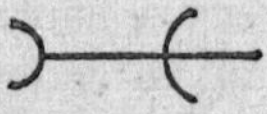

When I myself am in question – and this happens frequently, for they have done everything possible to exterminate my noble Kuath and me – the signs

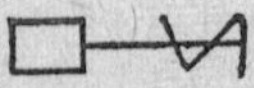

have invariably been exchanged – among others, like the word or

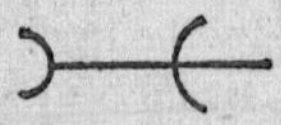

phrase given above. The usual calling sign is

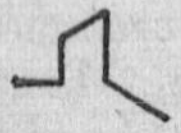

and this makes the receiving individual hasten up. When the Xipehuz are invited to a general meeting, I have never failed to observe a signal of this form

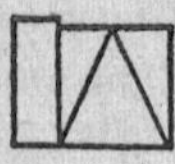

representing the triple appearance of these beings.

In addition, the Xipehuz have more complicated signs not relating to actions similar to ours but to a completely extraordinary order of things, and these I have been unable to decipher. One can hardly entertain any doubt of their ability to exchange *ideas* of an abstract order, probably the equivalents of human ideas, for they are capable of standing motionless for long periods, doing nothing but conversing, which indicates real accumulations of thoughts.

In spite of their metamorphoses (whose laws differ for each, only very slightly, but characteristically enough for a determined observer), during my long sojourn among them I learned to know a number of Xipehuz rather intimately by recognizing the peculiarities among their individual differences. (Should I say among their characters?) I have known taciturn ones, who almost never traced a word; voluble ones who wrote veritable discourses; attentive ones; gossips who spoke at the same time, one interrupting the other. Some were of a retiring nature and preferred a solitary life; others obviously sought company; some were fierce, constantly hunting birds and beasts; and some merciful, often sparing animals and letting them live in peace. Does not all this open an enormous avenue to the imagination? Does it not lead us to imagine diversities of aptitude, strength, and intelligence analogous to those of the human race?

They practise education. How many times have I not seen an old Xipehuz, seated in the midst of many young ones, irradiating them with signs which they then repeated one after another – and which he made them do over when their repetition was imperfect! These lessons were indeed marvellous to my eyes, and in all that concerns the Xipehuz, there is nothing that has more often fixed my attention, nothing that has preoccupied me more during my nights of insomnia. It seemed to me that here, in the morning of the race, the veil of mystery might open, that some simple, primitive idea might spring forth and illuminate for me a corner of this profound darkness. No, nothing discouraged me; year after year I watched that education, and I tried innumerable interpretations. How many times have I thought to grasp a fugitive glimmer of the essential nature of the Xipehuz, an invisible light, a pure abstraction, which, alas! my poor flesh-burdened faculties could never follow.

I have said previously that for a long time I believed the Xipehuz to be immortal. Having abandoned this belief, after seeing the violent deaths which followed some encounters between Xipehuz, I was naturally led to seek their vulnerable points, and devoted all my days from that time forward to the search for means of destruction. For the Xipehuz were growing in numbers, to such a point that, having emerged from the forest of Kzur in the south, west, and north, they were beginning to encroach upon the plains in the direction of the Levant. Alas! in a few cycles they would have dispossessed man from his earthly abode.

Accordingly, I armed myself with a sling, and whenever a Xipehuz emerged from the forest within my range, I took aim and hurled my stone at him. I obtained no result in this way, although I had struck my targets on every part of their surface, even including the luminous point. They appeared entirely insensible to my blows, and none ever turned aside to avoid one of my projectiles. After a month's trial I could only conclude that nothing could be done against them with the sling, and I abandoned that weapon.

I took up the bow. With the first arrows I shot, the Xipehuz betrayed an intense fear, for they turned aside, stayed out of range, and avoided me as much as possible. For a week I did not succeed in striking one. On the eighth day, a party of Xipehuz, carried away I suppose by their enthusiasm for the hunt, passed fairly close to me in pursuit of a fine gazelle. I quickly shot several arrows, *without any apparent effect*, and the party dispersed, I pursuing them and using up my ammunition. I had barely shot my last arrow when they all turned back at full speed, from different directions, surrounding me on three sides, and I would have lost my life if not for the prodigious speed of my valiant Kuath.

This adventure left me full of hope and uncertainty; for a week I did nothing, lost in the oceanic depths of my meditations, in a subtle, absorbing, sleep-dispelling problem which filled me with joy and anguish. Why did the Xipehuz fear my arrows? Why, again, among the great number of projectiles with which I had struck the hunters, had none produced any effect? My knowledge of the enemy's intelligence ruled out the hypothesis of a terror without cause. On the contrary, everything I knew compelled me to believe that the *arrow*, under the proper conditions, must be a formidable weapon against them. But what were these conditions? What was the vulnerable point of the Xipehuz? Suddenly the thought came to me that it was the *star* that I must strike. For a moment I held this as a certainty, a blind, impassioned certainty.

Then I was seized by doubt. With a sling, had I not aimed at and struck this point many times? Why should the arrow be luckier than the stone?

Now the night had come, the measureless abyss, with its marvellous lamps strewn above the earth. And I sat lost in thought, my head in my hands, my spirit darker than the night.

A lion began to roar, jackals were running across the plain, and once again a spark of hope was born. It had just come to my mind that the slingstone was relatively large, and the Xipehuz' star so tiny! Perhaps it was necessary to penetrate deeply, to pierce with a sharp point, and then their fear of the bow became understandable!

But Vega was turning slowly around the pole, dawn was near, and for a few hours weariness conquered my thoughts with sleep.

In the days that followed, armed with the bow, I was in constant pursuit of the Xipehuz, as deep in their territory as prudence would permit. But they all avoided my assault, keeping at a distance, out of range. Lying in ambush was not to be considered; their mode of perception enabled them to detect my presence behind obstacles.

Towards the end of the fifth day an event occurred which, in itself, proved that the Xipehuz, like men, are fallible creatures. That evening, at twilight, a Xipehuz deliberately approached me with that constantly accelerating speed they use in attack. Surprised, my heart beating fast, I drew my bow. He, steadily advancing, like a column of turquoise in the growing dusk, came almost within bowshot. Then, as I made ready to loose my arrow, I was stunned to see him turn his body, hiding his star, while he continued to hurtle towards me. I had barely time to put Kuath into a gallop and retreat out of reach of this formidable adversary.

Now this simple manoeuvre, which no Xipehuz appeared to have thought of before, in addition to demonstrating once more the individuality and personal inventiveness of the enemy, suggested two ideas: first, it was probable that I had reasoned correctly about the vulnerability of the Xipehuz' star; second, less encouraging, the same tactic, if adopted by all, would render my task extraordinarily difficult, perhaps impossible.

Nevertheless, having laboured so long to learn the truth, I felt my courage grow in the face of this obstacle, and I dared to hope that my ingenuity would be great enough to surmount it.[3]

VI

I returned to my wilderness. Anakhre, the third son of my wife Tepai, was a mighty maker of weapons. I ordered him to carve a bow of extraordinary size. He took a branch of the tree Waham, hard as iron, and the bow he cut from it was four times stronger than that of the shepherd Zankann, the mightiest archer of the thousand tribes. No man living could have bent it. But I had thought of an artifice and, Anakhre having wrought according to my plan, it came about that the immense bow could be bent and loosed by a woman.

Now I had always been skilled in casting darts and arrows, and in a few days I learned so perfectly the use of the weapon made by my son Anakhre that I never missed a target, be it as small as a fly or moving as swiftly as a falcon.

Having done all this, I returned to Kzur, mounted on my flame-eyed Kuath, and once more began to prowl around the enemies of man.

In order to give them confidence, I loosed many arrows with my customary bow each time one of their parties approached the frontier, and my arrows fell far short of them. Thus they learned to know the exact range of the weapon, and from this to believe themselves absolutely out of danger

3. In the following chapters, of a narrative character, I have adhered closely to the literal translation of Professor Dessault, without, however, feeling bound to follow the tiresome division into verses, or the needless repetitions.

at a certain distance. Nevertheless they remained mistrustful; this caused them to be mobile and agitated when they were not sheltered by the forest, and to hide their stars from my view.

By dint of patience I wore out their suspicions. On the morning of the sixth day a troop of them took up a position facing me, beneath a great chestnut tree at a distance of three ordinary bowshots. At once I loosed a cloud of useless arrows. Then their vigilance lessened more and more, and their movements became as free as in the early days of my sojourn.

It was the decisive moment. My heart beat so loudly that at first I felt myself strengthless. I waited, for the future hung upon a single arrow. If it failed to strike its target, never again, perhaps, would the Xipehuz offer themselves to my experiments, and then how would it be possible to know whether they were vulnerable to the blows of men?

Nevertheless, little by little, my will triumphed, quieted my heart, made my limbs supple and strong and my eye steady. Then, slowly, I raised the bow of Anakhre. There, in the distance, a great cone of emerald stood motionless in the shade of the tree, its sparkling star turned toward me. The enormous bow bent; the arrow flew whistling across space ... and the Xipehuz *fell, shrank, and petrified*.

A resounding cry of triumph burst from my lips. Stretching out my arms in ecstasy, I gave thanks to the One.

So, then, they were vulnerable to human weapons, these terrible Xipehuz! We could hope to destroy them!

Now, without fear, I let my heart murmur, I gave myself up to the beating of the music of gladness: I, who had so greatly despaired of the future of my race, who beneath the stars in their courses, beneath the blue crystal of the abyss, had so often calculated that in two centuries the vast world's limits would have burst before the Xipehuz invasion.

And yet when it came again, the well-beloved Night, the pensive Night, a shadow fell over my happiness, the sorrow that man and Xipehuz could not exist together, that the annihilation of one was the grim condition of the other's survival.

VII

The priests, the elders and the chiefs had listened marvelling to my story; couriers had carried the good news into the depths of the wilderness. The great council had ordered the warriors to gather in the sixth moon of the year 22,649, in the plain of Mehur-Asar, and the prophets had preached a holy war. More than a hundred thousand Zahelal warriors came, and many members of foreign races – Dzums, Sahrs, Khaldes – drawn by rumour, came to offer themselves to the great nation.

Kzur was surrounded by a tenfold ring of archers, but all their arrows failed against the tactics of the Xipehuz, and incautious warriors perished in great numbers.

Then for several weeks great fear prevailed among men...

On the third day of the eighth moon, armed with a sharp-pointed knife, I announced to the multitudes that I would go to fight the Xipehuz alone, in the hope of laying to rest the doubts which had begun to arise concerning the truth of my story.

My sons Lum, Demja, and Anakhre were violently opposed to this project and offered to go in my place. And Lum said: 'You cannot go, for once you are dead, all will believe the Xipehuz are invulnerable and the human race will perish.'

Demja, Anakhre, and many of the chiefs having echoed these words, I found their reasons good and withdrew.

Then Lum, taking my horn-handled knife, crossed the frontier. The Xipehuz hastened up. One, swifter by far than the rest, was about to rush upon him, but Lum, more agile than a leopard, sprang aside, circled the Xipehuz, then with a giant bound closed in again and stabbed with his sharp point.

The waiting throng saw his adversary *collapse, dwindle, and petrify*. A hundred thousand voices rose to the blue dawn, and already Lum was returning, crossing the frontier. The glory of his name spread throughout the armies.

The year 22,649 of the world, the seventh day of the eighth moon.

At daybreak the horns sounded; hammers beat brazen bells for the great battle. A hundred black buffalo and two hundred stallions were sacrificed by the priests, and my fifteen sons and I prayed to the One.

The globe of the sun was engulfed in the red dawn, the chiefs galloped in the forefront of their armies, the clamour of the attack swelled in the headlong rush of a hundred thousand warriors.

The tribe of Nazzum was first to encounter the enemy in bitter combat. Powerless at first, mowed down by invisible lightning bolts, the warriors soon learned the art of striking the Xipehuz and destroying them. Then all the nations, Zahelals, Dzums, Sahrs, Khaldes, Xisoastres, Pjarvanns, roaring like oceans, invaded the plain and the forest, everywhere surrounding the silent enemy.

For a long time the battle was in chaos; messengers came continuously to tell the priests that men were dying by hundreds, but that their deaths were being avenged.

In the heat of midday my swift-footed son Surdar, sent by Lum, came to tell me that for each Xipehuz destroyed, a dozen of ours had perished. My spirit was dark and my heart weak, but my lips murmured, 'Let it be as the Father wills!'

In recalling to my mind the numbers of the armies, which added together gave a sum of a hundred and forty thousand, and knowing that the numbers of Xipehuz amounted to about four thousand, I told myself that more than a third of the vast army would perish, but that the earth would belong to man.

'It is a victory, then,' I murmured sadly.

But as I pondered on these things, the clamour of the battle shook the forest more violently; then great masses of warriors reappeared, all with cries of distress, fleeing towards the frontier.

Then I saw the Xipehuz emerge at the border, not separate from one another as they had been in the morning, but in groups of twenty formed into circles, with their stars turned inward. In this array, invulnerable, they advanced on our helpless warriors and massacred them.

It was defeat.

The boldest warriors thought of nothing but flight. Nevertheless, in spite of the sorrow that weighed down my spirit, I patiently observed the fatal encounters in the hope of finding some remedy in the very heart of misfortune, for often the venom and the antidote are found side by side.

For this confidence in the power of thought, destiny repaid me with two discoveries. I remarked, first, that in places where our tribes were massed in multitudes and the Xipehuz were in small numbers, the slaughter, immeasurable at first, lessened by degrees. The strength of the enemy's blows grew *less and less*, many of the victims rising again after a moment's dizziness. The strongest resisted the shock completely, continuing to flee after repeated blows. The same phenomenon being evident in various parts of the field of battle, I dared to conclude that the Xipehuz were growing weary, that their powers of destruction were not unlimited.

The second observation, which aptly complemented the first, was furnished to me by a group of Khaldes. These unfortunate men, surrounded on all sides by Xipehuz and losing confidence in their short knives, pulled up bushes and made clubs of them, with which they tried to beat their way to freedom. To my great surprise, their attempt succeeded. I saw the Xipehuz topple by the dozen under these blows, and about half the Khaldes escaped through the hole they had opened in this way. But, curiously, those who made use of bronze implements instead of bushes (as in the case of several chiefs) killed themselves in striking the enemy. I must point out further that the blows from these clubs gave no apparent hurt to the Xipehuz, for those who fell rose again promptly and took up the pursuit. Nevertheless, I considered my double discovery of the greatest importance for future battles.

Meanwhile, the rout continued. The earth resounded to the flight of the vanquished. By nightfall, only our dead remained within the Xipehuz boundaries, and a few hundred warriors who had taken refuge in trees. The fate of these latter was terrible, for the Xipehuz burned them alive, concentrating a thousand fires in the branches which sheltered them. Their frightful cries echoed for hours under the vast firmament.

The next day, the tribes counted their survivors. It was found that the battle had cost nine thousand human lives or thereabout. A moderate estimate put the loss of Xipehuz at six hundred. Thus the death of each enemy had cost us fifteen men.

Despair settled in the hearts of the tribesmen, many crying out against the chiefs and talking of giving up the terrible enterprise. Then, under these complaints, I strode into the middle of the camp and loudly reproached the warriors for their faintheartedness. I asked them if it were better to let all men perish, or to sacrifice a part. I showed them that in ten years the Zahelal country would be invaded by the Shapes, and in twenty the country of the Khaldes, the Sahrs, the Pjarvanns and the Xisoastres. Then, having reawakened their conscience in this way, I reminded them that already a sixth of the disputed territory had been reconquered, that on three sides the enemy had been driven back into the forest. Finally I told them of my observations, and made them understand that the Xipehuz were not tireless, that clubs of wood could topple them and force them to expose their vulnerable points.

Silence fell across the plain; hope returned to the hearts of the multitude who heard me. And to strengthen their confidence I described the contrivances of wood which I had thought of, suited both for attack and defence. With renewed enthusiasm the people applauded my words, and the chiefs laid their sceptres of command at my feet.

In the days that followed, I had a great number of trees cut down, and displayed a model of a light, portable barrier, of which a brief description follows. A framework, six cubits long and two cubits wide, fastened by crossbars to an interior framework, one cubit wide and five cubits long. Six men (two porters, two warriors armed with heavy, blunt wooden spears, two others also armed with wooden spears having sharp metal points, and furnished in addition with bows and arrows) could stand within it comfortably and could roam the forest, protected from the direct attack of the Xipehuz. Once within range of the enemy, the warriors armed with blunt spears were to strike and overturn them, force them to expose themselves, and the archer-spearmen were to aim at the stars, with bow or spear according to circumstance. Since the average height of the Xipehuz was a little more than a cubit and a half, I had arranged the crossbars in such a way that the exterior framework, while being carried, would reach a height above the ground of no more than a cubit and a quarter, and for this it sufficed to incline somewhat the supports by which it was attached to the interior framework. In addition, since the Xipehuz were unable to surmount any steep obstacle or to move in any way except upright, the barrier thus devised was sufficient to give shelter against their direct assaults. Undoubtedly they would attempt to burn these new weapons, and in some cases they would succeed; but since their fires were almost ineffective out of bowshot they would be forced to expose themselves in order to do so. Besides, since these fires did not take effect instantaneously, it would be possible to avoid them in many cases by rapid movement.

The year 22,649 of the world, the eleventh day of the eighth moon. On this day the second battle with the Xipehuz took place, and the chiefs gave me the supreme command. Then I divided the people into three armies. Shortly before dawn I sent against Kzur forty thousand warriors armed with the barrier devices. This attack was less confused than that of the seventh day. The tribes entered the forest slowly, in small bands disposed in good order. The encounter began. During the first hour the advantage was entirely ours, the Xipehuz being caught off guard by the new tactics; more than a hundred Shapes were slain, while only a dozen of our warriors perished. But, once over their surprise, the Xipehuz applied themselves to burning the barriers. In some circumstances they were able to do so. A more dangerous manoeuvre was the one they adopted towards the fourth hour of the day. Taking advantage of their swiftness, groups of Xipehuz tightly pressed together, hurled themselves at the barriers and succeeded in overturning them. In this fashion great numbers of men perished, so many that, the enemy having regained the advantage, a part of our army fell into despair.

Toward the fifth hour, the Zahelal tribes of Khemar and Djoh, and part of the Xisoastres and Sahrs began to flee. Wishing to avert a catastrophe, I sent messengers protected by strong barriers to promise reinforcements. At the same time, I disposed the second army for the attack. But first I gave new orders. The barriers were to cluster in groups, as thickly as movement in the forest would permit, and to arrange themselves in compact squares whenever a large band of Xipehuz approached. This was to be done without giving up the offensive.

After this, I gave the signal, and in a short time I had the pleasure of seeing the battle turn in our favour. At length, towards the middle of the day, an approximate reckoning – which brought the number of our losses to two thousand men, and of the Xipehuz to three hundred – decisively showed the progress we had accomplished and strengthened the hearts of all.

Nevertheless, the proportion changed somewhat to our disadvantage during the fourth hour, the tribes then having lost four thousand warriors and the Xipehuz five hundred.

It was then that I sent in the third army. The battle reached its greatest intensity. The warriors' enthusiasm rose from minute to minute, until the hour when the sun was about to sink into the west.

At that moment the Xipehuz took the offensive again to the north of Kzur. A retreat of the Dzums and Pjarvanns gave me uneasiness. Judging that in any case the darkness would be more favourable to the enemy than to us, I signalled the end of the battle. The troops returned calm and victorious; much of the night was passed in celebrating our successes. These were considerable: eight hundred Xipehuz had succumbed; their sphere of action was reduced to two-thirds of Kzur. It is true that we had left seven thousand slain in the forest, but these losses were much smaller, in proportion to the result, than in the first battle. Thus, filled with hope, I dared to conceive the plan of a more decisive attack against the two thousand six hundred Xipehuz still living.

The year 22,649 of the world, the fifteenth day of the eighth moon.

When the red star rose over the eastern hills, the tribes were in battle array before Kzur. With my heart full of hope, I gave my last instructions to the chiefs. The horns sounded. The bells set up their brazen clangour and the first army marched against the forest.

Our barriers now were stronger and somewhat larger, enclosing twelve men instead of six, except for about a third which were constructed according to the old design. Thus they were more difficult either to set on fire or to overturn.

The beginning of the battle was promising. After the third hour, four hundred Xipehuz had been exterminated, and we lost only two thousand men. Encouraged by the good news, I sent in the second army. The fury of the battle on both sides grew appalling, our warriors being flushed with triumph, their adversaries resisting with the stubbornness of a noble kingdom. From the fourth to the eighth hour we sacrificed no less than ten thousand lives; but the Xipehuz paid with a thousand of theirs, so that only a thousand remained in the depths of Kzur.

From this moment, I knew that man would possess the world. My last misgivings faded.

Nevertheless, at the ninth hour, a great shadow fell over our victory. At this time the Xipehuz appeared only in enormous masses in the clearings, concealing their stars, and it became almost impossible to overthrow them. In the heat of the battle, many of our warriors hurled themselves upon these masses. Then, with a rapid movement, a party of Xipehuz would detach itself, overthrowing and slaughtering these foolhardy men.

A thousand perished thus, without any perceptible loss to the enemy. Seeing this, the Pjarvanns cried that all was lost, and a panic began which put more than ten thousand men to flight, many being so imprudent as to abandon their barriers in order to run faster. It cost them dear. A hundred pursuing Xipehuz cut down more than two thousand Pjarvanns and Zahelals. Terror was beginning to spread throughout our lines.

When the messengers brought me this dismal news I knew that the day was lost, unless by some swift manoeuvre I succeeded in retaking the abandoned positions. At once I gave the chiefs of the third army the order to attack, and I announced that I would assume command. I then quickly brought these reserves to the place from which the others had fled. Shortly we found ourselves face to face with the pursuing Xipehuz. Carried away by the passion of their slaughter, they did not regroup quickly enough, and in a few moments we had surrounded them. Few escaped. The great acclamation for our victory went far to restore the courage of our men.

From that time on I had no trouble in re-forming the attack. Our methods were limited to detaching segments of the enemy groups, then surrounding these segments and annihilating them. Soon, realizing how greatly these tactics worked to their disfavour, the Xipehuz once more took up the assault in small groups, and the massacre of the two kingdoms, neither of which could survive except by the annihilation of the other, redoubled dreadfully. But all doubt of the final issue had vanished from the faintest hearts. By the fourteenth hour there remained hardly five hundred Xipehuz against more than a hundred thousand men, and this small number of the enemy was more and more hemmed in by narrow frontiers, about a sixth of the forest of Kzur, which greatly facilitated our movements.

Meanwhile, the red light of sunset streamed through the trees, and fearing ambushes in the shadows, I broke off the battle.

The immensity of our victory swelled every heart; the chiefs talked of offering me the kingship of the nations. I counselled them never to confide the destinies of so many men to one poor fallible creature, and to take *Wisdom* for their earthly master.

The earth belongs to man. Two days of combat have annihilated the Xipehuz; the whole domain occupied by the last two hundred of them has been razed, every tree, every plant, every blade of grass has been cut down. And I, aided by my sons Lum, Azah and Simbo, have finished inscribing this history upon tablets of granite for the instruction of future nations.

And now I am alone, at the edge of Kzur, in the pale night. A coppery half-moon hangs over the west. Lions are roaring at the stars. The brook wanders slowly among the willows; its eternal voice speaks of time passing, of the melancholy of perishable things. And I have buried my face in my hands, and my heart mourns. For, now that the Xipehuz are no more, my soul laments for them, and I ask the One what Fatality demanded that the splendour of Life be tarnished by the Shadow of Murder!

THEODORE STURGEON

THE OTHER CELIA

If you live in a cheap enough rooming-house and the doors are made of cheap enough pine, and the locks are old-fashioned single-action jobs and the hinges are loose, and if you have a hundred and ninety lean pounds to operate with, you can grasp the knob, press the door sidewise against its hinges, and slip the latch. Further, you can lock the door the same way when you come out.

Slim Walsh lived in, and was, and had, and did these things partly because he was bored. The company doctors had laid him up – not off, up – for three weeks (after his helper had hit him just over the temple with a fourteen-inch crescent wrench) pending some more X-rays. If he was going to get just sick-leave pay, he wanted to make it stretch. If he was going to get a big fat settlement – all to the good; what he saved by living in this firetrap would make the money look even better. Meanwhile, he felt fine and had nothing to do all day.

'Slim isn't dishonest,' his mother used to tell Children's Court some years back. 'He's just curious.'

She was perfectly right.

Slim was constitutionally incapable of borrowing your bathroom without looking into your medicine chest. Send him into your kitchen for a saucer and when he came out a minute later, he'd have inventoried your refrigerator, your vegetable bin, and (since he was six feet three inches tall) he would know about a mouldering jar of maraschino cherries in the back of the top shelf that you'd forgotten about.

Perhaps Slim, who was not impressed by his impressive size and build, felt that a knowledge that you secretly use hair restorer, or are one of those strange people who keep a little mound of unmated socks in your second drawer, gave him a kind of superiority. Or maybe security is a better word. Or maybe it was an odd compensation for one of the most advanced cases of gawking, gasping shyness ever recorded.

Whatever it was, Slim liked you better if, while talking to you, he knew how many jackets hung in your closet, how old that unpaid phone bill was, and just where you'd hidden those photographs. On the other hand, Slim didn't insist on knowing bad or even embarrassing things about you. He just wanted to know things about you, period.

His current situation was, therefore, a near paradise. Flimsy doors stood in rows, barely sustaining vacuum on aching vacuum of knowledge; and one by one they imploded at the nudge of his curiosity. He touched nothing (or if he did, he replaced it carefully) and removed nothing, and within a week he knew Mrs Koyper's roomers far better than she could, or cared to. Each secret visit to the rooms gave him a starting point; subsequent ones taught him more. He knew not only what these people had, but what they did, where, how much, *for* how much, and how often. In almost every case, he knew why as well.

Almost every case. Celia Sarton came.

Now, at various times, in various places, Slim had found strange things in other people's rooms. There was an old lady in one shabby place who had an electric train under her bed. Used it, too. There was an old spinster in this very building who collected bottles, large and small, of any value or capacity, providing they were round and squat and with long necks. A man on the second floor secretly guarded his desirables with the unloaded .25 automatic in his top bureau drawer, for which he had a half-box of .38 cartridges.

There was a (to be chivalrous) girl in one of the rooms who

kept fresh cut flowers before a photograph on her night table – or, rather, before a frame in which were stacked eight photographs, one of which held the stage each day. Seven days, eight photographs. Slim admired the system. A new love every day and, predictably, a different love on successive Wednesdays. And all of them movie stars.

Dozens of rooms, dozens of imprints, marks, impressions, overlays, atmospheres of people. And they needn't be odd ones. A woman moves into a room, however standardized; the instant she puts down her dusting powder on top of the flush tank, the room is *hers*. Something stuck in the ill-fitting frame of a mirror, something draped over the long-dead gas jet, and the samest of rooms begins to shrink towards its occupant as if it wished, one day, to be a close-knit, form-fitting, individual integument as intimate as a skin.

But not Celia Sarton's room.

Slim Walsh got a glimpse of her as she followed Mrs Koyper up the stairs to the third floor. Mrs Koyper, who hobbled, slowed any follower sufficiently to afford the most disinterested witness a good look, and Slim was anything but disinterested. Yet for days he could not recall her clearly. It was as if Celia Sarton had been – not invisible, for that would have been memorable in itself – but translucent or, chameleonlike, drably reradiating the drab wall colour, carpet colour, woodwork colour.

She was – how old? Old enough to pay taxes. How tall? Tall enough. Dressed in ... whatever women cover themselves with in their statistical thousands. Shoes, hose, skirt, jacket, hat.

She carried a bag. When you go to the baggage window at a big terminal, you notice a suitcase here, a steamer trunk there; and all around, high up, far back, there are rows and ranks and racks of luggage not individually noticed but just *there*. This bag, Celia Sarton's bag, was one of them.

And to Mrs Koyper, she said – she said – she said whatever is necessary when one takes a cheap room; and to find her voice, divide the sound of a crowd by the number of people in it.

So anonymous, so unnoticeable was she that, aside from being aware that she left in the morning and returned in the evening, Slim let two days go by before he entered her room; he simply could not remind himself about her. And when he did, and had inspected it to his satisfaction, he had his hand on the knob, about to leave, before he recalled that the room was, after all, occupied. Until that second, he had thought he was giving one of the vacancies the once-over. (He did this regularly; it gave him a reference point.)

He grunted and turned back, flicking his gaze over the room. First he had to assure himself that he was in the right room, which, for a man of his instinctive orientations, was extraordinary. Then he had to spend a moment of disbelief in his own eyes, which was all but unthinkable. When that passed, he stood in astonishment, staring at the refutation of everything his – hobby – had taught him about people and the places they live in.

The bureau drawers were empty. The ashtray was clean. No toothbrush, toothpaste, soap. In the closet, two wire hangers and one wooden one covered with dirty quilted silk, and nothing else. Under the grime-grey dresser scarf, nothing. In the shower stall, the medicine chest, nothing and nothing again, except what Mrs Koyper had grudgingly installed.

Slim went to the bed and carefully turned back the faded coverlet. Maybe she had slept in it, but very possibly not; Mrs Koyper specialized in unironed sheets of such a ground-in grey that it wasn't easy to tell. Frowning, Slim put up the coverlet again and smoothed it.

Suddenly he struck his forehead, which yielded him a flash of pain from his injury. He ignored it. 'The bag!'

It was under the bed, shoved there, not hidden there. He looked at it without touching it for a moment, so that it could be returned exactly. Then he hauled it out.

It was a black Gladstone, neither new nor expensive, of that nondescript rusty colour acquired by untended leatherette. It had a worn zipper closure and was not locked. Slim opened it. It contained a cardboard box, crisp and new, for a thousand virgin sheets of cheap white typewriter paper surrounded by a glossy bright blue band bearing a white diamond with the legend: *Nonpareil the writer's friend 15% cotton fibre trade mark registered.*

Slim lifted the paper out of the box, looked under it, riffled a thumbful of the sheets at the top and the same from the bottom, shook his head, replaced the paper, closed the box, put it back into the bag and restored everything precisely as he had found it. He paused again in the middle of the room, turning slowly once, but there was simply nothing else to look at. He let himself out, locked the door, and went silently back to his room.

He sat down on the edge of his bed and at last protested, 'Nobody *lives* like that!'

His room was on the fourth and topmost floor of the old house. Anyone else would have called it the worst room in the place. It was small, dark, shabby and remote and it suited him beautifully. Its door had a transom, the glass of which had many times been painted over.

By standing on the foot of his bed, Slim could apply one eye to the peephole he had scratched in the paint and look straight down the stairs to the third-floor landing. On this landing, hanging to the stub of one of the ancient gas jets, was a cloudy mirror surmounted by a dust-mantled gilt eagle and surrounded by a great many rococo carved flowers. By careful propping with folded cigarette wrappers, innumerable tests and a great deal of silent mileage up and down the stairs, Slim had arranged the exact tilt necessary in the mirror so that it covered the second floor landing as well.

And just as a radar operator learns to translate glowing pips and masses into aircraft and weather, so Slim became expert at the interpretation of the fogged and distant image it afforded him. Thus he had the comings and goings of half the tenants under surveillance without having to leave his room.

It was in this mirror, at twelve minutes past six, that he

saw Celia Sarton next, and as he watched her climb the stairs, his eyes glowed.

The anonymity was gone. She came up the stairs two at a time, with a gait like bounding. She reached the landing and whirled into her corridor and was gone, and while a part of Slim's mind listened for the way she opened her door (hurriedly rattling the key against the lock-plate, banging the door open, slamming it shut), another part studied a mental photograph of her face.

What raised its veil of the statistical ordinary was its set purpose. Here were eyes only superficially interested in cars, curbs, stairs, doors. It was as if she had projected every important part of herself into that empty room of hers and waited there impatiently for her body to catch up. There was something in the room, or something she had to do there, which she could not, would not, wait for. One goes this way to a beloved after a long parting, or to a deathbed in the last, precipitous moments. This was not the arrival of one who wants, but of one who needs.

Slim buttoned his shirt, eased his door open and sidled through it. He poised a moment on his landing like a great moose sensing the air before descending to a waterhole, and then moved downstairs.

Celia Sarton's only neighbour in the north corridor – the spinster with the bottles – was settled for the evening; she was a woman of very regular habits and Slim knew them well.

Completely confident that he would not be seen, he drifted to the girl's door and paused.

She was there, all right. He could see the light around the edges of the ill-fitting door, could sense that difference between an occupied room and an empty one, which exists however silent the occupant might be. And this one *was* silent. Whatever it was that had driven her into the room with such headlong urgency, whatever it was she was doing (*had* to do) was being done with no sound or motion that he could detect.

For a long time – six minutes, seven – Slim hung there,

open-throated to conceal the sound of his breath. At last, shaking his head, he withdrew, climbed the stairs, let himself into his own room and lay down on the bed, frowning.

He could only wait. Yet he *could* wait. No one does any single thing for very long. Especially a thing not involving movement. In an hour, in two—

It was five. At half past eleven, some faint sound from the floor below brought Slim, half-dozing, twisting up from the bed and to his high peephole in the transom. He saw the Sarton girl come out of the corridor slowly, and stop, and look around at nothing in particular, like someone confined too long in a ship's cabin who has emerged on deck, not so much for the lungs' sake, but for the eyes'. And when she went down the stairs, it was easily and without hurry, as if (again) the important part of her was in the room. But the something was finished with her for now and what was ahead of her wasn't important and could wait.

Standing with his hand on his own doorknob, Slim decided that he, too, could wait. The temptation to go straight to her room was, of course, large, but caution also loomed. What he had tentatively established as her habit patterns did not include midnight exits.

He could not know when she might come back and it would be foolish indeed to jeopardize his hobby – not only where it included her, but all of it – by being caught. He sighed, mixing resignation with anticipatory pleasure, and went to bed.

Less than fifteen minutes later, he congratulated himself with a sleepy smile as he heard her slow footsteps mount the stair below. He slept.

There was nothing in the closet, there was nothing in the ashtray, there was nothing in the medicine chest or under the dresser scarf. The bed was made, the dresser drawers were empty, and under the bed was the cheap Gladstone. In it was a box containing a thousand sheets of typing paper surrounded by a glossy blue band. Without disturbing this, Slim riffled the sheets, once at the top, once at the bottom.

He grunted, shook his head and then proceeded, automatically but meticulously, to put everything back as he had found it.

'Whatever it is this girl does at night,' he said glumly, 'it leaves tracks like it makes noise.'

He left.

The rest of the day was unusually busy for Slim. In the morning he had a doctor's appointment, and in the afternoon he spent hours with a company lawyer who seemed determined to (a) deny the existence of any head injury and (b) prove to Slim and the world that the injury must have occurred years ago. He got absolutely nowhere. If Slim had another characteristic as consuming and compulsive as his curiosity, it was his shyness; these two could stand on one another's shoulders, though, and still look upward at Slim's stubbornness. It served its purpose. It took hours, however, and it was after seven when he got home.

He paused at the third-floor landing and glanced down the corridor. Celia Sarton's room was occupied and silent. If she emerged around midnight, exhausted and relieved, then he would know she had again raced up the stairs to her urgent, motionless task, whatever it was ... and here he checked himself. He had long ago learned the uselessness of cluttering up his busy head with conjectures. A thousand things might happen; in each case, only one would. He would wait, then, and could.

And again, some hours later, he saw her come out of her corridor. She looked about, but he knew she saw very little; her face was withdrawn and her eyes wide and unguarded. Then, instead of going out, she went back into her room.

He slipped downstairs half an hour later and listened at her door, and smiled. She was washing her lingerie in the handbasin. It was a small thing to learn, but he felt he was making progress. It did not explain why she lived as she did, but indicated how she could manage without so much as a spare handkerchief.

Oh, well, maybe in the morning.

In the morning, there was no maybe. He found it, he found it, though he could not know what it was he'd found. He laughed at first, not in triumph, but wryly, calling himself a clown. Then he squatted on his heels in the middle of the floor (he would not sit on the bed, for fear of leaving wrinkles of his own on those Mrs Koyper supplied) and carefully lifted the box of paper out of the suitcase and put it on the floor in front of him.

Up to now, he had contented himself with a quick riffle of the blank paper, a little at the top, a little at the bottom. He had done just this again, without removing the box from the suitcase, but only taking the top off and tilting up the banded ream of *Nonpareil-the-writer's-friend*. And almost in spite of himself, his quick eye had caught the briefest flash of pale blue.

Gently, he removed the band, sliding it off the pack of paper, being careful not to slit the glossy finish. Now he could freely riffle the pages, and when he did, he discovered that all of them except a hundred or so, top and bottom, had the same rectangular cutout, leaving only a narrow margin all the way around. In the hollow space thus formed, something was packed.

He could not tell what the something was, except that it was pale tan, with a tinge of pink, and felt like smooth untextured leather. There was a lot of it, neatly folded so that it exactly fitted the hole in the ream of paper.

He puzzled over it for some minutes without touching it again, and then, scrubbing his fingertips against his shirt until he felt that they were quite free of moisture and grease, he gently worked loose the top corner of the substance and unfolded a layer. All he found was more of the same.

He folded it down flat again to be sure he could, and then brought more of it out. He soon realized that the material was of an irregular shape and almost certainly of one piece, so that folding it into a tight rectangle required care and great skill. Therefore he proceeded very slowly, stopping every now and then to fold it up again, and it took him more than an hour to get enough of it out so that he could identify it.

Identify? It was completely unlike anything he had ever seen before.

It was a human skin, done in some substance very like the real thing. The first fold, the one which had been revealed at first, was an area of the back, which was why it showed no features. One might liken it to a balloon, except that a deflated balloon is smaller in every dimension than an inflated one. As far as Slim could judge, this was life-sized – a little over five feet long and proportioned accordingly. The hair was peculiar, looking exactly like the real thing until flexed, and then revealing itself to be one piece.

It had Celia Sarton's face.

Slim closed his eyes and opened them, and found that it was still true. He held his breath and put forth a careful, steady forefinger and gently pressed the left eyelid upward. There was an eye under it, all right, light blue and seemingly moist, but flat.

Slim released the breath, closed the eye and sat back on his heels. His feet were beginning to tingle from his having knelt on the floor for so long.

He looked all round the room once, to clear his head of strangeness, and then began to fold the thing up again. It took a while, but when he was finished, he knew he had it right. He replaced the typewriter paper in the box and the box in the bag, put the bag away and at last stood in the middle of the room in the suspension which overcame him when he was deep in thought.

After a moment of this, he began to inspect the ceiling. It was made of stamped tin, like those of many old-fashioned houses. It was grimy and flaked and stained; here and there, rust showed through, and in one or two places, edges of the tin sheets had sagged. Slim nodded to himself in profound satisfaction, listened for a while at the door, let himself out, locked it and went upstairs.

He stood in his own corridor for a minute, checking the position of doors, the hall window, and his accurate orientation of the same things on the floor below. Then he went into his own room.

His room, though smaller than most, was one of the few in the house which was blessed with a real closet instead of a rickety off-the-floor wardrobe. He went into it and knelt, and grunted in satisfaction when he found how loose the ancient, unpainted floorboards were. By removing the side baseboard, he found it possible to get at the air-space between the fourth floor and the third-floor ceiling.

He took out boards until he had an opening perhaps fourteen inches wide, and then, working in almost total silence, he began cleaning away dirt and old plaster. He did this meticulously, because when he finally pierced the tin sheeting, he wanted not one grain of dirt to fall into the room below. He took his time and it was late in the afternoon when he was satisfied with his preparations and began, with his knife, on the tin.

It was thinner and softer than he had dared to hope; he almost overcut on the first try. Carefully he squeezed the sharp steel into the little slot he had cut, lengthening it. When it was somewhat less than an inch long, he withdrew all but the point of the knife and twisted it slightly, moved it a sixteenth of an inch and twisted again, repeating this all down the cut until he had widened it enough for his purposes.

He checked the time, then returned to Celia Sarton's room for just long enough to check the appearance of his work from that side. He was very pleased with it. The little cut had come through a foot away from the wall over the bed and was a mere pencil line lost in the baroque design with which the tin was stamped and the dirt and rust that marred it. He returned to his room and sat down to wait.

He heard the old house coming to its evening surge of life, a voice here, a door there, footsteps on the stairs. He ignored them all as he sat on the edge of his bed, hands folded between his knees, eyes half-closed, immobile like a machine fuelled, oiled, tuned and ready, lacking only the right touch on the right control. And like that touch, the faint sound of Celia Sarton's footsteps moved him.

To use his new peephole, he had to lie on the floor half in and half out of the closet, with his head in the hole, actually below floor level. With this he was perfectly content, any amount of discomfort being well worth his trouble – an attitude he shared with many another ardent hobbyist, mountain-climber or speleologist, duck-hunter or bird-watcher.

When she turned on the light, he could see her splendidly, as well as most of the floor, the lower third of the door and part of the washbasin in the bathroom.

She had come in hurriedly, with that same agonized haste he had observed before. At the same second she turned on the light, she had apparently flung her handbag towards the bed; it was in mid-air as the light appeared. She did not even glance its way, but hastily fumbled the old Gladstone from under the bed, opened it, and removed the box, opened it, took out the paper, slipped off the blue band and removed the blank sheets of paper which covered the hollowed-out ream.

She scooped out the thing hidden there, shaking it once like a grocery clerk with a folded paper sack, so that the long limp thing straightened itself out. She arranged it carefully on the worn linoleum of the floor, arms down at the side, legs slightly apart, face up, neck straight. Then she lay down on the floor, too, head-to-head with the deflated thing. She reached up over her head, took hold of the collapsed image of herself about the region of the ears, and for a moment did some sort of manipulation of it against the top of her own head.

Slim heard faintly a sharp, chitinous click, like the sound one makes by snapping the edge of a thumbnail against the edge of a fingernail.

Her hands slipped to the cheeks of the figure and she pulled at the empty head as if testing a connexion. The head seemed now to have adhered to hers.

Then she assumed the same pose she had arranged for

this other, letting her hands fall wearily to her sides on the floor, closing her eyes.

For a long while, nothing seemed to be happening, except for the odd way she was breathing, very deeply but very slowly, like the slow-motion picture of someone panting, gasping for breath after a long hard run. After perhaps ten minutes of this, the breathing became shallower and even slower, until, at the end of a half-hour, he could detect none at all.

Slim lay there immobile for more than an hour, until his body shrieked protest and his head ached from eyestrain. He hated to move, but move he must. Silently he backed out of the closet, stood up and stretched. It was a great luxury and he deeply enjoyed it. He felt moved to think over what he had just seen, but clearly and consciously decided not to – not yet, anyway.

When he was unkinked again, he crept back into the closet, put his head in the hole and his eye to the slot.

Nothing had changed. She still lay quiet, utterly relaxed, so much so that her hands had turned palm upward.

Slim watched and he watched. Just as he was about to conclude that this was the way the girl spent her entire nights and that there would be nothing more to see, he saw a slight and sudden contraction about the region of the solar plexus, and then another. For a time, there was nothing more, and then the empty thing attached to the top of her head began to fill.

And Celia Sarton began to empty.

Slim stopped breathing until it hurt and watched in total astonishment.

Once it had started, the process progressed swiftly. It was as if something passed from the clothed body of the girl to this naked empty thing. The something, whatever it might be, had to be fluid, for nothing but a fluid would fill a flexible container in just this way, or make a flexible container slowly and evenly flatten out like this. Slim could see the fingers, which had been folded flat against the palms, inflate and move until they took on the normal relaxed curl of a normal hand. The elbows shifted a little to lie more normally against the body. And yes, it was a body now.

The other one was not a body any more. It lay foolishly limp in its garments, its sleeping face slightly distorted by its flattening. The fingers fell against the palms by their own limp weight. The shoes thumped quietly on their sides, heels together, toes pointing in opposite directions.

The exchange was done in less than ten minutes and then the newly filled body moved.

It flexed its hands tentatively, drew up its knees and stretched its legs out again, arched its back against the floor. Its eyes flickered open. It put up its arms and made some deft manipulation at the top of its head. Slim heard another version of the soft-hard click and the now-empty head fell flat to the floor.

The new Celia Sarton sat up and sighed and rubbed her hands lightly over her body, as if restoring circulation and sensation to a chilled skin. She stretched as comfortingly and luxuriously as Slim had a few minutes earlier. She looked rested and refreshed.

At the top of her head, Slim caught a glimpse of a slit through which a wet whiteness showed, but it seemed to be closing. In a brief time, nothing showed there but a small valley in the hair, like a normal parting.

She sighed again and got up. She took the clothed thing on the floor by the neck, raised it and shook it twice to make the clothes fall away. She tossed it to the bed and carefully picked up the clothes and deployed them about the room, the undergarments in the washbasin, the dress and slip on a hanger in the wardrobe.

Moving leisurely but with purpose, she went into the bathroom and, except for her shins down, out of Slim's range of vision. There he heard the same faint domestic sounds he had once detected outside her door, as she washed her underclothes. She emerged in due course, went to the wardrobe for some wire hangers, and took them into the bathroom. Back she came with the underwear folded on the hangers, which she hooked to the top of the open wardrobe door. Then she took the deflated integument which lay crumpled on the bed, shook it again, rolled it up into a ball and took it into the bathroom.

Slim heard more water running and sudsing noises, and, by ear, followed the operation through a soaping and two rinses. Then she came out again, shaking out the object which had apparently just been wrung, pulled it through a wooden clothes hanger, arranged it creaselessly depending from the crossbar of the hanger with the bar about its waistline, and hung it with the others on the wardrobe door.

Then she lay down on the bed, not to sleep or to read or even to rest – she seemed very rested – but merely to wait until it was time to do something else.

By now, Slim's bones were complaining again, so he wormed noiselessly backward out of his lookout point, got into his shoes and a jacket, and went out to get something to eat. When he came home an hour later and looked, her light was out and he could see nothing. He spread his overcoat carefully over the hole in the closet so no stray light from his room would appear in the little slot in the ceiling, closed the door, read a comic book for a while, and went to bed.

The next day, he followed her. What strange occupation she might have, what weird vampiric duties she might disclose, he did not speculate on. He was doggedly determined to gather information first and think later.

What he found out about her daytime activities was, if anything, more surprising than any wild surmise. She was a clerk in a small five-and-ten on the East Side. She ate in the store's lunch bar at lunchtime – a green salad and a surprising amount of milk – and in the evening she stopped at a hot-dog stand and drank a small container of milk, though she ate nothing.

Her steps were slowed by then and she moved wearily, speeding up only when she was close to the rooming-house, and then apparently all but overcome with eagerness to get home and ... into something more comfortable. She was watched in this process, and Slim, had he disbelieved his own eyes the first time, must believe them now.

So it went for a week, three days of which Slim spent in shadowing her, every evening in watching her make her strange toilet. Every twenty-four hours, she changed bodies, carefully washing, drying, folding and putting away the one she was not using.

Twice during the week, she went out for what was apparently a constitutional and nothing more – a half-hour around midnight, when she would stand on the walk in front of the rooming-house, or wander around the block.

At work, she was silent but not unnaturally so; she spoke, when spoken to, in a small, unmusical voice. She seemed to have no friends; she maintained her aloofness by being uninteresting and by seeking no one out and by needing no one. She evinced no outside interests, never going to the movies or to the park. She had no dates, not even with girls. Slim thought she did not sleep, but lay quietly in the dark waiting for it to be time to get up and go to work.

And when he came to think about it, as ultimately he did, it occurred to Slim that within the anthill in which we all live and have our being, enough privacy can be exacted to allow for all sorts of strangeness in the members of society, providing the strangeness is not permitted to show. If it is a man's pleasure to sleep upside down like a bat, and if he so arranges his life that no one ever sees him sleeping, or his sleeping-place, why, batlike he may sleep all the days of his life.

One need not, by these rules, even *be* a human being. Not if the mimicry is good enough. It is a measure of Slim's odd personality to report that Celia Sarton's ways did not frighten him. He was, if anything, less disturbed by her now that he'd been before he had begun to spy on her. He knew what she did in her room and how she lived. Before, he had not known. Now he did. This made him much happier.

He was, however, still curious. His curiosity would never drive him to do what another man might – to speak to her on the stairs or on the street, get to know her and more about her. He was too shy for that. Nor was he moved to report to anyone the odd practice he watched each evening. It wasn't his business to report. She was doing no harm as far as he could see. In his cosmos, everybody had a right to live and make a buck if they could.

Yet his curiosity, its immediacy taken care of, did undergo a change. It was not in him to wonder what sort of being this was and whether its ancestors had grown up among human beings, living with them in caves and in tents, developing and evolving along with *homo sap* until it could assume the uniform of the smallest and most invisible of wage-workers. He would never reach the conclusion that in the fight for survival, a species might discover that a most excellent characteristic for survival among human beings might be not to fight them but to join them.

No, Slim's curiosity was far simpler, more basic and less informed than any of these conjectures. He simply changed the field of his wonderment from *what* to *what if*?

So it was that on the eighth day of his survey, a Tuesday, he went again to her room, got the bag, opened it, removed the box, opened it, removed the ream of paper, slid the blue band off, removed the covering sheets, took out the second Celia Sarton, put her on the bed and then replaced paper, blue band, box-cover, box, and bag just as he had found them. He put the folded thing under his shirt and went out, carefully locking the door behind him in his special way, and went upstairs to his room. He put his prize under the four clean shirts in his bottom drawer and sat down to await Celia Sarton's homecoming.

She was a little late that night – twenty minutes, perhaps. The delay seemed to have increased both her fatigue and her eagerness; she burst in feverishly, moved with the rapidity of near-panic. She looked drawn and pale and her hands shook. She fumbled the bag from under the bed, snatched out the box and opened it, contrary to her usual measured movements, by inverting it over the bed and dumping out its contents.

When she saw nothing there but sheets of paper, some

with a wide rectangle cut from them and some without, she froze. She crouched over that bed without moving for an interminable two minutes. Then she straightened up slowly and glanced about the room. Once she fumbled through the paper, but resignedly, without hope. She made one sound, a high, sad whimper, and, from that moment on, was silent.

She went to the window slowly, her feet dragging, her shoulders slumped. For a long time, she stood looking out at the city, its growing darkness, its growing colonies of lights, each a symbol of life and life's usages. Then she drew down the blind and went back to the bed.

She stacked the papers there with loose uncaring fingers and put the heap of them on the dresser. She took off her shoes and placed them neatly side by side on the floor by the bed. She lay down in the same utterly relaxed pose she affected when she made her change, hands down and open, legs a little apart.

Her face looked like a death mask, its tissues sunken and sagging. It was flushed and sick-looking. There was a little of the deep regular breathing, but only a little. There was a bit of the fluttering contractions at the midriff, but only a bit. Then – nothing.

Slim backed away from the peephole and sat up. He felt very bad about this. He had been only curious; he hadn't wanted her to get sick, to die. For he was sure she had died. How could he know what sort of sleep-surrogate an organism like this might require, or what might be the results of a delay in changing? What could he know of the chemistry of such a being? He had thought vaguely of slipping down the next day while she was out and returning her property. Just to see. Just to know *what if*. Just out of curiosity.

Should he call a doctor?

She hadn't. She hadn't even tried, though she must have known much better than he did how serious her predicament was. (Yet if a species depended for its existence on secrecy, it would be species-survival to let an individual die undetected.) Well, maybe not calling a doctor meant that she'd be all right, after all. Doctors would have a lot of silly questions to ask. She might even tell the doctor about her other skin, and if Slim was the one who had fetched the doctor, Slim might be questioned about that.

Slim didn't want to get involved with anything. He just wanted to know things.

He thought, 'I'll take another look.'

He crawled back into the closet and put his head in the hole. Celia Sarton, he knew instantly, would not survive this. Her face was swollen, her eyes protruded, and her purpled tongue lolled far – too far – from the corner of her mouth. Even as he watched, her face darkened still more and the skin of it crinkled until it looked like carbon paper which has been balled up tight and then smoothed out.

The very beginnings of an impulse to snatch the thing she needed out of his shirt drawer and rush it down to her died within him, for he saw a wisp of smoke emerge from her nostrils and then—

Slim cried out, snatched his head from the hole, bumping it cruelly, and clapped his hands over his eyes. Put the biggest size flash-bulb an inch from your nose, and fire it, and you might get a flare approaching the one he got through his little slot in the tin ceiling.

He sat grunting in pain and watching, on the insides of his eyelids, migrations of flaming worms. At last they faded and he tentatively opened his eyes. They hurt and the after-image of the slot hung before him, but at least he could see.

Feet pounded on the stairs. He smelled smoke and a burned, oily unpleasant something which he could not identify. Someone shouted. Someone hammered on a door. Then someone screamed and screamed.

It was in the papers next day. Mysterious, the story said. Charles Fort, in *Lo!*, had reported many such cases and there had been others since – people burned to a crisp by a fierce heat which had nevertheless not destroyed clothes or bedding, while leaving nothing for autopsy. This was, said the paper, either an unknown kind of heat or heat of such intensity and such brevity that it would do such a thing. No known relatives, it said. Police mystified – no clues or suspects.

Slim didn't say anything to anybody. He wasn't curious about the matter any more. He closed up the hole in the closet that same night, and next day, after he read the story, he used the newspaper to wrap up the thing in his shirt drawer. It smelled pretty bad and, even that early, was too far gone to be unfolded. He dropped it into a garbage can on the way to the lawyer's office on Wednesday.

They settled his law suit that afternoon and he moved.

GORDON R. DICKSON

BLACK CHARLIE

You ask me, what is art? You expect me to have a logical answer at my fingertips, because I have been a buyer for museums and galleries long enough to acquire a plentiful crop of grey hairs. It's not that simple.

Well, what is art? For forty years I've examined, felt, admired and loved many things fashioned as hopeful vessels for that bright spirit we call art – and I'm unable to answer the question directly. The layman answers easily – beauty. But art is not necessarily beautiful. Sometimes it is ugly. Sometimes it is crude. Sometimes it is incomplete.

I have fallen back, as many men have in the business of making like decisions, on *feel*, for the judgement of art. You know this business of *feel*. Let us say that you pick up something. A piece of statuary – or better, a fragment of stone, etched and coloured by some ancient man of prehistoric times. You look at it. At first it is nothing, a half-developed reproduction of some wild animal, not even as good as a grade-school child could accomplish today.

But then, holding it, your imagination suddenly reaches through rock and time, back to the man himself, half-squatting before the stone wall of his cave – and you see there, not the dusty thing you hold in your hand – but what the man himself saw in the hour of its creation. You look beyond the physical reproduction to the magnificent accomplishment of his imagination.

This, then, may be called art – no matter what strange

guise it appears in – this magic which bridges all gaps between the artist and yourself. To it, no distance, or any difference is too great. Let me give you an example from my own experience.

Some years back, when I was touring the newer worlds as a buyer for one of our well-known art institutions, I received a communication from a man named Cary Longan, asking me, if possible, to visit a planet named Elman's World and examine some statuary he had for sale.

Messages rarely came directly to me. They were usually referred to me by the institution I was representing at the time. Since, however, the world in question was close, being of the same solar system as the planet I was then visiting, I spacegraphed my answer that I would come. After cleaning up what remained of my business where I was, I took an interworld ship and, within a couple of days, landed on Elman's World.

It appeared to be a very raw, very new planet indeed. The port we landed at was, I learned, one of the only two suitable for deep-space vessels. And the city surrounding it was scarcely more than a village. Mr Longan did not meet me at the port, so I took a cab directly to the hotel where I had made a reservation.

That evening, in my rooms, the annunciator rang, then spoke, giving me a name. I opened the door to admit a tall, brown-faced man, with uncut, dark hair and troubled, green-brown eyes.

'Mr Longan?' I asked.

'Mr Jones?' he countered. He shifted the unvarnished wooden box he was carrying to his left hand and put out his right to shake mine. I closed the door behind him and led him to a chair.

He put the box down, without opening it, on a small coffee table between us. It was then that I noticed his rough, bush-country clothes, breeches and tunic of drab plastic. Also an embarrassed air about him, like that of a man unused to city dealings. An odd sort of person to be offering art for sale.

'Your spacegram,' I told him, 'was not very explicit. The institution I represent . . .'

'I've got it here,' he said, putting his hand on the box.

I looked at it in astonishment. It was no more than half a metre square by twenty centimetres deep.

'There?' I said. I looked back at him, with the beginnings of a suspicion forming in my mind. I suppose I should have been more wary when the message had come direct, instead of through Earth. But you know how it is – something of a feather in your cap when you bring in an unexpected item. 'Tell me, Mr Longan,' I said, 'where does this statuary come from?'

He looked at me, a little defiantly. 'A friend of mine made them,' he said.

'A friend?' I repeated – and I must admit I was growing somewhat annoyed. It makes a man feel like a fool to be taken in that way. 'May I ask whether this friend of yours has ever sold any of his work before?'

'Well, no . . .' Longan hedged. He was obviously suffering – but so was I, when I thought of my own wasted time.

'I see,' I said, getting to my feet. 'You've brought me on a very expensive side-trip, merely to show me the work of some amateur. Goodbye, Mr Longan. And please take your box with you when you leave!'

'You've never seen anything like this before!' He was looking up at me with desperation.

'No doubt,' I said.

'Look. I'll show you. . . .' He fumbled, his fingers nervous on the hasp. 'Since you've come all this way, you can at least look.'

Because there seemed no way of getting him out of there, short of having the hotel manager eject him forcibly, I sat down with bad grace. 'What's your friend's name?' I demanded.

Longan's fingers hesitated on the hasp. 'Black Charlie,' he replied, not looking up at me.

I stared. 'I beg your pardon. Black – Charles Black?'

He looked up quite defiantly, met my eye and shook his

head. 'Just Black Charlie,' he said with sudden calmness. 'Just the way it sounds. Black Charlie.' He continued unfastening the box.

I watched rather dubiously, as he finally managed to loosen the clumsy, handmade wooden bolt that secured the hasp. He was about to raise the lid, then apparently changed his mind. He turned the box around and pushed it across the coffee table.

The wood was hard and uneven under my fingers. I lifted the lid. There were five small partitions, each containing a rock of finegrained grey sandstone of different but thoroughly incomprehensible shape.

I stared at them – then looked back at Longan, to see if this weren't some sort of elaborate joke. But the tall man's eyes were severely serious. Slowly, I began to take out the stones and line them up on the table.

I studied them one by one, trying to make some sense out of their forms. But there was nothing there, absolutely nothing. One vaguely resembled a regular-sided pyramid. Another gave a foggy impression of a crouching figure. The best that could be said of the rest was that they bore a somewhat disconcerting resemblance to the kind of stones people pick up for paperweights. Yet they all had obviously been worked on. There were noticeable chisel marks on each one. And, in addition, they had been polished as well as such soft, grainy rock could be.

I looked up at Longan. His eyes were tense with waiting. I was completely puzzled about his discovery – or what he felt as a discovery. I tried to be fair about his acceptance of this as art. It was obviously nothing more than loyalty to a friend, a friend no doubt as unaware of what constituted art as himself. I made my tone as kind as I could.

'What did your friend expect me to do with these, Mr Longan?' I asked gently.

'Aren't you buying things for that museum-place on Earth?' he said.

I nodded. I picked up the piece that resembled a crouching animal figure and turned it over in my fingers. It was an awkward situation. 'Mr Longan,' I said, 'I have been in this business many years . . .'

'I know,' he interrupted. 'I read about you in the newsfax when you landed on the next world. That's why I wrote you.'

'I see,' I said. 'Well, I've been in it a long time, as I say and, I think, I can safely boast that I know something about art. If there is art in these carvings your friend has made, I should be able to recognize it. And I do not.'

He stared at me, shock in his greenish-brown eyes.

'You're . . .' he said, finally. 'You don't mean that. You're sore because I brought you out here this way.'

'I'm sorry,' I said. 'I'm *not* sore and I *do* mean it. These things are not merely not good – there is nothing of value in them. Nothing! Someone has deluded your friend into thinking that he has talent. You'll be doing him a favour if you tell him the truth.'

He stared at me for a long moment, as if waiting for me to say something to soften the verdict. Then, suddenly, he rose from the chair and crossed the room in three long strides, staring tensely out the window. His calloused hands clenched and unclenched spasmodically.

I gave him a little time to wrestle it out with himself. Then I started putting the pieces of stone back into their sections of the box.

'I'm sorry,' I told him.

He wheeled about and came back to me, leaning down from his lanky height to look in my face. 'Are you?' he said. '*Are* you?'

'Believe me,' I said sincerely, 'I am.' And I was.

'Then will you do something for me?' The words came in a rush. 'Will you come and tell Charlie what you've told me? Will *you* break the news to him?'

'I . . .' I meant to protest, to beg off, but with his tortured eyes six inches from mine, the words would not come. 'All right,' I said.

The breath he had been holding came out in one long sigh. 'Thanks,' he said. 'We'll go out tomorrow. You don't know what this means. Thanks.'

I had ample time to regret my decision, both that night and the following morning, when Longan roused me at an early hour, furnished me with a set of bush clothes like his own, including high, impervious boots, and whisked me off in an old air-ground combination flyer that was loaded down with all kinds of bush-dweller's equipment. But a promise is a promise – and I reconciled myself to keeping mine.

We flew south along a high chain of mountains until we came to a coastal area and what appeared to be the swamp delta of some monster river. Here, we began to descend – much to my distaste. I have little affection for hot, muggy climates and could not conceive of anyone wanting to live under such conditions.

We set down lightly in a little open stretch of water – and Longan taxied the flyer across to the nearest bank, a tussocky mass of high brown weeds and soft mud. By myself, I would not have trusted the soggy ground to refrain from drawing me down like quicksand – but Longan stepped out onto the bank confidently enough, and I followed. The mud yielded, little pools of water springing up around my boot soles. A hot rank smell of decaying vegetation came to my nose. Under a thin but uniform blanket of cloud, the sky looked white and sick.

'This way,' said Longan, and led off to the right.

I followed him along a little trail and into a small, swamp clearing with dome-shaped huts of woven branches, plastered with mud, scattered about it. And, for the first time, it struck me that Black Charlie might be something other than an expatriate Earthman – might, indeed, be a native of this planet, though I had heard of no other humanlike race on other worlds before. My head spinning, I followed Longan to the entrance of one of the huts and halted as he whistled.

I don't remember now what I expected to see. Something vaguely humanoid, no doubt. But what came through the entrance in response to Longan's whistle was more like a large otter, with flat, muscular grasping pads on the ends of its four limbs, instead of feet. It was black, with glossy, dampish hair all over it. About four feet in length, I judged, with no visible tail and a long, snaky neck. The creature must have weighed one hundred to, perhaps, one hundred and fifty pounds. The head on its long neck was also long and narrow, like the head of a well-bred collie – covered with the same black hair, with bright, intelligent eyes and a long mouth.

'This is Black Charlie,' said Longan.

The creature stared at me and I returned his gaze. Abruptly, I was conscious of the absurdity of the situation. It would have been difficult for any ordinary person to think of this being as a sculptor. To add to this necessity, an obligation, to convince it that it was *not* a sculptor – mind you, I could not be expected to know a word of its language – was to pile Pelion upon Ossa in a madman's farce. I swung on Longan.

'Look here,' I began with quite natural heat, 'how do you except me to tell—'

'He understands you,' interrupted Longan.

'Speech?' I said, increduously. 'Real human speech?'

'No,' Longan shook his head. 'But he understands actions.' He turned from me abruptly and plunged into the weeds surrounding the clearing. He returned immediately with two objects that looked like gigantic puffballs, and handed one to me.

'Sit on this,' he said, doing so himself. I obeyed.

Black Charlie – I could think of nothing else to call him – came closer, and we sat down together. Charlie was half-squatting on ebony haunches. All this time, I had been carrying the wooden box that contained his sculptures and, now that we were seated, his bright eyes swung inquisitively towards it.

'All right,' said Longan, 'give it to me.'

I passed him the box, and it drew Black Charlie's eyes like a magnet. Longan took it under one arm and pointed towards the lake with the other – to where we had landed the flyer. Then his arm rose in the air in a slow, impressive circle and pointed northwards, from the direction we had come.

Black Charlie whistled suddenly. It was an odd note, like the cry of a loon – a far, sad sound.

Longan struck himself on the chest, holding the box with one hand. Then he struck the box and pointed to me. He looked at Black Charlie, looked back at me – then put the box into my numb hands.

'Look them over and hand them back,' he said, his voice tight. Against my will, I looked at Charlie.

His eyes met mine. Strange, liquid, black inhuman eyes, like two tiny pools of pitch. I had to tear my own gaze away.

Torn between my feeling of foolishness and a real sympathy for the waiting creature, I awkwardly opened the box and lifted the stones from their compartments. One by one, I turned them in my hand and put them back. I closed the box and returned it to Longan, shaking my head, not knowing if Charlie would understand that.

For a long moment, Longan merely sat facing me, holding the box. Then, slowly, he turned and set it, still open, in front of Charlie.

Charlie did not react at first. His head, on its long neck, dropped over the open compartments as if he was sniffing them. Then, surprisingly, his lips wrinkled back, revealing long, chisel-shaped teeth. Daintily, he reached into the box with these and lifted out the stones, one by one. He held them in his forepads, turning them this way and that, as if searching for the defects of each. Finally, he lifted one – it was the stone that faintly resembled a crouching beast. He lifted it to his mouth – and with his gleaming teeth, made slight alterations in its surface. Then he brought it to me.

Helplessly I took it in my hands and examined it. The changes he had made in no way altered it towards something recognizable. I was forced to hand it back, with another headshake, and a poignant pause fell between us.

I had been desperately turning over in my mind some way to explain, through the medium of pantomime, the reasons for my refusal. Now, something occurred to me. I turned to Longan.

'Can he get me a piece of unworked stone?' I asked.

Longan turned to Charlie and made motions as if he were breaking something off and handing it to me. For a moment, Charlie sat still, as if considering this. Then he went into his hut, returning a moment later with a chunk of rock the size of my hand.

I had a small pocket knife, and the rock was soft. I held the rock out towards Longan and looked from him to it. Using my pocket knife, I whittled a rough, lumpy caricature of Longan, seated on the puffball. When I was finished, I put the two side by side, the hacked piece of stone insignificant on the ground beside the living man.

Black Charlie looked at it. Then he came up to me – and, peering up into my face, cried softly, once. Moving so abruptly that it startled me, he turned smoothly, picked up in his teeth the piece of stone I had carved. Soon he disappeared back into his hut.

Longan stood up stiffly, like a man who has held one position too long. 'That's it,' he said. 'Let's go.'

We made our way to the combination and took off once more, headed back towards the city and the spaceship that would carry me away from this irrational world. As the mountains commenced to rise, far beneath us, I stole a glance at Longan, sitting beside me at the controls of the combination. His face was set in an expression of stolid unhappiness.

The question came from my lips before I had time to debate internally whether it was wise or not to ask it.

'Tell me, Mr Longan,' I said, 'has – er – Black Charlie some special claim on your friendship?'

The tall man looked at me with something close to amazement.

'Claim!' he said. Then, after a short pause, during which he seemed to search my features to see if I was joking. 'He saved my life.'

'Oh,' I said. 'I see.'

'You do, do you?' he countered. 'Suppose I told you it was just after I'd finished killing his mate. They mate for life, you know.'

'No, I didn't know,' I answered feebly.

'I forget people don't know,' he said in a subdued voice. I said nothing, hoping that, if I did not disturb him, he would say more. After a while he spoke. 'This planet's not much good.'

'I noticed,' I answered. 'I didn't see much in the way of plants and factories. And your sister world – the one I came from – is much more populated and built up.'

'There's not much here,' he said. 'No minerals to speak of. Climate's bad, except on the plateaux. Soil's not much good.' He paused. It seemed to take effort to say what came next. 'Used to have a novelty trade in furs, though.'

'Furs!' I echoed.

'Off Charlie's people,' he went on, fiddling with the combination's controls. 'Trappers and hunters used to be after them, at first, before they knew. I was one of them.'

'You!' I said.

'Me!' His voice was flat. 'I was doing fine, too, until I trapped Charlie's mate. Up till then, I'd been getting them out by themselves. They did a lot of travelling in those swamps. But, this time, I was close to the village. I'd just clubbed her on the head when the whole tribe jumped me.' His voice trailed off, then strengthened. 'They kept me under guard for a couple of months.

'I learned a lot in that time. I learned they were intelligent. I learned it was Black Charlie who kept them from killing me right off. Seems he took the point of view that I was a reasonable being and, if he could just talk things over with me, we could get together and end the war.' Longan laughed, a little bitterly. 'They called it a war, Charlie's people did.' He stopped talking.

I waited. And when he remained quiet, I prompted him. 'What happened?' I asked.

'They let me go, finally,' he said. 'And I went to bat for them. Clear up to the Commissioner sent from Earth. I got them recognized as people instead of animals. I put an end to the hunting and trapping.'

He stopped again. We were still flying through the upper air of Elman's World, the sun breaking through the clouds at last, revealing the ground below like a huge green relief map.

'I see,' I said, finally.

Longan looked at me stonily.

We flew back to the city.

I left Elman's World the next day, fully believing that I had heard and seen the last of both Longan and Black Charlie. Several years later, at home in New York, I was visited by a member of the government's Foreign Service. He was a slight, dark man, and he didn't beat about the bush.

'You don't know me,' he said. I looked at his card – *Antonio Walters*. 'I was Deputy Colonial Representative on Elman's World at the time you were there.'

I looked up at him, surprised. I had forgotten Elman's World by that time.

'Were you?' I asked, feeling a little foolish, unable to think of anything better to say. I turned his card over several times, staring at it, as a person will do when at a loss. 'What can I do for you, Mr Walters?'

'We've been requested by the local government on Elman's World to locate you, Mr Jones,' he answered. 'Cary Longan is dying—'

'*Dying!*' I said.

'Lung fungus, unfortunately,' said Walters. 'You catch it in the swamps. He wants to see you before the end – and, since we're very grateful to him out there for the work he's been doing all these years for the natives, a place has been kept for you on a government courier ship leaving for Elman's World right away – if you're willing to go.'

'Why, I . . .' I hesitated. In common decency, I could not refuse. 'I'll have to notify my employers.'

'Of course,' he said.

Luckily, the arrangements I had to make consisted of a few business calls and packing my bags. I was, as a matter of fact, between trips at the time. As an experienced traveller, I could always get under way with a minimum of fuss. Walters and I drove out to Government Port, in northern New Jersey and, from there on, the authorities took over.

Less than a week later, I stood by Longan's bedside in the hospital of the same city I had visited years before. The man was now nothing more than a barely living skeleton, the hard vitality all but gone from him, hardly able to speak a few words at a time. I bent over to catch the whispered syllables from his wasted lips.

'Black Charlie . . .' he whispered.

'Black Charlie,' I repeated. 'Yes, what about him?'

'He's done something new,' whispered Longan. 'That carving of yours started him off, copying things. His tribe don't like it.'

'They don't?' I said.

'They,' whispered Longan, 'don't understand. It's not normal, the way they see it. They're afraid . . .'

'You mean they're superstitious about what he carves?' I asked.

'Something like that. Listen – he's an artist . . .'

I winced internally at the last word, but held my tongue for the sake of the dying man.

'. . . an artist. But they'll kill him for it, now that I'm gone. You can save him, though.'

'Me?' I said.

'You!' The man's voice was like a wind rustling through dry leaves. 'If you go out – take this last thing from him – act pleased . . . then they'll be scared to touch him. But hurry. Every day is that much closer. . . .'

His strength failed him. He closed his eyes and his straining throat muscles relaxed to a little hiss of air that puffed between his lips. The nurse hurried me from his room.

The local government helped me. I was surprised, and not a little touched, to see how many people knew Longan. How many of them admired his attempts to pay back the natives by helping them in any way he could. They located Charlie's tribe on a map for me and sent me out with a pilot who knew the country.

We landed on the same patch of slime. I went alone towards the clearing. With the brown weeds still walling it about, the locale showed no natural change, but Black

Charlie's hut appeared broken and deserted. I whistled and waited. I called. And, finally, I got down on my hands and knees and crawled inside. But there was nothing there save a pile of loose rock and a mass of dried weeds. Feeling cramped and uncomfortable, for I am not used to such gymnastics, I backed out, to find myself surrounded by a crowd.

It looked as if all the other inhabitants of the village had come out of their huts and congregated before Charlie's. They seemed agitated, milling about, occasionally whistling at each other on that one low, plaintive note which was the only sound I had ever heard Charlie make. Eventually, the excitement seemed to fade, the group fell back and one individual came forward alone. He looked up into my face for a brief moment, then turned and glided swiftly on his pads towards the the edge of the clearing.

I followed. There seemed nothing else to do. And, at that time, it did not occur to me to be afraid.

My guide led me deep into the weed patch, then abruptly disappeared. I looked around surprised and undecided, half-inclined to turn about and retrace my steps by the trail of crushed weeds I had left in my floundering advance. Then, a low whistle sounded close by. I went forward and found Charlie.

He lay on his side in a little circular open area of crushed weeds. He was too weak to do more than raise his head and look at me, for the whole surface of his body was crisscrossed and marked with the slashings of shallow wounds, from which dark blood seeped slowly and stained the reeds in which he lay. In Charlie's mouth, I had seen the long, chisel-teeth of his kind, and I knew what had made those wounds. A gust of rage went through me, and I stooped to pick him up in my arms.

He came up easily, for the bones of his kind are cartilaginous, and their flesh is far lighter than our human flesh. Holding him, I turned and made my way back to the clearing.

The others were waiting for me as we came out into the

open. I glared at them – and then the rage inside me went out like a blown candle. For there was nothing there to hate. *They* had not hated Charlie. They had merely feared him – and their only crime was ignorance.

They moved back from me, and I carried Charlie to the door of his own hut. There I laid him down. The chest and arms of my jacket were soaked from his dark body fluid, and I saw that his blood was not clotting as our own does.

Clumsily, I took off my shirt and, tearing it into strips, made a poor attempt to bind up the torn flesh. But the blood came through in spite of my first-aid. Charlie, lifting his head from the ground with a great effort picked feebly at the bandages with his teeth, so that I gave up and removed them.

I sat down beside him then, feeling sick and helpless. In spite of Longan's care and dying effort, in spite of all the scientific developments of my own human race, I had come too late. Numbly, I sat and looked down at him and wondered why I could not have come one day earlier.

From this half-stupor of self-accusation. I was roused by Charlie's attempts to crawl back into his hut. My first reaction was to restrain him. But, from somewhere, he seemed to have dredged up a remnant of his waning strength – and he persisted. Seeing this, I changed my mind and, instead of hindering, helped. He dragged himself through the entrance, his strength visibly waning.

I did not expect to see him emerge. I believed some ancient instinct had called him, that he would die then and there. But, a few moments later, I heard a sound as of stones rattling from within – and, in a few seconds, he began to back out. Halfway through the entrance, his strength finally failed him. He lay still for a minute, then whistled weakly.

I went to him and pulled him out the rest of the way. He turned his head towards me, holding in his mouth what I first took to be a ball of dried mud.

I took it from him and began to scrape the mud off with my fingernails. Almost immediately, the grain and surface of the sandstone he used for his carvings began to emerge – and my hands started to shake so hard that, for a moment, I had to put the stone down while I got myself under control. For the first time, the true importance to Charlie of these things he had chewed and bitten into shape got home to me. In that moment, I swore that whatever bizarre form this last and greatest work of his might possess, I would make certain that it was accorded a place in some respectable museum as a true work of art. After all, it had been conceived in honesty and executed in the love that took no count of labour, provided the end was achieved.

And then, the rest of the mud came free in my hands. I saw what it was, and I could have cried and laughed at the same time. For, of all the shapes he could have chosen to work in stone, he had picked the one that no critic would have selected as the choice of an artist of his race. For he had chosen no plant or animal, no structure or natural shape out of his environment, to express the hungry longing of his spirit. None of these had he chosen – instead, with painful clumsiness, he had fashioned an image from the soft and grainy rock: a statue of a standing man.

And I knew what man it was.

Charlie lifted his head from the stained ground and looked towards the lake where my flyer waited. I am not an intuitive man – but, for once, I was able to understand the meaning of a look. He wanted me to leave while he was still alive. He wanted to see me go, carrying the thing he had fashioned. I got to my feet, holding it and stumbled off. At the edge of the clearing I looked back. He still watched. And the rest of his people still hung back from him. I did not think they would bother him now.

And so I came home.

But there is one thing more to tell. For a long time, after I returned from Elman's World, I did not look at the crude statuette. I did not want to, for I knew that seeing it would only confirm what I had known from the start, that all the longing and desires in the world cannot create art where there is no talent, no true visualization. But at the end of one year I was cleaning up all the little details of my office. And, because I believe in system and order – and also, because I was ashamed of myself for having put it off so long – I took the statuette from a bottom drawer of my desk, unwrapped it and set it on the desk's polished surface.

I was alone in my office at the time, at the end of a day, when the afternoon sun, striking red through the tall window beside my desk, touched everything between the walls with a clear, amber light. I ran my fingers over the grainy sandstone and held it up to look at it.

And then – for the first time – I saw it, saw through the stone to the image beyond, saw what Black Charlie had seen, with Black Charlie's eyes, when he looked at Longan. I saw men as Black Charlie's kind saw men – and I saw what the worlds of men meant to Black Charlie. And, above all, overriding all, I saw art as Black Charlie saw it, through his bright alien eyes – saw the beauty he had sought at the price of his life, and had half-found.

But, most of all, I saw that this crude statuette was *art*.

One more word. Amid the mud and weeds of the swamp, I had held the carving in my hands and promised myself that this work would one day stand on display. Following that moment of true insight in my office, I did my best to place it with the institution I represented, then with others who knew me as a reputable buyer.

But I could find no takers. No one, although each trusted me individually, was willing to exhibit such a poor-looking piece of work on the strength of a history that I, alone, could vouch for. There are people, close to any institution, who are only too ready to cry, 'Hoax!' For several years, I tried without success.

Eventually, I gave up on the true story and sold the statuette, along with a number of other odd pieces, to a dealer of minor reputation, representing it as an object whose history I did not know.

Curiously, the statuette has justified my belief in what is art, by finding a niche for itself. I traced it from the dealer, after a time, and ran it to Earth quite recently. There is a highly respectable art gallery on this planet which has an extensive display of primitive figures of early American Indian origin.

And Black Charlie's statuette is among them. I will not tell which or where it is.

III OTHER DIMENSIONS

A. J. DEUTSCH

A SUBWAY NAMED MOBIUS

In a complex and ingenious pattern, the subway had spread out from a focus at Park Street. A shunt connected the Lechmere line with the Ashmont for trains southbound, and with the Forest Hills line for those northbound. Harvard and Brookline had been linked with a tunnel that passed through Kenmore Under, and during rush hours every other train was switched through the Kenmore Branch back to Egleston. The Kenmore Branch joined the Maverick Tunnel near Fields Corner. It climbed a hundred feet in two blocks to connect Copley Over with Scollay Square, then it dipped down again to join the Cambridge line at Boylston. The Boylston shuttle had finally tied together the seven principal lines on four different levels. It went into service, you remember, on March 3rd. After that, a train could travel from any one station to any other station in the whole system.

There were 227 trains running the subways every weekday, and they carried about a million and a half passengers. The Cambridge-Dorchester train that disappeared on March 4th was Number 86. Nobody missed it at first. During the evening rush, the traffic was a little heavier than usual on that line. But a crowd is a crowd. The ad posters at the Forest Hills yards looked for 86 about 7.30, but neither of them mentioned its absence until three days later. The controller at the Milk Street Cross-Over called the Harvard checker for an extra train after the hockey game that night, and the

Harvard checker relayed the call to the yards. The dispatcher there sent out 87, which had been put to bed at ten o'clock, as usual. He didn't notice that 86 was missing.

It was near the peak of the rush the next morning that Jack O'Brien, at the Park Street Control, called Warren Sweeney at the Forest Hills yards and told him to put another train on the Cambridge run. Sweeney was short, so he went to the board and scanned it for a spare train and crew. Then, for the first time, he noticed that Gallagher had not checked in the night before. He put the tag up and left a note. Gallagher was due in at ten. At ten-thirty, Sweeney was down looking at the board again, and he noticed Gallagher's tag still up, and the note where he had left it. He groused to the checker and asked if Gallagher had come in late. The checker said he hadn't seen Gallagher at all that morning. Then Sweeney wanted to know who was running 86. A few minuutes later he noted that Dorkin's card was still up, although it was Dorkin's day off. It was 11.30 before he finally realized that he had lost a train.

Sweeney spent the next hour and a half on the phone, and he quizzed every dispatcher, controller, and checker on the whole system. When he finished his lunch at 1.30, he covered the whole net again. At 4.40, just before he left for the day, he reported the matter, with some information to Central Traffic. The phones buzzed through the tunnels and shops until nearly midnight before the general manager was finally notified at his home.

It was the engineer on the main switchbank who, late in the morning of the 6th, first associated the missing train with the newspaper stories about the sudden rash of missing persons. He tipped off the *Transcript*, and by the end of the lunch-hour three papers had extras on the streets. That was the way the story got out.

Kelvin Whyte, the general manager, spent a good part of that afternoon with the police. They checked Gallagher's wife, and Dorkin's. The motorman and the conductor had not been home since the morning of the 4th. By mid-afternoon, it was clear to the police that three hundred and fifty

Bostonians, more or less, had been lost with the train. The System closed, and Whyte nearly expired with simple exasperation. But the train was not found.

Roger Tupelo, the Harvard mathematician, stepped into the picture the evening of the 6th. He reached Whyte by phone, late, at his home, and told him he had some ideas about the missing train. Then he taxied to Whyte's home in Newton and had the first of many talks with Whyte about Number 86.

Whyte was an intelligent man, a good organizer, and not without imagination. 'But I don't know what you're talking about!' he expostulated.

Tupelo was resolved to be patient. 'This is a very hard thing for *anybody* to understand, Mr Whyte,' he said. 'I can see why you are puzzled. But it's the only explanation. The train has vanished, and the people on it. But the System is closed. Trains are conserved. It's somewhere on the System!'

Whyte's voice grew louder again. 'And I tell you, Dr Tupelo, that train is *not* on the System! It is *not!* You can't overlook a seven-car train carrying four hundred passengers. The System has been combed. Do you think I'm trying to *hide* the train?'

'Of course not. Now look, let's be reasonable. We know the train was en route to Cambridge at 8.40 AM on the 4th. At least twenty of the missing people probably boarded the train a few minutes earlier at Washington, and forty more at Park Street Under. A few got off at both stations. And that's the last. The ones who were going to Kendall, to Central, to Harvard – they never got there. The train did not get to Cambridge.'

'I know that, Dr Tupelo,' Whyte said savagely. 'In the tunnel under the river, the train turned into a boat. It left the tunnel and sailed for Africa.'

'No, Mr Whyte. I'm trying to tell you. It hit a node.'

Whyte was livid. 'What is a node!' he exploded. 'The System keeps the tracks clear. Nothing on the tracks but trains, no nodes left lying around—'

'You still don't understand. A node is not an obstruction. It's a singularity. A pole of high order.'

Tupelo's explanations that night did not greatly clarify the situation for Kelvin Whyte. But at two in the morning, the general manager conceded to Tupelo the privilege of examining the master maps of the System. He put in a call first to the police, who could not assist him with his first attempt to master topology, and then, finally, to Central Traffic. Tupelo taxied down there alone, and pored over the maps till morning. He had coffee and a snail, and then went to Whyte's office.

He found the general manager on the telephone. There was a conversation having to do with another, more elaborate inspection of the Dorchester-Cambridge tunnel under the Charles River. When the conversation ended, Whyte slammed the telephone into its cradle and glared at Tupelo. The mathematician spoke first.

'I think probably it's the new shuttle that did this,' he said.

Whyte gripped the edge of his desk and prowled silently through his vocabulary until he had located some civil words. 'Dr Tupelo,' he said. 'I have been awake all night going over your theory. I don't understand it all. I don't know what the Boylston shuttle has to do with this.'

'Remember what I was saying last night about the connective properties of networks?' Tupelo asked quietly. 'Remember the Mobius band we made – the surface with one face and one edge? Remember this?—' and he removed a little glass Klein bottle from his pocket and placed it on the desk.

Whyte sat back in his chair and stared wordlessly at the mathematician. Three emotions marched across his face in quick successes – anger, bewilderment, and utter dejection. Tupelo went on.

'Mr Whyte, the System is a network of amazing topological complexity. It was already complex before the Boylston shuttle was installed, and of a high order of connectivity. But this shuttle makes the network absolutely unique. I don't fully understand it, but the situation seems to be something like this: the shuttle has made the connectivity of the whole System of an order so high that I don't know how to calculate it. I suspect the connectivity has become infinite.'

The general manager listened as though in a daze. He kept his eyes glued to the little Klein bottle.

'The Mobius band,' Tupelo said, 'has unusual properties because it has a singularity. The Klein bottle, with two singularities, manages to be inside of itself. The topologists know surfaces with as many as a thousand singularities, and they have properties that make the Mobius band and the Klein bottle both look simple. But a network with infinite connectivity must have an infinite number of singularities. Can you imagine what the properties of that network could be?'

After a long pause, Tupelo added, 'I can't either. To tell the truth, the structure of the System, with the Boylston shuttle, is completely beyond me. I can only guess.'

Whyte swivelled his eyes up from the desk at a moment when anger was the dominant feeling within him. 'And you call yourself a mathematician, Professor Tupelo!' he said.

Tupelo almost laughed aloud. The incongruousness, the absolute foolishness of the situation, all but overwhelmed him. He smiled thinly, and said, 'I'm no topologist. Really, Mr Whyte, I'm a tyro in the field – not much better acquainted with it than you are. Mathematics is a big pasture. I happen to be an algebraist.'

His candour softened Whyte a little. 'Well, then,' he ventured, 'if you don't understand it, maybe we should call in a topologist. Are there any in Boston?'

'Yes and no,' Tupelo answered. 'The best in the world is at Tech.'

Whyte reached for the telephone. 'What's his name?' he asked. 'I'll call him.'

'Merritt Turnbull. He can't be reached. I've tried for three days.'

'Is he out of town?' Whyte asked. 'We'll send for him – emergency.'

'I don't know. Professor Turnbull is a bachelor. He lives alone at the Brattle Club. He has not been seen since the morning of the 4th.'

Whyte was uncommonly perceptive. 'Was he on the train?' he asked tensely.

'I don't know,' the mathematician replied. 'What do you think?'

There was a long silence. Whyte looked alternately at Tupelo and at the glass object on the desk. 'I don't understand it,' he said finally. 'We've looked everywhere on the System. There was no way for the train to get out.'

'The train didn't get out. It's still on the System,' Tupelo said.

'Where?'

Tupelo shrugged. 'The train has no real "where". The whole System is without real "whereness". It's double-valued, or worse.'

'How can we find it?'

'I don't think we can,' Tupelo said.

There was another long silence. Whyte broke it with a loud exclamation. He rose suddenly, and sent the Klein bottle flying across the room. 'You are crazy, Professor!' he shouted. 'Between midnight tonight and 6.00 AM tomorrow, we'll get every train out of the tunnels. I'll send in three hundred men, to comb every inch of the tracks – every inch of the one hundred eighty-three miles. We'll find the train! Now, please excuse me.' He glared at Tupelo.

Tupelo left the office. He felt tired, completely exhausted. Mechanically, he walked along Washington Street towards the Essex Station. Halfway down the stairs, he stopped abruptly, looked around him slowly. Then he ascended again to the street and hailed a taxi. At home, he helped himself to a double shot. He fell into bed.

At 3.30 that afternoon he met his class in Algebra of Fields and Rings. After a quick supper at the Crimson Spa, he went to his apartment and spent the evening in a second attempt to analyse the connective properties of the System. The attempt was vain, but the mathematician came to a few important conclusions. At eleven o'clock he telephoned Whyte at Central Traffic.

'I think you might want to consult me during tonight's search,' he said. 'May I come down?'

The general manager was none too gracious about Tupelo's offer of help. He indicated that the System would solve this little problem without any help from harebrained professors who thought that whole subway trains could jump off into the fourth dimension. Tupelo submitted to Whyte's unkindness, then went to bed. At about 4.00 AM the telephone awakened him. His caller was a contrite Kelvin Whyte.

'Perhaps I was a bit hasty last night, Professor,' he stammered. 'You may be able to help us after all. Could you come down to the Milk Street Cross-Over?'

Tupelo agreed readily. He felt none of the satisfaction he had anticipated. He called a taxi, and in less than half an hour was at the prescribed station. At the foot of the stairs, on the upper level, he saw that the tunnel was brightly lighted, as during normal operation of the System. But the platforms were deserted except for a tight little knot of seven men near the far end. As he walked toward the group, he noticed that two were policemen. He observed a one-car train on the track beside the platform. The forward door was open, the car brightly lit, and empty. Whyte heard his footsteps and greeted him sheepishly.

'Thanks for coming down, Professor,' he said, extending his hand. 'Gentlemen, Dr Roger Tupelo, of Harvard. Dr Tupelo, Mr Kennedy, our chief engineer; Mr Wilson, representing the Mayor; Dr Gannot of Mercy Hospital.' Whyte did not bother to introduce the motorman and the two policemen.

'How do you do,' said Tupelo. 'Any results, Mr Whyte?'

The general manager exchanged embarrassed glances with his companions. 'Well . . . yes, Dr Tupelo,' he finally answered. 'I think we do have some results, of a kind.'

'Has the train been seen?'

'Yes,' said Whyte. 'That is, practically seen. At least, we

know it's somewhere in the tunnels.' The six others nodded their agreement.

Tupelo was not surprised to learn that the train was still on the System. After all, the System was closed. 'Would you mind telling me just what happened?' Tupelo insisted.

'I hit a red signal,' the motorman volunteered. 'Just outside the Copley junction.'

'The tracks have been completely cleared of all trains,' Whyte explained, 'except for this one. We've been riding it, all over the System, for four hours now. When Edmunds, here, hit a red light at the Copley junction, he stopped, of course. I thought the light must be defective, and told him to go ahead. But then we heard another train pass the junction.'

'Did you see it?' Tupelo asked.

'We couldn't see it. The light is placed just behind a curve. But we all heard it. There's no doubt the train went through the junction. And it must be Number 86, because our car was the only other one on the tracks.'

'What happened then?'

'Well, then the light changed to yellow, and Edmunds went ahead.'

'Did he follow the other train?'

'No. We couldn't be sure which way it was going. We must have guessed wrong.'

'How long ago did this happen?'

'At 1.38, the first time—'

'Oh,' said Tupelo, 'then it happened again later?'

'Yes. But not at the same spot, of course. We hit another red signal near South Station at 2.15. And then at 3.28—'

Tupelo interrupted the general manager. 'Did you see the train at 2.15?'

'We didn't even hear it, that time. Edmunds tried to catch it, but it must have turned off onto the Boylston shuttle.'

'What happened at 3.28?'

'Another red light. Near Park Street. We heard it up ahead of us.'

'But you didn't see it?'

'No. There is a little slope beyond the light. But we all heard it. The only thing I don't understand, Dr Tupelo, is how that train could run the tracks for nearly five days without anybody seeing—'

Whyte's words trailed off into silence, and his right hand went up in a peremptory gesture for quiet. In the distance, the low metallic thunder of a fast-rolling train swelled up suddenly into a sharp, shrill roar of wheels below. The platform vibrated perceptibly as the train passed.

'Now we've got it!' Whyte exclaimed. 'Right past the men on the platform below!' He broke into a run towards the stairs to the lower level. All the others followed him, except Tupelo. He thought he knew what was going to happen. It did. Before Whyte reached the stairs, a policeman bounded up to the top.

'Did you see it, now?' he shouted.

Whyte stopped in his tracks, and the others with him.

'Did you see that train?' the policeman from the lower level asked again, as two more men came running up the stairs.

'What happened?' Wilson wanted to know.

'Didn't *you* see it?' snapped Kennedy.

'Sure not,' the policeman replied. 'It passed through up here.'

'It did *not*.' roared Whyte. 'Down there!'

The six men with Whyte glowered at the three from the lower level. Tupelo walked to Whyte's elbow. 'The train can't be seen, Mr Whyte,' he said quietly.

Whyte looked down at him in utter disbelief. 'You heard it yourself. It passed right below—'

'Can we go to the car, Mr Whyte!' Tupelo asked. 'I think we ought to talk a little.'

Whyte nodded dumbly, then turned to the policeman and the others who had been watching at the lower level. 'You really didn't see it?' he begged them.

'We heard it,' the policeman answered. 'It passed up here, going that way, I think,' and he gestured with his thumb.

'Get back downstairs, Maloney,' one of the policemen

with Whyte commanded. Maloney scratched his head, turned, and disappeared below. The two other men followed him. Tupelo led the original group to the car beside the station platform. They went in and took seats, silently. Then they all watched the mathematician and waited.

'You didn't call me down here tonight just to tell me you'd found the missing train,' Tupelo began, looking at Whyte. 'Has this sort of thing happened before?'

Whyte squirmed in his seat and exchanged glances with the chief engineer. 'Not exactly like this,' he said, evasively, 'but there have been some funny things.'

'Like what?' Tupelo snapped.

'Well, like the red lights. The watchers near Kendall found a red light at the same time we hit the one near South Station.'

'Go on.'

'Mr Sweeney called me from Forest Hills at Park Street Under. He heard the train there just two minutes after we heard it at the Copley junction. Twenty-eight track miles away.'

'As a matter of fact, Dr Tupelo,' Wilson broke in, 'several dozen men have seen lights go red, or have heard the train, or both, inside of the last four hours. The thing acts as though it can be in several places at once.'

'It can,' Tupelo said.

'We keep getting reports of watchers seeing the thing,' the engineer added. 'Well, not exactly seeing it, either, but everything except that. Sometimes at two or even three places, far apart, at the same time. It's sure to be on the tracks. Maybe the cars are uncoupled.'

'Are you really sure it's on the tracks, Mr Kennedy?' Tupelo asked.

'Positive,' the engineer said. 'The dynamometers at the power house show that it's drawing power. It's been drawing power all night. So at 3.30 we broke the circuits. Cut the power.'

'What happened?'

'Nothing,' Whyte answered. 'Nothing at all. The power

was off for twenty minutes. During that time, not one of the two hundred fifty men on the tunnels saw a red light or heard a train. But the power wasn't on for five minutes before we had two reports again – one from Arlington, the other from Egleston.'

There was a long silence after Whyte finished speaking. In the tunnel below, one man could be heard calling something to another. Tupelo looked at his watch. The time was 5.20.

'In short, Dr Tupelo,' the general manager finally said, 'we are compelled to admit that there may be something in your theory.' The others nodded agreement.

'Thank you, gentlemen,' Tupelo said.

The physician cleared his throat. 'Now about the passengers,' he began. 'Have you any idea what?—'

'None,' Tupelo interrupted.

'What should we do, Dr Tupelo?' the mayor's representative asked.

'I don't know. What can you do?'

'As I understand it from Mr Whyte,' Wilson continued, 'the train has . . . well, it has jumped into another dimension. It isn't really on the System at all. It's just gone. Is that right?'

'In a manner of speaking.'

'And this . . . er . . . peculiar behaviour has resulted from certain mathematical properties associated with the new Boylston shuttle?'

'Correct.'

'And there is nothing we can do to bring the train back to . . . uh . . . this dimension?'

'I know of nothing.'

Wilson took the bit in his teeth. 'In this case, gentlemen,' he said, 'our course is clear. First, we must close off the new shuttle, so this fantastic thing can never happen again. Then, since the missing train is really gone, in spite of all these red lights and noises, we can resume normal operation of the System. At least there will be no danger of collision – which has worried you so much, Whyte. As for the missing train and the people on it—' He gestured them into infinity. 'Do you agree, Dr Tupelo?' he asked the mathematician.

Tupelo shook his head slowly. 'Not entirely, Mr Wilson,' he responded. 'Now, please keep in mind that I don't fully comprehend what has happened. It's unfortunate that you won't find anybody who can give a good explanation. The one man who might have done so is Professor Turnbull, of Tech, and he was on the train. But in any case, you will want to check my conclusions against those of some competent topologists. I can put you in touch with several.

'Now, with regard to the recovery of the missing train, I can say that I think this is not hopeless. There is a finite probability, as I see it, that the train will eventually pass from the non-spatial part of the network, which it now occupies, back to the spatial part. Since the non-spatial part is wholly inaccessible, there is unfortunately nothing we can do to bring about this transition, or even to predict when or how it will occur. But the possibility of the transition will vanish if the Boylston shuttle is taken out. It is just this section of the track that gives the network its essential singularities. If the singularities are removed, the train can never reappear. Is this clear?'

It was not clear, of course, but the seven listening men nodded agreement. Tupelo continued.

'As for the continued operation of the System while the missing train is in the non-spatial part of the network, I can only give you the facts as I see them and leave to your judgement the difficult decision to be drawn from them. The transition back to the spatial part is unpredictable, as I have already told you. There is no way to know when it will occur, or where. In particular, there is a fifty per cent probability that, if and when the train reappears, it will be running on the wrong track. Then there will be a collision, of course.'

The engineer asked, 'To rule out this possibility, Dr Tupelo, couldn't we leave the Boylston shuttle open, but send no trains through it? Then, when the missing train reappears on the shuttle, it cannot meet another train.'

'That precaution would be ineffective, Mr Kennedy,'

Tupelo answered. 'You see, the train can reappear anywhere on the System. It is true that the System owes its topological complexity to the new shuttle. But, with the shuttle in the System, it is now the whole System that possesses infinite connectivity. In other words, the relevant topological property is a property *derived* from the shuttle, but *belonging* to the whole System. Remember that the train made its first transition at a point between Park and Kendall, more than three miles away from the shuttle.

'There is one question more you will want answered. If you decide to go on operating the System, with the Boylston shuttle left in until the train reappears, can this happen again, to another train? I am not certain of the answer, but I think it is: No. I believe an exclusion principle operates here, such that only one train at a time can occupy the non-spatial network.'

The physician rose from his seat. 'Dr Tupelo,' he began, timorously, 'when the train does reappear, will the passengers?—'

'I don't know about the people on the train,' Tupelo cut in. 'The topological theory does not consider such matters.' He looked quickly at each of the seven tired, querulous faces before him. 'I am sorry, gentlemen,' he added, somewhat more gently. 'I simply do not know.' To Whyte, he added, 'I think I can be of no more help tonight. You know where to reach me.' And, turning on his heel, he left the car and climbed the stairs. He found dawn spilling over the street, dissolving the shadows of night.

That impromptu conference in a lonely subway car was never reported in the papers. Nor were the full results of the night-long vigil over the dark and twisted tunnels. During the week that followed, Tupelo participated in four more formal conferences with Kelvin Whyte and certain city officials. At two of these, other topologists were present. Ornstein was imported to Boston from Philadelphia, Kashta from Chicago, and Michaelis from Los Angeles. The mathematicians were unable to reach a concensus. None of the three would fully endorse Tupelo's conclusions, although Kashta indicated that there *might* be something to them. Ornstein averred that a finite network could not possess infinite connectivity, although he could not prove this proposition and could not actually calculate the connectivity of the System. He insisted that if the train could not be found on the System then the System must be open, or at least must once have been open.

But the more deeply Tupelo analysed the problem, the more fully he was convinced of the essential correctness of his first analysis. From the point of view of topology, the System soon suggested whole families of multiple-valued networks, each with an infinite number of infinite discontinuities. But a definite discussion of these new spatio-hyperspatial networks somehow eluded him. He gave the subject his full attention for only a week. Then his other duties compelled him to lay the analysis aside. He resolved to go back to the problem later in the spring, after courses were over.

Meanwhile, the System was operated as though nothing untoward had happened. The general manager and the mayor's representative had somehow managed to forget the night of the search, or at least to reinterpret what they had seen and not seen. The newspapers and the public at large speculated wildly, and they kept continuing pressure on Whyte. A number of suits were filed against the System on behalf of persons who had lost a relative. The state stepped into the affair and prepared its own thorough investigation. Recriminations were sounded in the halls of Congress. A garbled version of Tupelo's theory eventually found its way into the press. He ignored it, and it was soon forgotten.

The weeks passed, and then a month. The state's investigation was completed. The newspaper stories moved from the first page to the second; to the twenty-third; and then stopped. The missing persons did not return. In the large, they were no longer missed.

One day in mid-April, Tupelo travelled by subway again, from Charles Street to Harvard. He sat stiffly in the front of the first car, and watched the tracks and grey tunnel walls hurl themselves at the train. Twice the train stopped for a red light, and Tupelo found himself wondering whether the other train was really just ahead, or just beyond space. He half-hoped, out of curiosity, that his exclusion principle was wrong, that the train might make the transition. But he arrived at Harvard on time. Only he among the passengers had found the trip exciting.

The next week he made another trip by subway, and again the next. As experiments, they were unsuccessful, and much less tense than the first ride in mid-April. Tupelo began to doubt his own analysis. Sometime in May, he reverted to the practice of commuting by subway between his Beacon Hill apartment and his office at Harvard. His mind stopped racing down the knotted grey caverns ahead of the train. He read the morning newspaper, or the abstracts in *Reviews of Modern Mathematics*.

Then there was one morning when he looked up from the newspaper and sensed something. He pushed panic back on its stiff, quivering spring, and looked quickly out the window at his right. The lights of the car showed the black and grey lines of wall-spots streaking by. The tracks ground out their familiar steely dissonance. The train rounded a curve and crossed a junction that he remembered. Swiftly, he recalled boarding the train at Charles, noting the girl on the ice-carnival poster at Kendall, meeting the southbound train going into Central.

He looked at the man sitting beside him, with a lunch box on his lap. The other seats were filled, and there were a dozen or so straphangers. A mealy-faced youth near the front door smoked a cigarette, in violation of the rules. Two girls behind him across the aisle were discussing a club meeting. In the seat ahead, a young woman was scolding her little son. The man on the aisle, in the seat ahead of that, was reading the paper. The Transit-ad above him extolled Florida oranges.

He looked again at the man two seats ahead and fought down the terror within. He studied that man. What was it? Brunet, greying hair; a roundish head; wan complexion;

rather flat features; a thick neck, with the hairline a little low, a little ragged; a grey, pin-stripe suit. While Tupelo watched, the man waved a fly away from his left ear. He swayed a little with the train. His newspaper was folded vertically down the middle. His *newspaper!* It was last March's!

Tupelo's eyes swivelled to the man beside him. Below his lunch box was a paper. Today's. He turned in his seat and looked behind him. A young man held the *Transcript* open to the sports pages. The date was March 4th. Tupelo's eyes raced up and down the aisle. There were a dozen passengers carrying papers ten weeks old.

Tupelo lunged out of his seat. The man on the aisle muttered a curse as the mathematician crowded in front of him. He crossed the aisle in a bound and pulled the cord above the windows. The brakes sawed and screeched at the tracks, and the train ground to a stop. The startled passengers eyed Tupelo with hostility. At the rear of the car, the door flew open and a tall, thin man in a blue uniform burst in. Tupelo spoke first.

'Mr Dorkin?' he called, vehemently.

The conductor stopped short and groped for words.

'There's been a serious accident, Dorkin,' Tupelo said, loudly, to carry over the rising swell of protest from the passengers. 'Get Gallagher back here right away!'

Dorkin reached up and pulled the cord four times. 'What happened?' he asked.

Tupelo ignored the question, and asked one of his own. 'Where have you been, Dorkin?'

The conductor's face was blank. 'In the next car, but—'

Tupelo cut him off. He glanced at his watch, then shouted at the passengers. 'It's ten minutes to nine on May 17th!'

The announcement stilled the rising clamour for a moment. The passengers exchanged bewildered glances.

'Look at your newspapers!' Tupelo shouted. 'Your newspapers!'

The passengers began to buzz. As they discovered each other's papers, the voices rose. Tupelo took Dorkin's arm and led him to the rear of the car. 'What time is it?' he asked.

'8.21,' Dorkin said, looking at his watch.

'Open the door,' said Tupelo, motioning ahead. 'Let me out. Where's the phone?'

Dorkin followed Tupelo's directions. He pointed to a niche in the tunnel wall a hundred yards ahead. Tupelo vaulted to the ground and raced down the narrow lane between the cars and the wall. 'Central Traffic!' he barked at the operator. He waited a few seconds, and saw that a train had stopped at the red signal behind his train. Flashlights were advancing down the tunnel. He saw Gallagher's legs running down the tunnel on the other side of 86. 'Get me Whyte!' he commanded, when Central Traffic answered. 'Emergency!'

There was a delay. He heard voices rising from the train beside him. The sound was mixed – anger, fear, hysteria.

'Hello!' he shouted. 'Hello! Emergency! Get me Whyte!'

'I'll take it,' a man's voice said at the other end of the line. 'Whyte's busy!'

'Number 86 is back,' Tupelo called. 'Between Central and Harvard now. Don't know when it made the jump. I caught it at Charles ten minutes ago, and didn't notice it till a minute ago.'

The man at the other end gulped hard enough to carry over the telephone. 'The passengers?' he croaked.

'All right, the ones that are left,' Tupelo said. 'Some must have got off already at Kendall and Central.'

'Where have they been?'

Tupelo dropped the receiver from his ear and stared at it, his mouth wide open. Then he slammed the receiver onto the hook and ran back to the open door.

Eventually, order was restored, and within a half-hour the train proceeded to Harvard. At the station, the police took all passengers into protective custody. Whyte himself arrived at Harvard before the train did. Tupelo found him on the platform.

Whyte motioned weakly towards the passengers. 'They're really all right?' he asked.

'Perfectly,' said Tupelo. 'Don't know they've been gone.'

'Any sign of Professor Turnbull?' asked the general manager.

'I didn't see him. He probably got off at Kendall, as usual.'

'Too bad,' said Whyte. 'I'd like to see him!'

'So would I!' Tupelo answered. 'By the way, now is the time to close the Boylston shuttle.'

'Now is too late,' Whyte said. 'Train 143 vanished twenty-five minutes ago between Egleston and Dorchester.'

Tupelo stared past Whyte, and down and down the tracks.

'We've got to find Turnbull,' Whyte said.

Tupelo looked at Whyte and smiled thinly.

'Do you really think Turnbull got off this train at Kendall?' he asked.

'Of course!' answered Whyte: 'Where else?'

POUL ANDERSON

THE MAN WHO CAME EARLY

Yes, when a man grows old he has heard so much that is strange there's little more can surprise him. They say the king in Miklagard has a beast of gold before his high seat which stands up and roars. I have it from Eilif Eiriksson, who served in the guard down yonder, and he is a steady fellow when not drunk. He has also seen the Greek fire used, it burns on water.

So, priest, I am not unwilling to believe what you say about the White Christ. I have been in England and France myself, and seen how the folk prosper. He must be a very powerful god, to ward so many realms . . . and did you say that everyone who is baptized will be given a white robe? I would like to have one. They mildew, of course, in this cursed wet Iceland weather, but a small sacrifice to the house elves should—No sacrifices? Come now! I'll give up horseflesh if I must, my teeth not being what they were, but every sensible man knows how much trouble the elves make if they're not fed.

—Well, let's have another cup and talk about it. How do you like the beer? It's my own brew, you know. The cups I got in England, many years back. I was a young man then . . . time goes, time goes. Afterwards I came back and inherited this, my father's steading, and have not left it since. Well enough to go in viking as a youth, but grown older you see where the real wealth lies: here, in the land and the cattle.

Stoke up the fires, Hjalti. It's getting cold. Sometimes I think the winters are colder than when I was a boy. Thorbrand of the Salmondale says so, but he believes the gods are angry because so many are turning from them. You'll have trouble winning Thorbrand over, priest. A stubborn man. Myself I am open-minded, and willing to listen at least.

—Now, then. There is one point on which I must set you right. The end of the world is not coming in two years. This I know.

And if you ask me how I know, that's a very long tale, and in some ways a terrible one. Glad I am to be old, and safe in the earth before that great tomorrow comes. It will be an eldritch time before the frost giants fare loose . . . oh, very well, before the angel blows his battle horn. One reason I hearken to your preaching is that I know the White Christ will conquer Thor. I know Iceland is going to be Christian ere long, and it seems best to range myself on the winning side.

No, I've had no visions. This is a happening of five years ago, which my own household and neighbours can swear to. They mostly did not believe what the stranger told; I do, more or less, if only because I don't think a liar could wreak so much harm. I loved my daughter, priest, and after the trouble was over I made a good marriage for her. She did not naysay it, but now she sits out on the nessfarm with her husband and never a word to me; and I hear he is ill pleased with her silence and moodiness, and spends his nights with an Irish leman. For this I cannot blame him, but it grieves me.

Well, I've drunk enough to tell the whole truth now, and whether you believe it or not makes no odds to me. Here . . . you, girls! . . . fill these cups again, for I'll have a dry throat before I finish the telling.

It begins, then, on a day in early summer, five years ago. At that time, my wife Ragnhild and I had only two unwed children still living with us: our youngest son Helgi, of seventeen winters, and our daughter Thorgunna, of eighteen. The girl, being fair, had already had suitors. But she refused them, and I am not one who would compel his daughter. As for Helgi, he was ever a lively one, good with his hands but a breakneck youth. He is now serving in the guard of King Olaf of Norway. Besides these, of course, we had about ten housefolk – two thralls, two girls to help with the women's work, and half a dozen hired carles. This is not a small garth.

You have seen how my land lies. A couple of miles to the west is the bay; the thorps at Reykjavik are some five miles south. The land rises towards the Long Jökull, so that my acres are hilly; but it's good hay-land, and we often find driftwood on the beach. I've built a shed down there for it, as well as a boathouse.

We had had a storm the night before – a wild huge storm with lightning flashes across heaven, such as you seldom get in Iceland – so Helgi and I were going down to look for drift. You, coming from Norway, do not know how precious wood is to us here, who have only a few scrubby trees and must get our timber from abroad. Back there men have often been burned in their houses by their foes, but we count that the worst of deeds, though it's not unheard of.

As I was on good terms with my neighbours, we took only hand weapons. I bore my axe, Helgi a sword, and the two carles we had with us bore spears. It was a day washed clean by the night's fury, and the sun fell bright on long wet grass. I saw my garth lying rich around its courtyard, sleek cows and sheep, smoke rising from the roofhole of the hall, and knew I'd not done so ill in my lifetime. My son Helgi's hair fluttered in the low west wind as we left the steading behind a ridge and neared the water. Strange how well I remember all that happened that day, somehow it was a sharper day than most.

When we came down to the strand, the sea was beating heavy, white and grey out to the world's edge, smelling of salt and kelp. A few gulls mewed above us, frightened off a cod washed onto the shore. I saw a litter of no few sticks, even a baulk of timber . . . from some ship carrying it that broke up during the night, I suppose. That was a useful find, though as a careful man I would later sacrifice to be sure the owner's ghost wouldn't plague me.

We had fallen to and were dragging the baulk towards the shed when Helgi cried out. I ran for my axe as I looked the way he pointed. We had no feuds then, but there are always outlaws.

This newcomer seemed harmless, though. Indeed, as he stumbled nearer across the black sand I thought him quite unarmed and wondered what had happened. He was a big man and strangely clad – he wore coat and breeches and shoes like anyone else, but they were of odd cut and he bound his trousers with leggings rather than crossgaiters. Nor had I ever seen a helmet like his: it was almost square, and came down to ward his neck, but it had no nose guard. And this you may not believe, but it was not metal yet had been cast in one piece!

He broke into a staggering run as he drew close, flapped his arms and croaked something. The tongue was none I had heard, and I have heard many; it was like dogs barking. I saw that he was clean-shaven and his black hair cropped short, and thought he might be French. Otherwise he was a young man, and good-looking, with blue eyes and regular features. From his skin I judged that he spent much time indoors. However, he had a fine manly build.

'Could he have been shipwrecked?' asked Helgi.

'His clothes are dry and unstained,' I said, 'nor has he been wandering long, for no stubble is on his chin. Yet I've heard of no strangers guesting hereabouts.'

We lowered our weapons and he came up to us and stood gasping. I saw that his coat and the shirt behind were fastened with bonelike buttons rather than laces, and were of heavy weave. About his neck he had fastened a strip of cloth tucked into his coat. These garments were all in greenish-brownish hues. His shoes were of a sort new to me, very well stitched. Here and there on his coat were bits of brass, and he had three broken stripes on each sleeve; also a black band with white letters, the same letters being on his helmet. Those were not runes, but Roman – thus: MP. He wore a broad belt, with a small clublike thing of metal in a sheath at the hip and also a real club.

'I think he must be a warlock,' muttered my carle Sigurd. 'Why else so many tokens?'

'They may only be ornament, or to ward against witchcraft,' I soothed him. Then, to the stranger, 'I hight Ospak Ulfsson of Hillstead. What is your errand?'

He stood with his chest heaving and a wildness in his eyes. He must have run a long way. At last he moaned and sat down and covered his face.

'If he's sick, best we get him to the house,' said Helgi. I heard eagerness; we see few new faces here.

'No . . . no . . .' The stranger looked up. 'Let me rest a moment—'

He spoke the Norse tongue readily enough, though with a thick accent not easy to follow and with many foreign words I did not understand.

The other carle, Grim, hefted his spear. 'Have Vikings landed?' he asked.

'When did Vikings ever come to Iceland?' I snorted. 'It's the other way around.'

The newcomer shook his head, as if it had been struck. He got shakily to his feet. 'What happened?' he said. 'What became of the town?'

'What town?' I asked reasonably.

'Reykjavik!' he cried. 'Where is it?'

'Five miles south, the way you came – unless you mean the bay itself,' I said.

'No! There was only a beach, and a few wretched huts, and—'

'Best not let Hjalmar Broadnose hear you call his thorp that,' I counselled.

'But there was a town!' he gasped. 'I was crossing the street, in a storm, and heard a crash and then I stood on the beach and the town was gone!'

'He's mad,' said Sigurd, backing away. 'Be careful. If he starts to foam at the mouth, it means he's going berserk.'

'Who are you?' babbled the stranger. 'What are you doing in those clothes? Why the spears?'

'Somehow,' said Helgi, 'he does not sound crazed, only frightened and bewildered. Something evil has beset him.'

'I'm not staying near a man under a curse!' yelped Sigurd, and started to run away.

'Come back!' I bawled. 'Stand where you are or I'll cleave your louse-bitten head.'

That stopped him, for he had no kin who would avenge him; but he would not come closer. Meanwhile the stranger had calmed down to the point where he could talk somewhat evenly.

'Was it the *aitsjbom*?' he asked. 'Has the war started?'

He used that word often, *aitsjbom*, so I know it now, though unsure of what it means. It seems to be a kind of Greek fire. As for the war, I knew not which war he meant, and told him so.

'We had a great thunderstorm last night,' I added. 'And you say you were out in one too. Maybe Thor's hammer knocked you from your place to here.'

'But where is here?' he answered. His voice was more dulled than otherwise, now that the first terror had lifted.

'I told you. This is Hillstead, which is on Iceland.'

'But that's where I was!' he said. 'Reykjavik . . . what happened? Did the *aitsjbom* destroy everything while I lay witless?'

'Nothing has been destroyed,' I said.

'Does he mean the fire at Olafsvik last month?' wondered Helgi.

'No, no, no!' Again he buried his face in his hands. After a while he looked up and said, 'See here. I am *Sardjant* Gerald Robbins of the United States Army base on Iceland. I was in Reykjavik and got struck by lightning or something. Suddenly I was standing on the beach, and lost my head and ran. That's all. Now, can you tell me how to get back to the base?'

Those were more or less his words, priest. Of course, we did not grasp half of them, and made him repeat several times and explain. Even then we did not understand, save that he was from some country called the United States of America, which he said lies beyond Greenland to the west, and that he and some others were on Iceland to help our folk against their foes. This I did not consider a lie – more a mistake or imagining. Grim would have cut him down for thinking us stupid enough to swallow that tale, but I could see that he meant it.

Talking cooled him further. 'Look here,' he said, in too calm a tone for a feverish man, 'maybe we can get at the truth from your side. Has there been no war you know of? Nothing which – Well, look here. My country's men first came to Iceland to guard it against the Germans. Now it is the Russians, but then it was the Germans. When was that?'

Helgi shook his head. 'That never happened that I know of,' he said. 'Who are these Russians?' We found out later that the Gardariki folk were meant. 'Unless,' Helgi said, 'the old warlocks—'

'He means the Irish monks,' I explained. 'A few dwelt here when the Norsemen came, but they were driven out. That was, hm, somewhat over a hundred years ago. Did your kingdom once help the monks?'

'I never heard of them!' he said. The breath sobbed in his throat. 'You . . . didn't you Icelanders come from Norway?'

'Yes, about a hundred years ago,' I answered patiently. 'After King Harald Fairhair laid the Norse lands under him and—'

'*A hundred years ago!*' he whispered. I saw whiteness creep up beneath his skin. 'What year is this?'

We gaped at him. 'Well, it's the second year after the great salmon catch,' I tried.

'What year after Christ, I mean,' he prayed hoarsely.

'Oh, so you are a Christian? Hm, let me think. . . I talked with a bishop in England once, we were holding him for ransom, and he said . . . let me see . . . I think he said this Christ man lived a thousand years ago, or maybe a little less.'

'A thousand—' Something went out of him. He stood with glassy eyes – yes, I have seen glass, I told you I am a travelled man – he stood thus, and when we led him towards the garth he went like a small child.

You can see for yourself, priest, that my wife Ragnhild is still good to look upon even in eld, and Thorgunna took after her. She was – is – tall and slim, with a dragon's hoard of golden hair. She being a maiden then, the locks flowed loose over her shoulders. She had great blue eyes and a heart-shaped face and very red lips. Withal she was a merry one, and kind-hearted, so that she was widely loved. Sverri Snorrason went in Viking when she refused him and was slain, but no one had the wit to see that she was unlucky.

We led this Gerald Samsson – when I asked, he said his father was named Sam – we led him home, leaving Sigurd and Grim to finish gathering the driftwood. Some folk would not have a Christian in their house, for fear of witchcraft, but I am a broadminded man and Helgi, at his age, was wild for anything new. Our guest stumbled over the fields as if blind, but seemed to rouse when we entered the yard. His eyes went around the buildings that enclose it, from the stables and sheds to the smokehouse, the brewery, the kitchen, the bath house, the god-shrine, and thence to the hall. And Thorgunna was standing in the doorway.

Their gazes locked for a little, and I saw her colour but thought nothing of it then. Our shoes rang on the flagging as we crossed the yard and kicked the dogs aside. My two thralls halted in cleaning the stables to gawp, until I got them back to work with the remark that a man good for naught else was always a pleasing sacrifice. That's one useful practice you Christians lack; I've never made a human offering myself, but you know not how helpful is the fact that I could do so.

We entered the hall and I told the folk Gerald's name and how we had found him. Ragnhild set her maids hopping, to stoke up the fire in the middle trench and fetch beer, while I led Gerald to the high seat and sat down by him. Thorgunna brought us the filled horns. His standing was not like yours, for whom we use our outland cups.

Gerald tasted the brew and made a face. I felt somewhat offended, for my beer is reckoned good, and asked him if aught was wrong. He laughed with a harsh note and said no, but he was used to beer that foamed and was not sour.

'And where might they make such?' I wondered testily.

'Everywhere,' he said. 'Iceland, too – no. . .' He stared before him in an empty wise. 'Let's say . . . in Vinland.'

'Where is Vinland?' I asked.

'The country to the west whence I came. I thought you knew . . . Wait a bit.' He frowned. 'Maybe I can find out something. Have you heard of Leif Eiriksson?'

'No,' I said. Since then it has struck me that this was one proof of his tale, for Leif Eiriksson is now a well-known chief; and I also take more seriously those yarns of land seen by Bjarni Herjulfsson.

'His father, Eirik the Red?' went on Gerald.

'Oh, yes,' I said. 'If you mean the Norseman who came hither because of a manslaughter, and left Iceland in turn for the same reason, and has now settled with his friends in Greenland.'

'Then this is . . . a little before Leif's voyage,' he muttered. 'The late tenth century.'

'See here,' broke in Helgi, 'we've been forbearing with you, but now is no time for riddles. We save those for feasts and drinking bouts. Will you not say plainly whence you come and how you got here?'

Gerald looked down at the floor, shaking.

'Let the man alone, Helgi,' said Thorgunna. 'Can you not see he's troubled?'

He raised his head and gave her the look of a hurt dog that someone has patted. The hall was dim; enough light seeped in the loft-windows that no candles were lit, but not enough to see well by. Nevertheless, I marked a reddening in both their faces.

Gerald drew a long breath and fumbled about. His clothes were made with pockets. He brought out a small parchment box and from it took a little white stick that he put in his mouth. Then he took out another box, and a wooden stick therefrom which burst into flame when scratched. With the fire he kindled the stick in his mouth, and sucked in the smoke.

We stared. 'Is that a Christian rite?' asked Helgi.

'No . . . not just so.' A wry, disappointed smile twisted his lips. 'I thought you'd be more surprised, even terrified.'

'It's something new,' I admitted, 'but we're a sober folk on Iceland. Those fire-sticks could be useful. Did you come to trade in them?'

'Hardly.' He sighed. The smoke he breathed in seemed to steady him, which was odd, because the smoke in the hall had made him cough and water at the eyes. 'The truth is, well, something you will not believe. I can hardly believe it myself.'

We waited. Thorgunna stood leaning forward, her lips parted.

'That lightning bolt—' Gerald nodded wearily. 'I was out in the storm, and somehow the lightning must have smitten me in just the right way, a way that happens only once in many thousands of times. It threw me back into the past.'

Those were his words, priest. I did not understand, and told him so.

'It's hard to grasp,' he agreed. 'God give that I'm merely dreaming. But if this is a dream, I must endure till I awaken . . . well, look. I was born one thousand, nine hundred and thirty-three years after Christ, in a land to the west which you have not yet found. In the twenty-fourth year of my life, I was in Iceland with my country's war-host. The lightning struck me, and now, it is less than one thousand years after Christ, and yet I am here – almost a thousand years before I was born, I am here!'

We sat very still. I signed myself with the Hammer and took a long pull from my horn. One of the maids whimpered, and Ragnhild whispered so fiercely I could hear: 'Be still. The poor fellow's out of his head. There's no harm in him.'

I thought she was right, unless maybe in the last part. The

gods can speak through a madman, and the gods are not always to be trusted. Or he could turn berserker, or he could be under a heavy curse that would also touch us.

He slumped, gazing before him. I caught a few fleas and cracked them while I pondered. Gerald noticed and asked with some horror if we had many fleas here.

'Why, of course,' said Thorgunna. 'Have you none?'

'No.' He smiled crookedly. 'Not yet.'

'Ah,' she sighed, 'then you *must* be sick.'

She was a level-headed girl. I saw her thought, and so did Ragnhild and Helgi. Clearly, a man so sick that he had no fleas could be expected to rave. We might still fret about whether we could catch the illness, but I deemed this unlikely; his woe was in the head, maybe from a blow he had taken. In any case, the matter was come down to earth now, something we could deal with.

I being a godi, a chief who holds sacrifices, it behoved me not to turn a stranger out. Moreover, if he could fetch in many of those fire-kindling sticks, a profitable trade might be built up. So I said Gerald should go to rest. He protested, but we manhandled him into the shutbed and there he lay tired and was soon asleep. Thorgunna said she would take care of him.

The next eventide I meant to sacrifice a horse, both because of the timber we had found and to take away any curse that might be on Gerald. Furthermore, the beast I picked was old and useless, and we were short of fresh meat. Gerald had spent the morning lounging moodily around the garth, but when I came in at noon to eat I found him and my daughter laughing.

'You seem to be on the road to health,' I said.

'Oh, yes. It . . . could be worse for me.' He sat down at my side as the carles set up the trestle table and the the maids brought in the food. 'I was ever much taken with the age of the Vikings, and I have some skills.'

'Well,' I said, 'if you have no home, we can keep you here for a while.'

'I can work,' he said eagerly. 'I'll be worth my pay.'

Now I knew he was from afar, because what chief would work on any land but his own, and for hire at that? Yet he had the easy manner of the high-born, and had clearly eaten well throughout his life. I overlooked that he had made me no gifts; after all, he was shipwrecked.

'Maybe you can get passage back to your United States,' said Helgi. 'We could hire a ship. I'm fain to see that realm.'

'No,' said Gerald bleakly. 'There is no such placc. Not yet.'

'So you still hold to that idea you came from tomorrow?' grunted Sigurd. 'Crazy notion. Pass the pork.'

'I do,' said Gerald. Calm had come upon him. 'And I can prove it.'

'I don't see how you speak our tongue, if you hail from so far away,' I said. I would not call a man a liar to his face, unless we were swapping friendly brags, but—

'They speak otherwise in my land and time,' he said, 'but it happens that in Iceland the tongue changed little since the old days, and because my work had me often talking with folk, I learned it when I came here.'

'If you are a Christian,' I said, 'you must bear with us while we sacrifice tonight.'

'I've naught against that,' he said. 'I fear I never was a very good Christian. I'd like to watch. How is it done?'

I told him how I would smite the horse with a hammer before the god, and cut its throat, and sprinkle the blood about with willow twigs; thereafter we would butcher the carcass and feast. He said hastily:

'Here's my chance to prove what I am. I have a weapon that will kill the horse with a flash of lightning.'

'What is it?' I wondered. We crowded around while he took the metal club out of its sheath and showed it to us. I had my doubts; it looked well enough for hitting a man, I reckoned, but had no edge, though a wondrously skillful smith had forged it. 'Well, we can try,' I said. You have seen how on Iceland we are less concerned to follow the rites exactly than they are in the older countries.

Gerald showed us what else he had in his pockets. There were some coins of remarkable roundness and sharpness, though neither gold nor true silver; a tiny key; a stick with lead in it for writing; a flat purse holding many bits of marked paper. When he told us gravely that some of this paper was money, Thorgunna herself had to laugh. Best was a knife whose blade folded into the handle. When he saw me admiring that, he gave it to me, which was well done for a shipwrecked man. I said I would give him clothes and a good axe, as well as lodging for as long as needful.

No, I don't have the knife now. You shall hear why. It's a pity, for that was a good knife, though rather small.

'What were you ere the war-arrow went out in your land?' asked Helgi. 'A merchant?'

'No,' said Gerald. 'I was an . . . *endjinir* . . . that is, I was learning how to be one. A man who builds things, bridges and roads and tools . . more than just an artisan. So I think my knowledge could be of great value here.' I saw a fever in his eyes. 'Yes, give me time and I'll be a king.'

'We have no king on Iceland,' I grunted. 'Our forefathers came hither to get away from kings. Now we meet at the Things to try suits and pass new laws, but each man must get his own redress as best he can.'

'But suppose the one in the wrong won't yield?' he asked.

'Then there can be a fine feud,' said Helgi, and went on to relate some of the killings in past years. Gerald looked unhappy and fingered his *gun*. That is what he called his fire-spitting club. He tried to rally himself with a joke about now, at last, being free to call it a gun instead of something else. That disquieted me, smacked of witchcraft, so to change the talk I told Helgi to stop his chattering of manslaughter as if it were sport. With law shall the land be built.

'Your clothing is rich,' said Thorgunna softly. 'Your folk must own broad acres at home.'

'No,' he said, 'our . . . our king gives each man in the host garments like these. As for my family, we owned no farm, we rented our home in a building where many other families also dwelt.'

I am not purse-proud, but it seemed to me he had not been honest, a landless man sharing my high seat like a chief. Thorgunna covered my huffiness by saying, 'You will gain a farm later.'

After sunset we went out to the shrine. The carles had built a fire before it, and as I opened the door the wooden Odin appeared to leap forth. My house has long invoked him above the others. Gerald muttered to my daughter that it was a clumsy bit of carving, and since my father had made it I was still more angry with him. Some folk have no understanding of the fine arts.

Nevertheless, I let him help me lead the horse forth to the altar stone. I took the blood-bowl in my hands and said he could now slay the beast if he would. He drew his gun, put the end behind the horse's ear, and squeezed. We heard a crack, and the beast jerked and dropped with a hole blown through its skull, wasting the brains. A clumsy weapon. I caught a whiff, sharp and bitter like that around a volcano. We all jumped, one of the women screamed, and Gerald looked happy. I gathered my wits and finished the rest of the sacrifice as was right. Gerald did not like having blood sprinkled over him, but then he was a Christian. Nor would he take more than a little of the soup and flesh.

Afterwards Helgi questioned him about the gun, and he said it could kill a man at bowshot distance but had no witchcraft in it, only use of some tricks we did not know. Having heard of the Greek fire, I believed him. A gun could be useful in a fight, as indeed I was to learn, but it did not seem very practical – iron costing what it does, and months of forging needed for each one.

I fretted more about the man himself.

And the next morning I found him telling Thorgunna a great deal of foolishness about his home, buildings as tall as mountains and wagons that flew or went without horses. He said there were eight or nine thousand thousands of folk in his town, a burgh called New Jorvik or the like. I enjoy a good brag as well as the next man, but this was too much and

I told him gruffly to come along and help me get in some strayed cattle.

After a day scrambling around the hills I saw that Gerald could hardly tell a cow's bow from her stern. We almost had the strays once, but he ran stupidly across their path and turned them so the whole work was to do again. I asked him with strained courtesy if he could milk, shear, wield scythe, or flail, and he said no, he had never lived on a farm.

'That's a shame,' I remarked, 'for everyone on Iceland does, unless he be outlawed.'

He flushed at my tone. 'I can do enough else,' he answered. 'Give me some tools and I'll show you good metalwork.'

That brightened me, for truth to tell, none of our household was a gifted smith. 'That's an honourable trade,' I said, 'and you can be of great help. I have a broken sword and several bent spearheads to be mended, and it were no bad idea to shoe the horses.' His admission that he did not know how to put on a shoe was not very dampening to me then.

We had returned home as we talked, and Thorgunna came angrily forward. 'That's no way to treat a guest, father,' she said. 'Making him work like a carle, indeed!'

Gerald smiled. 'I'll be glad to work,' he said. 'I need an . . . a stake . . . something to start me afresh. Also, I want to repay a little of your kindness.'

Those words made me mild towards him, and I said it was not his fault they had different ways in the United States. On the morrow he could begin in the smithy, and I would pay him, yet he would be treated as an equal since craftsmen are valued. This earned him black looks from the housefolk.

That evening he entertained us well with stories of his home; true or not, they made good listening. However, he had no real polish, being unable to compose a line of verse. They must be a raw and backward lot in the United States. He said his task in the war-host had been to keep order among the troops. Helgi said this was unheard of, and he must be bold who durst offend so many men, but Gerald said folk obeyed him out of fear of the king. When he added that the term of a levy in the United States was two years, and that men could be called to war even in harvest time, I said he was well out of a country with so ruthless and powerful a lord.

'No,' he answered wistfully, 'we are a free folk, who say what we please.'

'But it seems you may not do as you please,' said Helgi.

'Well,' Gerald said, 'we may not murder a man just because he aggrieves us.'

'Not even if he has slain your own kin?' asked Helgi.

'No. It is for the . . . the king to take vengeance, on behalf of the whole folk whose peace has been broken.'

I chuckled. 'Your yarns are cunningly wrought,' I said, 'but there you've hit a snag. How could the king so much as keep count of the slaughters, let alone avenge them? Why, he'd not have time to beget an heir!'

Gerald could say no more for the laughter that followed.

The next day he went to the smithy, with a thrall to pump the bellows for him. I was gone that day and night, down to Reykjavik to dicker with Hjalmar Broadnose about some sheep. I invited him back for an overnight stay, and we rode into my steading with his son Ketill, a red-haired sulky youth of twenty winters who had been refused by Thorgunna.

I found Gerald sitting gloomily on a bench in the hall. He wore the clothes I had given him, his own having been spoilt by ash and sparks; what had he awaited, the fool? He talked in a low voice with my daughter.

'Well,' I said as I trod in, 'how went the tasks?'

My man Grim snickered. 'He ruined two spearheads, but we put out the fire he started ere the whole smithy burned.'

'How's this?' I cried. 'You said you were a smith.'

Gerald stood up, defiant. 'I worked with different tools, and better ones, at home,' he replied. 'You do it otherwise here.'

They told me he had built up the fire too hot; his hammer

had struck everywhere but the place it should; he had wrecked the temper of the steel through not knowing when to quench it. Smithcraft takes years to learn, of course, but he might have owned to being not so much as an apprentice.

'Well,' I snapped, 'what can you do, then, to earn your bread?' It irked me to be made a ninny of before Hjalmar and Ketill, whom I had told about the stranger.

'Odin alone knows,' said Grim. 'I took him with me to ride after your goats, and never have I seen a worse horseman. I asked him if maybe he could spin or weave, and he said no.'

'That was no question to ask a man!' flared Thorgunna. 'He should have slain you for it.'

'He should indeed,' laughed Grim. 'But let me carry on the tale. I thought we would also repair your bridge over the foss. Well, he *can* barely handle a saw, but he nigh took his own foot off with the adze.'

'We don't use those tools, I tell you!' Gerald doubled his fists and looked close to tears.

I motioned my guests to sit down. 'I don't suppose you can butcher or smoke a hog, either,' I said, 'or salt a fish or turf a roof.'

'No.' I could hardly hear him.

'Well, then, man, whatever can you do?'

'I—' He could get no words out.

'You were a warrior,' said Thorgunna.

'Yes, that I was!' he said, his face kindling.

'Small use on Iceland when you have no other skills,' I grumbled, 'but maybe, if you can get passage to the eastlands, some king will take you in his guard.' Myself I doubted it, for a guardsman needs manners that will do credit to his lord; but I had not the heart to say so.

Ketill Hjalmarsson had plainly not liked the way Thorgunna stood close to Gerald and spoke for him. Now he flared and said, 'I might also doubt your skill in fighting.'

'That I have been trained for,' said Gerald grimly.

'Will you wrestle with me?' asked Ketill.

'Gladly!' spat Gerald.

Priest, what is a man to think? As I grow older, I find life to be less and less the good-and-evil, black-and-white thing you call it; we are each of us some hue of grey. This useless fellow, this spiritless lout who could be asked if he did women's work and not lift axe, went out into the yard with Ketill Hjalmarsson and threw him three times running. He had a trick of grabbing the clothes as Ketill rushed on him. . . I cried a stop when the youth was nearing murderous rage, praised them both, and filled the beer-horns. But Ketill brooded on the bench the whole evening.

Gerald said something about making a gun like his own, but bigger, a *cannon* he called it, that could sink ships and scatter hosts. He would need the help of smiths, and also various stuffs. Charcoal was easy, and sulphur could be found by the volcanoes, I suppose, but what is this saltpetre?

Too, being wary by now, I questioned him closely as to how he would make such a thing. Did he know just how to mix the powder? No, he admitted. What size must the gun be? When he told me – at least as long as a man – I laughed and asked him how a piece that size could be cast or bored, supposing we could scrape together so much iron. This he did not know either.

'You haven't the tools to make the tools to make the tools,' he said. I don't understand what he meant by that. 'God help me, I can't run through a thousand years of history by myself.'

He took out the last of his little smoke-sticks and lit it. Helgi had tried a puff earlier and gotten sick, though he remained a friend of Gerald's. Now my son proposed to take a boat in the morning and go with him and me to Ice Fjord, where I had some money outstanding I wanted to collect. Hjalmar and Ketill said they would come along for the trip, and Thorgunna pleaded so hard that I let her come too.

'An ill thing,' mumbled Sigurd. 'The land-trolls like not a woman aboard a vessel. It's unlucky.'

'How did your fathers bring women to this island?' I grinned.

Now I wish I had listened to him. He was not a clever man, but he often knew whereof he spoke.

At this time I owned a half share in a ship that went to Norway, bartering wadmal for timber. It was a profitable business until she ran afoul of Vikings during the uproar while Olaf Tryggvason was overthrowing Jarl Haakon there. Some men will do anything to make a living – thieves, cutthroats, they ought to be hanged, the worthless robbers pouncing on honest merchantmen. Had they any courage or honour they would go to Ireland, which is full of plunder.

Well, anyhow, the ship was abroad, but we had three boats and took one of these. Grim went with us others: myself, Helgi, Hjalmar, Ketill, Gerald, and Thorgunna. I saw how the castaway winced at the cold water as we launched her, yet afterwards took off his shoes and stockings to let his feet dry. He had been surprised to learn we had a bath house – did he think us savages? – but still, he was dainty as a girl and soon moved upwind of our feet.

We had a favouring breeze, so raised mast and sail. Gerald tried to help, but of course did not know one line from another and got them fouled. Grim snarled at him and Ketill laughed nastily. But ere long we were under weigh, and he came and sat by me where I had the steering oar.

He must have lain long awake thinking, for now he ventured shyly, 'In my land they have . . . will have a rig and rudder which are better than these. With them, you can sail so close to the wind that you can crisscross against it.'

'Ah, our wise sailor offers us redes,' sneered Ketill.

'Be still,' said Thorgunna sharply. 'Let Gerald speak.'

He gave her a look of humble thanks, and I was not unwilling to listen. 'This is something which could easily be made,' he said. 'While not a seaman, I've been on such boats myself and know them well. First, then, the sail should not be square and hang from a yardarm, but three-cornered, with the two bottom corners lashed to a yard swivelling fore and aft from the mast; and there should be one or two smaller headsails of the same shape. Next, your steering oar is in the wrong place. You should have a rudder in the stern, guided by a bar.' He grew eager and traced the plan with his fingernail on Thorgunna's cloak. 'With these two things, and a deep keel, going down about three feet for a boat this size, a ship can move across the wind . . . thus.'

Well, priest, I must say the idea has merits, and were it not for the fear of bad luck – for everything of his was unlucky – I might yet play with it. But the drawbacks were clear, and I pointed them out in a reasonable way.

'First and worst,' I said, 'this rudder and deep keel would make it impossible to beach the ship or go up a shallow river. Maybe they have many harbours where you hail from, but here a craft must take what landings she can find, and must be speedily launched if there should be an attack.'

'The keel can be built to draw up into the hull,' he said, 'with a box around so that water can't follow.'

'How would you keep dry rot out of the box?' I answered. 'No, your keel must be fixed, and must be heavy if the ship is not to capsize under so much sail as you have drawn. This means iron or lead, ruinously costly. Besides,' I said, 'this mast of yours would be hard to unstep when the wind dropped and oars came out. Furthermore, the sails are the wrong shape to stretch as an awning when one must sleep at sea.'

'The ship could lie out, and you go to land in a small boat,' he said. 'Also, you could build cabins aboard for shelter.'

'The cabins would get in the way of the oars,' I said, 'unless the ship were hopelessly broad-beamed or else the oarsmen sat below a deck; and, while I hear that galley slaves do this in the southlands, free men would never row in such foulness.'

'Must you have oars?' he asked like a very child.

Laughter barked along the hull. The gulls themselves, hovering to starboard where the shore rose dark, cried their scorn. 'Do they have tame winds in the place whence you came?' snorted Hjalmar. 'What happens if you're becalmed – for days, maybe, with provisions running out—'

'You could build a ship big enough to carry many weeks' provisions,' said Gerald.

'If you had the wealth of a king, you might,' said Helgi. 'And such a king's ship, lying helpless on a flat sea, would be swarmed by every Viking from here to Jomsborg. As for leaving her out on the water while you make camp, what would you have for shelter, or for defence if you should be trapped ashore?'

Gerald slumped. Thorgunna said to him, gently, 'Some folk have no heart to try anything new. I think it's a grand idea.'

He smiled at her, a weary smile, and plucked up the will to say something about a means for finding north in cloudy weather; he said a kind of stone always pointed north when hung from a string. I told him kindly that I would be most interested if he could find me some of this stone; or if he knew where it was to be had, I could ask a trader to fetch me a piece. But this he did not know, and fell silent. Ketill opened his mouth, but got such an edged look from Thorgunna that he shut it again. His face declared what a liar he thought Gerald to be.

The wind turned crank after a while, so we lowered the mast and took to the oars. Gerald was strong and willing, though awkward; however, his hands were so soft that ere long they bled. I offered to let him rest, but he kept doggedly at the work.

Watching him sway back and forth, under the dreary creak of the tholes, the shaft red and wet where he gripped it, I thought much about him. He had done everything wrong which a man could do – thus I imagined then, not knowing the future – and I did not like the way Thorgunna's eyes strayed to him and rested. He was no man for my daughter, landless and penniless and helpless. Yet I could not keep from liking him. Whether his tale was true or only a madness, I felt he was honest about it; and surely whatever way by which he came hither was a strange one. I noticed the cuts on his chin from my razor; he had said he was not used to our kind of shaving and would grow a beard. He had tried hard. I wondered how well I would have done, landing alone in this witch country of his dreams, with a gap of forever between me and my home.

Maybe that same wretchedness was what had turned Thorgunna's heart. Women are a kittle breed, priest, and you who have foresworn them belike understand them as well as I who have slept with half a hundred in six different lands. I do not think they even understand themselves. Birth and life and death, those are the great mysteries, which none will ever fathom, and a woman is closer to them than a man.

The ill wind stiffened, the sea grew grey and choppy under low leaden clouds, and our headway was poor. At sunset we could row no more, but must pull in to a small unpeopled bay and make camp as well as could be on the strand.

We had brought firewood and tinder along. Gerald, though staggering with weariness, made himself useful, his sulphury sticks kindling the blaze more easily than flint and steel. Thorgunna set herself to cook our supper. We were not much warded by the boat from a lean, whining wind; her cloak fluttered like wings and her hair blew wild above the streaming flames. It was the time of light nights, the sky a dim dusky blue, the sea a wrinkled metal sheet and the land like something risen out of dream-mists. We men huddled in our own cloaks, holding numbed hands to the fire and saying little.

I felt some cheer was needed, and ordered a cask of my best and strongest ale broached. An evil norn made me do that, but no man escapes his weird. Our bellies seemed the more empty now when our noses drank in the sputter of a spitted joint, and the ale went swiftly to our heads. I remember declaiming the death-song of Ragnar Hairybreeks for no other reason than that I felt like declaiming it.

Thorgunna came to stand over Gerald where he sat. I saw how her fingers brushed his hair, ever so lightly, and Ketill Hjalmarsson did too. 'Have they no verses in your land?' she asked.

'Not like yours,' he said, glancing up. Neither of them

looked away again. 'We sing rather than chant. I wish I had my *gittar* here – that's a kind of harp.'

'Ah, an Irish bard,' said Hjalmar Broadnose.

I remember strangely well how Gerald smiled, and what he said in his own tongue, though I know not the meaning: '*Only on me mither's side, begorra.*' I suppose it was magic.

'Well, sing for us,' laughed Thorgunna.

'Let me think,' he said. 'I shall have to put it in Norse words for you.' After a little while, still staring at her through the windy gloaming, he began a song. It had a tune I liked, thus:

From this valley they tell me you're leaving.
I will miss your bright eyes and sweet smile.
You will carry the sunshine with you
That has brightened my life all the while...

I don't remember the rest, save that it was not quite seemly.

When he had finished, Hjalmar and Grim went over to see if the meat was done. I spied a glimmer of tears in my daughter's eyes. 'That was a lovely thing,' she said.

Ketill sat straight. The flames splashed his face with wild, running red. A rawness was in his tone. 'Yes, we've found what this fellow can do. Sit about and make pretty songs for the girls. Keep him for that, Ospak.'

Thorgunna whitened, and Helgi clapped hand to sword. Gerald's face darkened and his voice grew thick. 'That was no way to talk. Take it back.'

Ketill rose. 'No,' he said. 'I'll ask no pardon of an idler living off honest yeomen.'

He was raging, but had kept sense enough to shift the insult from my family to Gerald alone. Otherwise he and his father would have had the four of us to deal with. As it was, Gerald stood too, fists knotted at his sides, and said, 'Will you step away from here and settle this?'

'Gladly!' Ketill turned and walked a few yards down the beach, taking his shield from the boat. Gerald followed.

Thorgunna stood stricken, then snatched his axe and ran after him.

'Are you going weaponless?' she shrieked.

Gerald stopped, looking dazed. 'I don't want anything like that,' he said. 'Fists—'

Ketill puffed himself up and drew sword. 'No doubt you're used to fighting like thralls in your land,' he said. 'So if you'll crave my pardon, I'll let this matter rest.'

Gerald stood with drooped shoulders. He stared at Thorgunna as if he were blind, as if asking her what to do. She handed him the axe.

'So you want me to kill him?' he whispered.

'Yes,' she answered.

Then I knew she loved him, for otherwise why should she have cared if he disgraced himself?

Helgi brought him his helmet. He put it on, took the axe, and went forward.

'Ill is this,' said Hjalmar to me. 'Do you stand by the stranger, Ospak?'

'No,' I said. 'He's no kin or oath-brother of mine. This is not my quarrel.'

'That's good,' said Hjalmar. 'I'd not like to fight with you. You were ever a good neighbour.'

We stepped forth together and staked out the ground. Thorgunna told me to lend Gerald my sword, so he could use a shield too, but the man looked oddly at me and said he would rather have the axe. They squared off before each other, he and Ketill, and began fighting.

This was no holmgang, with rules and a fixed order of blows and first blood meaning victory. There was death between those two. Drunk though the lot of us were, we saw that and so had not tried to make peace. Ketill stormed in with the sword whistling in his hand. Gerald sprang back, wielding the axe awkwardly. It bounced off Ketill's shield. The youth grinned and cut at Gerald's legs. Blood welled forth to stain the ripped breeches.

What followed was butchery. Gerald had never used a battle-axe before. Soon it turned in his grasp and he struck with the flat of the head. He would have been hewn down at once had Ketill's sword not been blunted on his helmet and had he not been quick on his feet. Even so, he was ere long lurching with a dozen wounds.

'Stop the fight!' Thorgunna cried and sped towards them. Helgi caught her arms and forced her back, where she struggled and kicked till Grim must help. I saw grief on my son's face but a wolfish glee on the carle's.

Ketill's blade came down and slashed Gerald's left hand. He dropped the axe. Ketill snarled and readied to finish him. Gerald drew his gun. It made a flash and a barking noise. Ketill fell. Blood gushed from him. His lower jaw was blown off and the back of his skull was gone.

A stillness came, where only the wind and the sea had voice.

Then Hjalmar trod forth, his mouth working but otherwise a cold steadiness over him. He knelt and closed his son's eyes, as token that the right of vengeance was his. Rising, he said: 'That was an evil deed. For that you shall be outlawed.'

'It wasn't witchcraft,' said Gerald in a stunned tone. 'It was like a . . . a bow. I had no choice. I didn't want to fight with more than my fists.'

I got between them and said the Thing must decide this matter, but that I hoped Hjalmar would take weregild for Ketill.

'But I killed him to save my own life!' protested Gerald.

'Nevertheless, weregild must be paid, if Ketill's kin will take it,' I explained. 'Because of the weapon, I think it will be doubled, but that is for the Thing to judge.'

Hjalmar had many other sons, and it was not as if Gerald belonged to a family at odds with his own, so I felt he would agree. However, he laughed coldly and asked where a man lacking wealth would find the silver.

Thorgunna stepped up with a wintry calm and said we would pay. I opened my mouth, but when I saw her eyes I nodded. 'Yes, we will,' I said, 'in order to keep the peace.'

'So you make this quarrel your own?' asked Hjalmar.

'No,' I answered. 'This man is no blood of mine. But if I choose to make him a gift of money to use as he wishes, what of it?'

Hjalmar smiled. Sorrow stood in his gaze, but he looked on me with old comradeship.

'One day he may be your son-in-law,' he said. 'I know the signs, Ospak. Then indeed he will be of your folk. Even helping him now in his need will range you on his side.'

'And so?' asked Helgi, most softly.

'And so, while I value your friendship, I have sons who will take the death of their brother ill. They'll want revenge on Gerald Samsson if only for the sake of their good names, and thus our two houses will be sundered and one manslaying will lead to another. It has happened often enough ere now.' Hjalmar sighed. 'I myself wish peace with you, Ospak, but if you take this killer's side it must be otherwise.'

I thought for a moment, thought of Helgi lying with his head cloven, of my other sons on their garths drawn to battle because of a man they had never seen, I thought of having to wear byrnies each time we went down for driftwood and never knowing when we went to bed if we would wake to find the house ringed in by spearmen.

'Yes,' I said, 'you are right, Hjalmar. I withdraw my offer. Let this be a matter between you and him alone.'

We gripped hands on it.

Thorgunna uttered a small cry and flew into Gerald's arms. He held her close. 'What does this mean?' he asked slowly.

'I cannot keep you any longer,' I said, 'but maybe some crofter will give you a roof. Hjalmar is a law-abiding man and will not harm you until the Thing has outlawed you. That will not be before they meet in fall. You can try to get passage out of Iceland ere then.'

'A useless one like me?' he replied in bitterness.

Thorgunna whirled free and blazed that I was a coward and a perjurer and all else evil. I let her have it out, before I laid my hands on her shoulders.

'I do this for the house,' I said. 'The house and the blood, which are holy. Men die and women weep, but while the kindred live our names are remembered. Can you ask a score of men to die for your hankerings?'

Long did she stand, and to this day I know not what her answer would have been. But Gerald spoke.

'No,' he said. 'I suppose you have right, Ospak . . . the right of your time, which is not mine.' He took my hand, and Helgi's. His lips brushed Thorgunna's cheek. Then he turned and walked out into the darkness.

I heard, later, that he went to earth with Thorvald Hallsson, the crofter of Humpback Feli, and did not tell his host what had happened. He must have hoped to go unnoticed until he could somehow get a berth on an eastbound ship. But of course word spread. I remember his brag that in the United States folk had ways to talk from one end of the land to another. So he must have scoffed at us, sitting in our lonely garths, and not known how fast news would get around. Thorvald's son Hrolf went to Brand Sealskin-Boots to talk about some matter, and mentioned the guest, and soon the whole western island had the tale.

Now if Gerald had known he must give notice of a manslaying at the first garth he found, he would have been safe at least till the Thing met, for Hjalmar and his sons are sober men who would not needlessly kill a man under the wing of the law. But as it was, his keeping the matter secret made him a murderer and therefore at once an outlaw. Hjalmar and his kin rode straight to Humpback Fell and haled him forth. He shot his way past them with the gun and fled into the hills. They followed him, having several hurts and one more death to avenge. I wonder if Gerald thought the strangeness of his weapon would unnerve us. He may not have understood that every man dies when his time comes, neither sooner nor later, so that fear of death is useless.

At the end, when they had him trapped, his weapon gave out on him. Then he took a dead man's sword and defended himself so valiantly that Ulf Hjalmarsson has limped ever since. That was well done, as even his foes admitted. They are an eldritch breed in the United States, but they do not lack manhood.

When he was slain, his body was brought back. For fear of the ghost, he having maybe been a warlock, it was burned, and everything he had owned was laid in the fire with him. Thus I lost the knife he gave me. The barrow stands out on the moor, north of here, and folk shun it though the ghost has not walked. Today, with so much else happening, he is slowly being forgotten.

And that is the tale, priest, as I saw it and heard it. Most men think Gerald Samsson was crazy, but I myself now believe he did come from out of time, and that his doom was that no man may ripen a field before harvest season. Yet I look into the future, a thousand years hence, when they fly through the air and ride in horseless wagons and smash whole towns with one blow. I think of this Iceland then, and of the young United States men come to help defend us in a year when the end of the world hovers close. Maybe some of them, walking about on the heaths, will see that barrow and wonder what ancient warrior lies buried there, and they may well wish they had lived long ago in his time when men were free.

MURRAY LEINSTER

THE OTHER NOW

It was self-evident nonsense. If Jimmy Patterson had told anybody but Haynes, calm men in white jackets would have taken him away for psychiatric treatment which undoubtedly would have been effective. He'd have been restored to sanity and common sense, and he'd probably have died of it. So to anyone who liked Jimmy and Jane, it is good that things worked out as they did. The facts are patently impossible, but they are satisfying.

Haynes, though, would like very much to know exactly why it happened in the case of Jimmy and Jane and nobody else. There must have been some specific reason, but there's absolutely no clue to it.

It began about three months after Jane was killed in that freak accident. Jimmy had taken her death hard. This night seemed no different from any other. He came home just as usual and his throat tightened a little, just as usual, as he went up to the door. It was still intolerable to know that Jane wouldn't be waiting for him.

The hurt in his throat was a familiar sensation which he was doggedly hoping would go away. But it was extra strong tonight and he wondered rather desperately if he'd sleep, or, if he did, whether he would dream. Sometimes he had dreams of Jane and was happy until he woke up, and then he wanted to cut his throat. But he wasn't at that point tonight. Not yet.

As he explained it to Haynes later, he simply put his key in the door and opened it and started to walk in. But he kicked the door instead, so he absently put his key in the door and opened it and started to walk in—

Yes, that is what happened. He was halfway through before he realized. He stared blankly. The door looked perfectly normal. He closed it behind him, feeling queer. He tried to reason out what had happened.

Then he felt a slight draught. The door wasn't shut. It was wide open. He had to close it again.

That was all that happened to mark this night off from any other, and there is no explanation why it happened – began, rather – this night instead of another. Jimmy went to bed with a taut feeling. He'd had the conviction that he'd opened the door twice. The same door. Then he'd had the conviction that he had had to close it twice. He'd heard of that feeling. Queer, but no doubt commonplace.

He slept, blessedly without dreams. He woke next morning and found his muscles tense. That was an acquired habit. Before he opened his eyes, every morning, he reminded himself that Jane wasn't beside him. It was necessary. If he forgot and turned contentedly – to emptiness – the ache of being alive, when Jane wasn't, was unbearable.

This morning he lay with his eyes closed to remind himself, and instead found himself thinking about that business of the door. He'd kicked the door between the two openings, so it wasn't only an illusion of repetition. He was puzzling over that repetition after closing the door, when he found he had to close it again. That proved to him it wasn't a standard mental vagary. It looked like a delusion. But his memory insisted that it had happened that way, whether it was possible or not.

Frowning, he went out and got his breakfast at a restaurant and rode to work. Work was blessed, because he had to think about it. The main trouble was that sometimes something turned up which Jane would have been amused to hear, and he had to remind himself that there was no use making a mental note to tell her. Jane was dead.

Today he thought a good deal about the door, but when

he went home he knew that he was going to have a black night. He wouldn't sleep, and oblivion would seem infinitely tempting, because the ache of being alive, when Jane wasn't, was horribly tedious and he could not imagine an end to it. Tonight would be a very bad one, indeed.

He opened the door and started in. He went crashing into the door. He stood still for an instant, and then fumbled for the lock. But the door was open. He'd opened it. There hadn't been anything for him to run into. Yet his forehead hurt where he'd bumped into the door which wasn't closed at all.

There was nothing he could do about it, though. He went in. He hung up his coat. He sat down wearily. He filled his pipe and grimly faced a night that was going to be one of the worst. He struck a match and lighted his pipe, and put the match in an ashtray. And he glanced in the tray. There were the stubs of cigarettes in it. Jane's brand. Freshly smoked.

He touched them with his fingers. They were real. Then a furious anger filled him. Maybe the cleaning woman had had the intolerable insolence to smoke Jane's cigarettes. He got up and stormed through the house, raging as he searched for signs of further impertinence. He found none. He came back, seething, to his chair. The ashtray was empty. And there'd been nobody around to empty it.

It was logical to question his own sanity, and the question gave him a sort of grim cheer. The matter of the recurrent oddities could be used to fight the abysmal depression ahead. He tried to reason them out, and always they added up to delusions only.

But he kept his mind resolutely on the problem. Work, during the day, was a godsend. Sometimes he was able to thrust aside for whole half-hours the fact that Jane was dead. Now he grappled relievedly with the question of his sanity or lunacy. He went to the desk where Jane had kept her household accounts. He'd set the whole thing down on paper and examine it methodically, checking this item against that.

Jane's diary lay on the desk-blotter, with a pencil between

two of its pages. He picked it up with a tug of dread. Some day he might read it – an absurd chronicle Jane had never offered him – but not now. Not now!

That was when he realized that it shouldn't be here. His hands jumped, and it fell open. He saw Jane's angular writing and it hurt. He closed it quickly, aching all over. But the printed date at the top of the page registered on his brain even as he snapped the cover shut.

He sat still for minutes, every muscle taut.

It was a long time before he opened the book again, and by that time he had a perfectly reasonable explanation. It must be that Jane hadn't restricted herself to assigned spaces. When she had something extra to write, she wrote it on past the page allotted for a given date.

Of course!

Jimmy fumbled back to the last written page, where the pencil had been, with a tense matter-of-factness. It was, as he'd noticed, today's date. The page was filled. The writing was fresh. It was Jane's handwriting.

'*Went to the cemetery,*' said the sprawling letters. '*It was very bad. Three months since the accident and it doesn't get any easier. I'm developing a personal enmity to chance. It doesn't seem like an abstraction any more. It was chance that killed Jimmy. It could have been me instead, or neither of us. I wish—*'

Jimmy went quietly mad for a moment or two. When he came to himself he was staring at an empty desk-blotter. There wasn't any book before him. There wasn't any pencil between his fingers. He remembered picking up the pencil and writing desperately under Jane's entry. '*Jane!*' he'd written – and he could remember the look of his scrawled script under Jane's – '*where are you? I'm not dead! I thought you were! In God's name, where are you?*'

But certainly nothing of the sort could have happened. It was delusion.

That night was particularly bad, but curiously not as bad as some other nights had been. Jimmy had a normal man's horror of insanity, yet this wasn't, so to speak, normal insanity. A lunatic has always an explanation for his delusions. Jimmy had none. He noted the fact.

Next morning he bought a small camera and a flash-bulb attachment and carefully memorized the directions for its use. This was the thing that would tell the story. And that night, when he got home, as usual after dark, he had the camera ready. He unlocked the door and opened it. He put his hand out tentatively. The door was still closed.

He stepped back and quickly snapped the camera. There was a sharp flash of the bulb. The glare blinded him. But when he put out his hand again, the door was open. He stepped into the living-room without having to unlock and open it a second time.

He looked at the desk as he turned the film and put in a new flash bulb. It was empty as he'd left it in the morning. He hung up his coat and settled down tensely with his pipe. Presently he knocked out the ashes. There were cigarette butts in the tray.

He quivered a little. He smoked again, carefully not looking at the desk. It was not until he knocked out the second pipeful of ashes that he let himself look where Jane's diary had been.

It was there again. The book was open. There was a ruler laid across it to keep it open.

Jimmy wasn't frightened, and he wasn't hopeful. There was absolutely no reason why this should happen to him. He was simply desperate and grim when he went across the room. He saw yesterday's entry, and his own hysterical message. And there was more writing beyond that.

In Jane's hand.

'Darling, maybe I'm going crazy. But I think you wrote me as if you were alive. Maybe I'm crazy to answer you. But please, darling, if you are alive somewhere and somehow—'

There was a tear blot here. The rest was frightened, and tender, and as desperate as Jimmy's own sensations.

He wrote, with trembling fingers, before he put the camera into position and pressed the shutter-control for the second time.

When his eyes recovered from the flash, there was nothing on the desk.

He did not sleep at all that night, nor did he work the next day. He went to a photographer with the film and paid an extravagant fee to have the film developed and enlarged at once. He got back two prints, quite distinct. Even very clear, considering everything. One looked like a trick shot, showing a door twice, once open and once closed, in the same photograph. The other was a picture of an open book and he could read every word on its pages. It was inconceivable that such a picture should have come out.

He walked around practically at random for a couple of hours, looking at the pictures from time to time. Pictures or no pictures, the thing was nonsense. The facts were preposterous. It must be that he only imagined seeing these prints. But there was a quick way to find out.

He went to Haynes. Haynes was his friend and reluctantly a lawyer – reluctantly because law practice interfered with a large number of unlikely hobbies.

'Haynes,' said Jimmy quietly, 'I want you to look at a couple of pictures and see if you see what I do. I may have gone out of my head.'

He passed over the picture of the door. It looked to Jimmy like two doors, nearly at right angles, in the same door-frame and hung from the same hinges.

Haynes looked at it and said tolerantly, 'Didn't know you went in for trick photography.' He picked up a reading glass and examined it in detail. 'A futile but highly competent job. You covered half the film and exposed with the door closed, and then exposed for the other half of the film with the door open. A neat job of matching, though. You've a good tripod.'

'I held the camera in my hand,' said Jimmy, with restraint.

'You couldn't do it that way, Jimmy,' objected Haynes. 'Don't try to kid me.'

'I'm trying not to fool myself,' said Jimmy. He was very pale. He handed over the other enlargement. 'What do you see in this?'

Haynes looked. Then he jumped. He read through what

was so plainly photographed on the pages of a diary that hadn't been before the camera. Then he looked at Jimmy in palpable uneasiness.

'Got any explanation?' asked Jimmy. He swallowed. 'I – haven't any.'

He told what had happened to date, baldly and without any attempt to make it reasonable. Haynes gaped at him. But before long the lawyer's eyes grew shrewd and compassionate. As noted hitherto, he had a number of unlikely hobbies, among which was a loud insistence on a belief in a fourth dimension and other esoteric ideas, because it was good fun to talk authoritatively about them. But he had common sense, had Haynes, and a good and varied law practice.

Presently he said gently, 'If you want it straight, Jimmy . . . I had a client once. She accused a chap of beating her up. It was very pathetic. She was absolutely sincere. She really believed it. But her own family admitted that she'd made the marks on herself – and the doctors agreed that she'd unconsciously blotted it out of her mind afterwards.'

'You suggest,' said Jimmy composedly, 'that I might have forged all that to comfort myself with, as soon as I could forget the forging. I don't think that's the case, Haynes. What possibilities does that leave?'

Haynes hesitated a long time. He looked at the pictures again, scrutinizing especially the one that looked like a trick shot.

'This is an amazingly good job of matching,' he said wrily. 'I can't pick the place where the two exposures join. Some people might manage to swallow this, and the theoretic explanation is a lot better. The only trouble is that it couldn't happen.'

Jimmy waited.

Haynes went on awkwardly. 'The accident in which Jane was killed. You were in your car. You came up behind a truck carrying structural steel. There was a long slim girder sticking way out behind, with a red rag on it. The truck had airbrakes. The driver jammed them on just after he'd passed over a bit of wet pavement. The truck stopped. Your car slid, even with the brakes locked. It's nonsense, Jimmy!'

'I'd rather you continued,' said Jimmy, white.

'You – ran into the truck, your car swinging a little as it slid. The girder came through the windshield. It could have hit you. It could have missed both of you. By pure chance, it happened to hit Jane.'

'And killed her,' said Jimmy very quietly. 'Yes. But it might have been me. That diary entry is written as if it had been me. Did you notice?'

There was a long pause in Haynes' office. The world outside the windows was highly prosaic and commonplace and normal. Haynes wriggled in his chair.

'I think,' he said unhappily, 'you did the same as my girl client – forged that writing and then forgot it. Have you seen a doctor yet?'

'I will,' said Jimmy. 'Systematize my lunacy for me first, Haynes. If it can be done.'

'It's not accepted science,' said Haynes. 'In fact, it's considered eyewash. But there have been speculations . . .' He grimaced. 'First point is that it was pure chance that Jane was hit. It was just as likely to be you instead, or neither of you. If it had been you—'

'Jane,' said Jimmy, 'would be living in our house alone, and she might very well have written that entry in the diary.'

'Yes,' agreed Haynes uncomfortably. 'I shouldn't suggest this, but – there are a lot of possible futures. We don't know which one will come about for us. Nobody except fatalists can argue with that statement. When today was in the future, there were a lot of possible todays. The present moment – now – is only one of any number of nows that might have been. So it's been suggested – mind you, this isn't accepted science, but pure charlatanry – it's been suggested that there may be more than one actual now. Before the girder actually hit, there were three nows in the possible future. One in which neither of you was hit, one in which you were hit, and one—'

He paused, embarrassed. 'So some people would say, how

do we know that the one in which Jane was hit is the only now? They'd say that the others could have happened and that maybe they did.'

Jimmy nodded.

'If that were true,' he said detachedly, 'Jane would be in a present moment, a now, where it was me who was killed. As I'm in a now where she was killed. Is that it?'

Haynes shrugged.

Jimmy thought, and said gravely, 'Thanks. Queer, isn't it?'

He picked up the two pictures and went out.

Haynes was the only one who knew about the affair, and he worried. But it is not easy to denounce someone as insane, when there is no evidence that he is apt to be dangerous. He did go to the trouble to find out that Jimmy acted in a reasonably normal manner, working industriously and talking quite sanely in the daytime. Only Haynes suspected that of nights he went home and experienced the impossible. Sometimes, Haynes suspected that the impossible might be the fact – that had been an amazingly good bit of trick photography – but it was too preposterous! Also, there was no reason for such a thing to happen to Jimmy.

For a week after Haynes' pseudoscientific explanation, however, Jimmy was almost light-hearted. He no longer had to remind himself that Jane was dead. He had evidence that she wasn't. She wrote to him in the diary which he found on her desk, and he read her messages and wrote in return. For a full week the sheer joy of simply being able to communicate with each other was enough.

The second week was not so good. To know that Jane was alive was good, but to be separated from her without hope was not. There was no meaning in a cosmos in which one could only write love letters to one's wife or husband in another now which only might have been. But for a while both Jimmy and Jane tried to hide this new hopelessness from each other.

Jimmy explained this carefully to Haynes before it was

all over. Their letters were tender and very natural and presently there was even time for gossip and actual bits of choice scandal. . .

Haynes met Jimmy on the street one day, after about two weeks. Jimmy looked better, but he was drawn very fine. Though he greeted Haynes without constraint, Haynes felt awkward. After a little he said, 'Er – Jimmy. That matter we were talking about the other day – those photographs—'

'Yes. You were right,' said Jimmy casually. 'Jane agrees. There is more than one now. In the now I'm in, Jane was killed. In the now she's in, I was killed.'

Haynes fidgeted. 'Would you let me see that picture of the door again?' he asked. 'A trick film like that simply can't be perfect! I'd like to enlarge that picture a little more. May I?'

'You can have the film,' said Jimmy. 'I don't need it any more.'

Haynes hesitated. Jimmy, quite matter-of-factly, told him most of what had happened to date. But he had no idea what had started it. Haynes almost wrung his hands.

'The thing can't be!' he said desperately. 'You *have* to be crazy, Jimmy!'

But he would not have said that to a man whose sanity he really suspected.

Jimmy nodded. 'Jane told me something, by the way. Did you have a near-accident night before last? Somebody almost ran into you out on the Saw Mill Road?'

Haynes started and went pale. 'I went around a curve and a car plunged out of nowhere on the wrong side of the road. We both swung hard. He smashed my fender and almost went off the road himself. But he went racing off without stopping to see if I'd gone in the ditch and killed myself. If I'd been five feet nearer the curve when he came out of it—'

'Where Jane is,' said Jimmy, 'you were. Just about five feet nearer the curve. It was a bad smash. Tony Shields was in the other car. It killed him – where Jane is.'

Haynes licked his lips. It was absurd, but he said, 'How about me?'

'Where Jane is,' Jimmy told him, 'you're in the hospital.'

Haynes swore in unreasonable irritation. There wasn't any way for Jimmy to know about that near-accident. He hadn't mentioned it, because he'd no idea who'd been in the other car.

'I don't believe it!' But he said pleadingly, 'Jimmy, it isn't so, is it? How in hell could you account for it?'

Jimmy shrugged. 'Jane and I – we're rather fond of each other.' The understatement was so patent that he smiled faintly. 'Chance separated us. The feeling we have for each other draws us together. There's a saying about two people becoming one flesh. If such a thing could happen, it would be Jane and me. After all, maybe only a tiny pebble or a single extra drop of water made my car swerve enough to get her killed – where I am, that is. That's a very little thing. So with such a trifle separating us, and so much pulling us together – why, sometimes the barrier wears thin. She leaves a door closed in the house where she is. I open that same door where I am. Sometimes I have to open the door she left closed, too. That's all.'

Haynes didn't say a word, but the question he wouldn't ask was so self-evident that Jimmy answered it.

'We're hoping,' he said. 'It's pretty bad being separated, but the – phenomena keep up. So we hope. Her diary is sometimes in the now where she is, and sometimes in this now of mine. Cigarette butts, too. Maybe—' That was the only time he showed any sign of emotion. He spoke as if his mouth were dry. 'If ever I'm in her now or she's in mine, even for an instant, all the devils in hell couldn't separate us again! – We hope.'

Which was insanity. In fact, it was the third week of insanity. He'd told Haynes quite calmly that Jane's diary was on her desk every night, and there was a letter to him in it, and he wrote one to her. He said quite calmly that the barrier between them seemed to be growing thinner. That at least once, when he went to bed, he was sure that there was one more cigarette stub in the ashtray than had been there earlier in the evening.

They were very near indeed. They were separated only by the difference between what was and what might have been. In one sense the difference was a pebble or a drop of water. In another, the difference was that between life and death. But they hoped. They convinced themselves that the barrier grew thinner. Once, it seemed to Jimmy that they touched hands. But he was not sure. He was still sane enough not to be sure. And he told all this to Haynes in a matter-of-fact fashion, and speculated mildly on what had started it all...

Then, one night, Haynes called Jimmy on the telephone. Jimmy answered.

He sounded impatient.

'Jimmy!' said Haynes. He was almost hysterical. 'I think I'm insane! You know you said Tony Shields was in the car that hit me?'

'Yes,' said Jimmy politely. 'What's the matter?'

'It's been driving me crazy,' wailed Haynes feverishly. 'You said he was killed – there. But I hadn't told a soul about the incident. So – so just now I broke down and phoned him. And it *was* Tony Shields! That near-crash scared him to death, and I gave him hell and – he's paying for my fender! I didn't tell him he was killed.'

Jimmy didn't answer. It didn't seem to matter to him.

'I'm coming over!' said Haynes feverishly. 'I've got to talk!'

'No,' said Jimmy. 'Jane and I are pretty close to each other. We've touched each other again. We're hoping. The barrier's wearing through. We hope it's going to break.'

'But it can't!' protested Haynes, shocked at the idea of improbabilities in the preposterous. 'It – it can't! What'd happen if you turned up where she is, or – or if she turned up here?'

'I don't know,' said Jimmy, 'but we'd be together.'

'You're crazy! You mustn't—'

'Goodbye,' said Jimmy politely. 'I'm hoping, Haynes. Something has to happen. It has to!'

His voice stopped. There was a noise in the room behind him; Haynes heard it. Only two words, and those faintly, and over a telephone, but he swore to himself that it was Jane's voice, throbbing with happiness. The two words Haynes thought he heard were, '*Jimmy! Darling!*'

Then the telephone crashed to the floor and Haynes heard no more. Even though he called back frantically again, Jimmy didn't answer.

Haynes sat up all that night, practically gibbering, and he tried to call Jimmy again next morning, and then tried his office, and at last went to the police. He explained to them that Jimmy had been in a highly nervous state since the death of his wife.

So finally the police broke into the house. They had to break in because every door and window was carefully fastened from the inside, as if Jimmy had been very careful to make sure nobody could interrupt what he and Jane hoped would occur. But Jimmy wasn't in the house. There was no trace of him. It was exactly as if he had vanished into the air.

Ultimately the police dragged ponds and such things for his body, but they never found any clues. Nobody ever saw Jimmy again. It was recorded that Jimmy simply left town, and everybody accepted that obvious explanation.

The thing that really bothered Haynes was the fact that Jimmy had told him who'd almost crashed into him on the Saw Mill Road, and it was true. That was, to understate, hard to take. And there was the double-exposure picture of Jimmy's front door, which was much more convincing than any other trick picture Haynes had ever seen. But on the other hand, if it did happen, why did it happen only to Jimmy and Jane? What set it off? What started it? Why, in effect, did those oddities start at that particular time, to those particular people, in that particular fashion? In fact, did anything happen at all?

Now, after Jimmy's disappearance, Haynes wished he could talk with him once more – talk sensibly, quietly, without fear and hysteria and this naggingly demanding wonderment.

For he had sketched to Jimmy, and Jimmy had accepted (hadn't he?) the possibility of the *other now* – but with that acceptance came still others. In one, Jane was dead. In one, Jimmy was dead. It was between these two that the barrier had grown so thin. . .

If he could talk to Jimmy about it!

There was also a now in which *both* had died, and another in which *neither* had died! And if it was togetherness that each wanted so desperately . . . *which was it?*

These were things that Haynes would have liked very much to know, but he kept his mouth shut, or calm men in white coats would have come and taken him away for treatment. As they would have taken Jimmy.

The only thing really sure was that it was all impossible. But to someone who liked Jimmy and Jane – and doubtless to Jimmy and to Jane themselves – no matter which barrier had been broken, it was a rather satisfying impossibility.

Haynes' car had been repaired. He could easily have driven out to the cemetery. For some reason, he never did.

IRA LEVIN

A KISS BEFORE DYING 25p

The all-time suspense classic and award-winning novel that has shocked, thrilled and fascinated critics and readers all over the world.
'Terrifyingly dramatic . . . it is bound to send the reader reeling' – MANCHESTER EVENING NEWS
'Don't read it in the train – you'll go past your stop' –
SUNDAY MIRROR

ROSEMARY'S BABY 25p

The book that topped US and British bestseller lists for months and was then made into a terrifying Paramount picture, starring Mia Farrow, John Cassavetes and Ralph Bellamy.
'At last I have got my wish. I am ridden by a book that plagues my mind and continues to squeeze my heart with fingers of bone. I swear that *Rosemary's Baby* is the most unnerving story I've read' –
KENNETH ALLSOP, EVENING NEWS

THIS PERFECT DAY 35p

'Not satisfied with scaring the bejabbers out of us by transplanting 16th century New York in *Rosemary's Baby*, Ira Levin has now concocted a futuristic nightmare' –
NEW YORK TIMES